The CAPE

Charles Whitecar Miskelly

Illustrated by Janet Rombough O'Neil

Published by Exit Zero Publishing, Inc.,
109 Sunset Boulevard, Suite D,
Cape May, NJ 08204
www.exitzero.us

Printed in Hong Kong

Foreword

By Jack Wright *Book Editor*

This book tells the story of a young British man, the sole survivor of a 17th-century shipwreck off the coast of South Jersey, who washes up on the shore of what is now Cape May. The story follows his integration into a tribe of Lenni-Lenape indians, the original inhabitants of the southern part of the state; his unlikely ascension to tribal chief; and his rollicking adventures as he takes on ruthless whalers who are drawn to the Cape. Eventually, our hero, John McJack, is forced to leave the Cape and lead his tribe north through Cumberland County, all the while fighting off the advances of ruthless white men who seek to exploit the land, *and* the people who had lived there for centuries before the ships started rolling in.

You'll have to read the book to find out more about the remarkable John McJack. In the meantime, let me tell you the equally remarkable story *behind* the story.

Around two years ago, a tall, silver-haired gentleman paid a visit to the offices of Exit Zero Publishing in Cape May. As usual, I was upstairs tapping away at my computer, wrestling with another project deadline (cue the violins) and, as usual, I was irked by having to walk downstairs to say hello to a stranger making a cold call (it happens often, and I should never complain, for great things can come from such chance encounters).

This time, I was greeted by a man with twinkling (they really do) blue eyes who told me his grandfather had written a book about this area a long time ago and would I like to read the manuscript? The man, George Carlisle, offered me a cardboard box that was torn at the edges and which at one time had contained Eagle-A typewriter paper made by the American Writing Paper Corporation, of Holyoke, Massachusetts.

Inside the box was a yellowed manuscript, the chapters held together by paper clips, many of which had rusted, leaving their outlines etched on the paper. Just how long ago was this story written, I asked George.

"Around the 1940s," he replied, adding that a prominent Philadelphia company, J. B. Lippincott & Co. (I later discovered that they published, among other great works, Harper Lee's *To Kill A Mockingbird* and Thomas Pynchon's *The Crying of Lot 49*), had wanted to publish the book back then, but that George's grandfather, Charles Whitecar Miskelly, had refused when Lippincott asked to make some (apparently minor) changes. A

In the name of the grandfather: George Carlisle at the offices of Exit Zero Publishing, with the original manuscript of this story, written by Charles Whitecar Miskelly.

curious thing since Mr Miskelly was a humble carpenter-turned-chicken farmer-turned-carpenter-again-when-the-chicken-business-crashed who presumably didn't receive these kinds of offers every day.

I was intrigued enough to take the box off George's hands and promised him I would get around to reading it. Back upstairs, I slid the box into one of 30 shelves in the huge hutch I had built by a local carpenter to resemble an old post office sorting desk. I pretend that it makes me more organized but, in reality, things go into those shelves and can disappear from my thoughts for quite a long time. Which is what happened to the old manuscript.

Around six months after George visited, he called to ask if I had read the story. I told him I hadn't but that I would get around to it. "No problem, Jack, I know you will read it. And I think you will really appreciate it," said George.

At least another six months went by before George called again. One of my colleagues picked up the phone and I thought about asking her to take a message, since I was embarrassed to admit I still hadn't got to the manuscript. But that would have been unworthy behavior, so I took the call. Again, George was upbeat and chirpy, not even a hint of impatience in his voice. "I know you're busy, and I know you will get around to it," said George.

And I did, about 18 months after George first visited me. One day last October I decided there would *never* be a time when I could feel unshackled enough to take the time to settle back in my office chair with a cup of tea in hand and leisurely work my way through the story, so I took it home and decided that no matter what, I would start the book that

Charles Miskelly (right) with his wife Ida, their daughter, son and daughter-in-law. Opposite page: Charles and Ida outside their home along the Maurice River in Cumberland County, NJ.

night. I figured I would read three or four chapters and quickly make up my mind about whether or not it was worth publishing. I'll admit — I went into it with very low expectations (the majority of submissions I receive from wannabe writers are on the mediocre side). But that night I read eight or nine of the 23 chapters and only stopped when sleep took over. As soon as I woke up the next morning, I read about six more. That night, I read another bunch, and finished the book the next morning.

I felt like I had discovered buried treasure. I didn't just love the story itself — I was also blown away by the beauty of the writing, by the remarkable detail in the descriptions of the landscape. One of my favorite writers is Thomas Hardy, the great 19th-century British novelist who made the environment a major character in almost all of his brilliant stories. Well, Charles Whitecar Miskelly did the same thing with the counties of Cape May and Cumberland (although they didn't exist when this story was set, in the 1600s). Shortly after finishing the book I called George, goosebumps appearing on my arms, and told him I would be delighted to publish the book. He was, naturally, thrilled — but not, I should say, surprised.

I followed up by sending George an email which explained the basics of how publishing works — I told him about the royalties we would offer and talked about the print run and distribution. I wrote the email as if he knew nothing about the publishing world, which is an assumption I had made. A big assumption.

Shortly after I wrote that email, I Googled George Carlisle just for the heck of it. All I knew is that he lived in Cambridge, Massachussets and loved to visit Cape May as often as possible (staying at the Chalfonte Hotel). Here's what I found in one story about him...

Carlisle, a University of Delaware graduate, received his Master of Fine Arts from the renowned Writing Workshop of the University of Iowa. He taught creative writing for 45 years

at St. Paul's School in Concord, NH — one of the top preparatory schools in the country — and was head of the English department for a period of time.

Turns out that George, who I had taken for a kindly old gentleman who simply wanted to do his grandfather a favor by having someone read his manuscript, had taught some very fine writers in his time, including the brilliant Nick Paumgarten, a staff writer for *The New Yorker*, and Rick Moody, an acclaimed novelist best known for *The Ice Storm*.

I was mortified and wrote another note to George, apologizing for what must have come across as a very patronizing email — here I was explaining the basics of the publishing industry to someone who seemed steeped in it. But he hadn't been offended in the least and was surprised I could even find him on Google. (George is as humble as he is charming.)

Later that year, George returned to our offices to tell us more about his grandfather, and that's when the story behind the writer became as intriguing as the book itself. Charles Whitecar Miskelly, for all his obvious skills with words, was no professional writer. He was born in 1880 and grew up in Millville, NJ. He became a carpenter, although he later gave that up to start a business breeding chickens. According to George, the enterprise didn't work out as Charles had hoped and sometime in the 1930s his grandfather lost everything. "He didn't have a cent to his name," said George, "so he went back into carpentry and did what he could to feed his family, but he definitely struggled."

George grew up in nearby Bridgeton and although he had more than a passing interest in writing, he didn't discuss literature with his grandfather. "We would go on fishing trips for the day — he loved to fish on the Maurice River. But he would never discuss writing. I was always aware that he wrote a lot, on a typewriter held together with fishing wire, but that was the extent of it." *On a typewriter held together with fishing wire.* You can see how easy it was to fall in love with the story of this book.

It was only after his grandfather passed away, in 1963 at the age of 83, that George discovered the manuscript and subsequently learned about the trip that Charles had made, with his uncle, to the Philadelphia office of J. B. Lippincott. "My grandfather was a shy man and he got cold feet about visiting the publisher, but my uncle apparently talked him into it," said George. "I don't know what happened in that office, but Lippincott were keen on putting the book on their fall print list. However, it all fell apart when they told Charles they wanted to make some changes. He was a proud man and I guess a stubborn one, too."

George kept the manuscript, along with other stories written by his grandfather, in a closet for a long time — more than 40 years. It was only when he retired, in 2008, that he decided to devote time to finally finding a publisher for Charles Whitecar Miskelly.

I feel proud, if I *can* be proud on behalf of a man who is no longer with us (and a man I never met), to finally present this compelling piece of work to the world, but full disclosure — I also felt guilty when I suggested to George that we had to change the title of his grandfather's manuscript, which was called *Moons of the Manitou*. George agreed with me that this title was too abstract, though I still wonder if Charles, even with the benefit of hindsight (and the gift of eternal life), would have agreed to such a change. I also made some minor changes to dialogue, tamping down some of the 17th-century lingo, which was a little overbearing in places. But other than that, the book is untouched, as impressive today as it was to the editors at J. B. Lippincott six or so decades ago.

For me, the most intriguing part of the story is the author's note, which you will find on the next page. My initial instinct was that Charles was using a bit of artistic licence, allowing the reader to believe that there was some truth to this story. But I changed my mind after I read the book — I was astonished by the detailed descriptions of the Lenni-Lenape way of life. This was someone who had either done a huge amount of research into Native American culture, or who had substantial personal experience of it. Given that Charles wrote this book in rural South Jersey (about 60 years before Google came along) and wasn't given to taking day trips to visit the Free Library of Philadelphia, for instance, it made me wonder how on earth he could have had access to this kind of information. It made George wonder, too. "It's a big mystery to everyone in the family how he would have known so much about the indian way of life," he said. "Sure, he would maybe go away fishing for the day, or walking in the woods. But that doesn't explain how he could have learned so much about the Lenni-Lenape people."

Does George think the author's note is genuine? That this story really *is* based on a true story passed along by tribal elders? Or could Charles have been the kind of man who would play a little fast and loose, trying to pass his manuscript off as an authentic story rooted in Lenni-Lenape tradition. "No, not at all," said George. "He was a serious man, a man of principles. The whole thing is fascinating to me. I wish he were still around to ask."

So do I.

By the way, I looked up the company who made the paper on which Charles typed his story — the American Writing Paper Corporation began operations in 1899 at Holyoke, MA, and at its peak controlled 75% of the country's fine paper output. The company went out of business in 1962. On the side of the box is a little blue stamp that says Cohanzick Office Supply Co., who were based in Bridgeton, which neighbors Charles' home town of Millville. I don't know who owned the office supply shop, but was curious to see that Bridgeton's zoo (the oldest in New Jersey) is named Cohanzick. After a little bit of keyboard research, I discovered that the zoo was named for the Cohanzick tribe of Lenni-Lenape indians who at one time lived alongside the Cohansey River in Bridgeton.

It made me wonder — did Charles Whitecar Miskelly buy the box of typewriter paper from an office supply company owned by a Lenni-Lenape family? Did he have connections to the tribe that even his own family didn't know about? Printer deadlines prevented me from digging any deeper, but if there's a reprint (a boy can dream), maybe I will be able to discover more about the story behind the story.

And now, that's more than enough musing from me... if I were you, I'd go ahead and read the story of John McJack.

AUTHOR'S NOTE

Many years ago, in the Cape May country of Southern New Jersey, the old people told fragments of a strange story. Now the old people are gone, and the younger generation has almost forgotten the story. From as many fragments as could be remembered, the author has, to the best of his ability, recreated it.

Its relation to written history is decidedly vague, inasmuch as the events occurred before the Cape was occupied by the whites, and its history was only recorded in the unwritten legends of the Lenni Lenape, "red people who live by the sea".

CHARLES WHITECAR MISKELLY, circa 1940

Chapter 1

THE first white man to see the mainland of what would later be New Jersey, and especially the southern end of it, was one Estevão Gomez in 1525, but nobody did anything about it for nearly a century. The land, between its bay and its ocean, lay as it had for ages. Its people, of the tribe of Lenni-Lenape, walked its woods and beaches, and where the brightly colored stones lay strewn upon the bar, they watched the sea and marveled at the winged ships that rode on the sea. But no ship, and no white man, ever came to their shore.

And then, one winter day when a change of wind blew the mists away to let the sun show red beyond the waters of the bay, a ship seemed to sail away from the land. From behind the point of the cape, where the land hooked its finger between the bay and the ocean to form a harbor, the ship sailed out to the sea. It left the shore where the little stream trickled down from the sweet-water pond among the cedar trees, where at the foot of the wooded slope a little band of red people lived, back a way from the beach.

There were a dozen wigwams or tepees, made of skins and bark, each with the totem of the turtle painted on its walls. Each home had its problems, of food and shelter and water. Commonplace things through commonplace ages, until that winter day when the strange ship moved through the east-wind mists and sailed away when the wind had changed to the west.

From the sandy and wooded bluff some five miles to the north, almost as far as the little creek which shoved its salted and twisting thread through the narrow and tree-girt meadow, Wawakna, chief of another band, saw the ship sail away. He stood on the bluff with his daughter, Minyanata, who was eight years old. Forgetting both dignity and daughter, Wawakna shouted and pointed. From the town among the trees, back a little from the bay, his people came running. And Lagunaka, too, the medicine man. All stood and wondered. They were frightened, too, because how could the ship sail away from the land without first having come to it?

No one had seen the ship come in, but Wawakna gravely explained that this was because of the mists. But Lagunaka pondered. Wise in the ways of devils and such, the magician doubted. He believed there was devilry in the wind. He would make a brew and sing a song and shake a rattle, and do what he could to fend off the evil.

However, because of the quarrel between the two camps, none could go down to the point to see what had happened. In the morning Wawakna would send a wampum down to seek the peace and learn the news. But the night wind shifted to the north of east; for four long days a blizzard blew; the snow piled high in the trails. The mystery of the ship could wait a while, and with the waiting the fear of the people lessened. Perhaps, the ship hadn't been leaving the harbor at all; more likely it had been sailing along the coast, as others had done. After his brew and his song, and especially after the blizzard had begun to blow, Lagunaka explained that the distance had been deceptive: the ship had sailed past the point of land and not from it.

Lagunaka, a jealous man, was extremely isolationist. The magician down by the pond would not agree with him on many matters, and this had been responsible for the neighborhood ill feeling. So things continued as they were until after warm weather had come. But the important point was this: what one ship had done another could do.

Other ships had passed the cape. One was the *Half Moon* of Captain Henry Hudson, exploring new waterways on his way to the great river and bay which would bear his name. Bypassing the cape, leaving the naming of it to Captain Cornelius Mey, of the ship *Glad Tidings*.

It was in April, eight years later, when Minyanata was sixteen and John McJack an uncertain 23 that McJack came ashore on a piece of timber, about a mile from the point of the cape and four miles below Wawakna's camp, up on the bluff.

For more than three hours McJack lay on the beach without even the strength to pull himself the rest of the way out of the water. Half unconscious, he lay with the waves lapping about his waist, then his knees, and then his ankles as the tide receded, leaving him on the hard-packed sand.

The skin of his arms was bloody from gripping a broken timber while the wind howled and the waves buried him in the rush of water. As he slowly moved his arms across the sand of the beach, he heard the crunch as the ship crashed the bar in the thunder squall, the cracking of the planking, and the screams of the crew.

McJack dug his hands into the sand and pulled them back painfully to his side and then stretched them over his head again as if he were swimming. He groaned, opened his eyes, and saw the beach, the marsh, the high ground, and the forest.

"Praise to god and all his saints who brought me through." He raised himself slowly to his knees and added, "And the saints help all who didn't make it," as he saw the litter from the wreck along the edge of the water. A few feet away from him lay the timber with the crooked handle of his adze emerging, its blade sunk deep in the wood.

"And what is this?" he asked himself as he drew his hand across the sand and collected shiny colored stones in his fingers. "Be I lucky enough to land on a bejeweled beach?"

But his exhaustion made his interest short-lived. The sun was setting, and he realized that soon the tide would come back in an effort to reclaim him. He crawled himself beyond the reach of the water where the sand was soft and soon fell asleep.

The next morning, stiff and sore from the night and starved after more than a day without food, he stood on the beach where the forest came clear to the shore, watching the birds come over the water. He was appalled by his loneliness. Except for the visible birds and the invisible beasts, his world seemed empty of living things. But McJack shrugged his shoulders and gave thanks for his adze to the saints an 'all, and raked some clams from among the stones. He wandered down the beach and drank from a little stream.

There was wreckage, broken boards and timbers and pieces of sail, but, thanking the saints again, no bodies. "Best they should rest where they be," McJack decided. "Mayhap they be better than me, at that." He had no doubt that the woods were full of wild animals, and probably wild men. Probably they were watching him that minute. He decided it was fortunate the saints were on his side.

He found some canvas and enough lumber to make himself a hut between the reach of the tide and the line of the forest. And that night falling asleep with an empty stomach, he was grateful for his canvas-covered shelter, though he crouched and shivered. There were strange sounds in the dark. An owl. A fox yelped shrilly. And once when McJack had dozed a little because the owl and the fox and the night were still, there came a scream from the dark.

"Saints help me now!" pleaded John McJack. "It's the devil let loose in the land, and all, to set me teeth a' chatter with the fright. Or mayhap it were the banshee call: Saints send the mornin' sun to shine and stop me shivers!"

Next morning, brave in the light of it, or desperate because of hunger, he ventured into the woods, frightened a cougar away from the carcass of a fawn, and broke his fast on raw venison, using the adze blade for a knife. The meat was young and not too tough, and the blood trickled down through the stubble on his chin.

"For a flint and steel I would pay, but I've naught with which to pay, so what I shall get I must take. I wonder why the land be so scarce with men? I had heard there were injuns in all of the coastlands. Mayhap some thing be wrong with this land. Mayhap that were a banshee call! McJack, be wise and wary! Ye must, whilst ye wander in the wood."

But that day, and in spite of his own advice, he did a foolish thing: he chased a tiny bear cub and brought the mother charging at him from a thicket. By a miracle, or by the grace of the saints and all, the battle was short. McJack drove the pin of the adze through the animal's skull. She reared and roared, spun round and round, the adze handle swaying. She pawed at the thing, and then her spine crumpled and she fell and slowly died while McJack, white-faced and shaking, stood and watched.

That was how he got his robe of stinking bear hide, and the cub for a pet. He christened it Saint Pat. It took until dusk to remove the great hide, and then he moved away from the carcass lest it draw other beasts in the night. He went back to the more open shore of the bay. At first the cub bit his fingers, but later it cuddled down in his arms.

"Sure," said McJack, "ye be something to talk to, though ye be too young and too dumb to sense that I murdered your mother, and to hold it against me. But this night we can sleep more warm in her hide, do we sleep at all. "And," he added, "Saints send yer daddy, if ye had one, some other place, else he should come searching. Saint Pat, me lad, quit yer squirming now, would ye know yer own dad did ye see him? Seems that I've heard ye would not at all. By all the laws of righteous men, I reckons yerself a bastard! Seems that a bear be like some men: he will get a wench with child and leave her to bear it. And fend for it too. Saints grant that I have not done that same; I cannot be sure!"

This set McJack to thinking of his sins. He made a little prayer for forgiveness, while he crouched in his sailcloth shack and heard the raindrops. Another April shower, and McJack slept a little under his stinking bear hide, cuddling Saint Pat lest he wander away. "Saint Pat, me lad," he told the cub, "I needs ye to talk to, lest me head be addled with the loneliness. I do, at that!"

Next day he went back to the carcass of the bear; some beasts had been at it. There were cat tracks in the sand, McJack nodded. "Mayhap it will lure the beasts from me," he reasoned. "I will search a bit further in the wood and stay away from here come night." And he hadn't gone more than a hundred yards inland when he came to a trail. It led down toward the point and up to the north. It was almost a yard wide, winding between the thickets and under the towering trees.

"It's a great highway of a sort, I will wager a wagon," said McJack to the cub. He grinned. "And do I win that wagon, we will climb aboard and ride." He scratched his head, felt meditatively his chin where the whiskers were sprouting. "Sure, the path were made by the feet of men, though no tracks show. Mayhap it's because of the rain in the night. Where it leads up yonder I cannot tell, but to the south it cannot go so far: it would be stopped by the sea. I will go down yon and learn, but slow, and takinh care. There may be injuns there. They may be good or bad. McJack, ye cannot wander long alone in the wood. Mayhap do ye find them, the Injuns will kill ye. Ye will take the path to the sea."

He went warily, pausing at every turn of the trail. Watching for footprints of men. But he found none, even when the way dipped down into a spot of marshland that wet his feet. On to the south for nearly a mile, through thicketed tunnels and open places, then beneath towering cedars. The path went through and crossed a tiny stream, two cedar logs for a bridge. These were old, beginning to rot, but McJack walked over, adze in his right hand and Saint Pat in his left arm, the pack strapped across his shoulders.

"This land be accursed," he muttered. "Almost I fears to go on, but go I must. This path leads to somewhere to be sure. I wonder what?"

There was a thicket of briars beyond the bridge and then the land sloped upward to pines and oaks and locust trees and to what had been a campsite. The stream under the bridge ran to a little pond; beyond stood the towering cedars, reflected in the water. Their tops swayed in the springtime breeze, but the water was still.

Not a soul was in sight, no wigwams nor tepees. McJack crossed himself and whispered a charm against pixies and elves and leprechauns... "or injuns, live ones or dead ones. More like it will be the dead, for the life has been burned from the very soil. Naught grows but trees where once the people lived. And there be dead cedars hung with the root ends up, about the camp. I wonder."

McJack walked warily across the campsite. The only sound at the moment was the sea; he could faintly hear the breakers on the ocean shore. Down the stream course he could glimpse the bay, for the marsh ran clear to the waters there.

McJack shivered. 'Saint Pat," said he, "we have a deadened world to our lonesome selves. We have at that! Where be the people that were here before? Why be the place so still?" And he dared the stillness with a loud "Ahoy!"

"Ahoy!" replied the echo from among the cedars. "Ahoy," it whispered from beyond the bridge, and McJack made the sign of the cross again. "There be naught in the place, and I be afeared of it," he confessed. "Sure, it did sound like a voice from the dead. I will not shout again at all. I will keep closed the mouth of me, for I've learned before now that this same mouth can bring me into trouble. What means that heap of soil over yon? What means these cedars hanging by their tails to swing in the wind?"

These cedar tips had touched and swept the ground. The heap in the center showed the ends of charred sticks. Pieces of pottery had been washed out by the rains. The shaft of an arrow protruded. And where some beast had dug in the soil were feathers, as from a bonnet. These were scorched a little.

McJack drew a deep breath. He glanced around and put the bear cub down. With his adze he dragged the bonnet from the sand.

"Aye, it were once a crown of some heathen sort," he surmised. "Did I dig in the dirt I might find the man as wore it, the which I shall not do at all. Saints ask the god to give these people peace — it seems the whole village has died, but, then, they could not cover in the sand. Two things be plain," he reasoned, "either some were left or others came and did it. A dead man, do he be alone, lies where he falls. As will I, mayhap. Which is not a glad thought at all; I will not think it. I be still alive; me hunger tells me so. Wait, what have I found?! A footprint of a man! He wears some sort of soften shoe. McJack, ye should be wary, for mayhap ye be seen! Ye cannot tell."

But although during the day he found more footprints he could not trail them nor find the man. "Mayhap he were but passing by, the same as myself," he conjectured as toward evening he stood by the bay to watch the lonely sunset. He inquired Saint Pat's opinion, but the bear only blinked, and McJack broke the shell of a clam for him, and the cub dined daintily.

"Ye would rather have milk," surmised McJack, "but that I cannot give ye; I never was shaped to that at all. So we will go back to the edge of this town for the night, for it's plain the injuns shun the spot and do not tarry there. Ghosts and goblins may be there, but we must risk them. They might fright the guts from a man, but a spirit be less deadly than a spear in the dark."

So he pitched his tent on the edge of the camp among some saplings and he and his bear cub huddled inside. By that time the bear skin was rank indeed, but the stink was better than the cold, for during the night the frost came down. The new moon was growing; it glinted on the frost and showed clear the surface of the pond, where the cedars reflected their blackness. The bare branches of the trees made serpentine marks on the sand of the campsite, and the sound of the surf sang faintly. No beasts made a sound, although the ducks in the bay seemed to quack at the moon at times. Perhaps these had awakened McJack.

Cramped by his sleeping and with an ache in his knees, he pushed aside his robe and crawled out of his tent. There he was among the saplings; when he stood his head was above them. He could see the pond, and the cedars, and the shapes on the sand among the boles of the trees, there in the glint of the frost. But he saw only dimly, because frost was still falling. He stooped to rub his knees, then stood upright again. He drew a sort of gasping breath and again he whispered his charm word. And he called on his saints. He shivered, for a chill worse than frost had gone up his spine.

Off in the camp among the shades, there where the sand was heaped in its pile, a gray shape showed. It walked slowly; had it not been a ghost it would have seemed feeble. It came toward McJack and stood in the moonlight. It wore a gray cloak, and its beard was white. It raised a hand as if pointing to the moon and, as if obedient, the moon went back behind a cloud. Then the gray thing vanished in the gloom.

"Saints Mary and Michael!" he whispered. "What be the thing, and all?" But nobody answered, and McJack kept his watch until dawn. The ghost didn't show again. It seemed to have vanished in the heap of sand where McJack was sure that the dead men lay. One, perhaps, had been restless; he had risen to walk the night.

"Can I but live to see the light," declared McJack, "I will leave this place far behind."

But in the morning, when he found fresh footprints where the thing had stood, his courage came back, with the warmth and light of the sun. So he tried to follow the tracks, but they led over pine needles and fallen leaves, and he lost them. After that he found some ducks' eggs, and he choked a little as he sucked them. Saint Pat ate an egg and some grubs that he found. He followed slowly while his master walked around the campsite and into the woods. Then they headed for the dunes behind the meadow.

They rounded a thicket of beach plums. And beyond it, squatting in the sun, clad in a long and ragged coat with woods leaves clinging to it, was the man. His long hair was white and his beard hung down on his chest, his head bowed in sleep. He was so thin that the coat pouched out in great wrinkles, and his hands showed the lines of their bones.

"God help the man!" whispered McJack. "He were no ghost at all. Mayhap he were cast ashore the same as I. He sleeps by day and walks the wood by night. The man looks daft, small wonder. How shall I wake him, now?"

He pondered a moment, looking up and down the shore for caution's sake. Then: "Ahoy, kind sir! Would ye wake and give yer greetings to a friend?"

The man slowly raised his head and opened his eyes; these were a faded blue and held a vacant stare.

McJack told him gently, "I be a friend; I means no harm at all. I gives ye greetings. And how come ye here?"

But the man didn't answer. He slowly got to his feet, and in his eyes was a look of disbelief. He came forward and seemed to grope for McJack's hand. He ran his fingers along his arm, he held his own head sideways to see McJack's face, and said strange words that made no sense at all, except for his sobbing.

McJack's eyes were misty; he stooped to put the bearcub down. St. Pat walked over to the edge of the thicket, as indifferent to what was going on as seemed the rest of the wild and empty world. The long beach where the waves rolled in, cresting and breaking from out in the sea. The endless thicketed forest there, the dunes and meadows up the shore. The sun which shone upon it all just as it had done for thousands of years.

McJack's voice was croaky: "I be a friend, though it's no wonder that ye weep for joy. Ye have not seen a living man for a long time, I'll warrant me. Can ye speak to me now? Can ye tell me how ye come, and how ye fared?

But convulsively, the man threw both hands above his head and fell. His body shuddered and was still. McJack stood watching, then felt for a heartbeat as he knelt beside him. He crossed himself. "The man be dead! Seems he has died of the muchness of his joy: it were too great for the poor old heart to stand. Saints pray to god for his soul!"

Already McJack had been long enough alone to sense what the other had suffered, and a chilling fear ran through his mind. "It may be thus with me."

He was as alone as the other had been, except for his bear cub. Saint Pat, still indifferent, lay down in the sun to snooze, and McJack was alone with the living mystery of the dead man there. A mystery without a sequel, it would seem, for had the man lived he could not have spoken to McJack. The latter sensed this from his speech. "Mayhap he were Dutch," he surmised. "I cannot tell."

McJack buried the man beside his hut, using the oar blade as a shovel. He thrust the scabbard into the ground, and the broken handle made a cross. He took for his own the deerskin roll and the flint and steel, and walked up the beach to further learn the lay of the land. There were the dunes and the meadows, and there must be a tidal stream too, he decided, because thousands of ducks rose into the air when an eagle flow over. Then McJack went back to the town site by the pond.

"In the morn I will tread that northern trail and see what I find. I will not sit and watch the sea for succor, and go daft with the watching as that other has done. Mayhap, being daft, he were the one who hung these cedars by their tails; I like not their looks at all."

So, next morning, before he left, he cut the thongs and let the trees fall. They crackled and bounced heavily. "And that be that," he concluded. "They made no sense hanging there at all."

Chapter 2

The trail to the north ran through mingled growths of gums and pines and elms and oaks and locust trees. Ancient trees that arched above John McJack's head. Or it went between thickets at the edges of little spots of marsh, where giant cedars thrust their branchless trunks like green crowned columns toward the sky, making midday dusk down near the ground. Along the edges of the marsh were bracken and fern and briar. Magnolia and huckleberry and what-not, too.

"It's a fruitful soil, said McJack. "It be a goodly land, for them as would like it. This be a mighty wood; there be timber here to build a score of London towns, yet never has an axe been laid upon a tree!" He shifted his pack by a shrug of a shoulder. Then, with a whimsical chuckle: "I will claim this land which no other seems to own. I will be Sir John McJack, the lord of it all! I will. Yon goes another highway; it leads across to the bay, branching off through me own fine park. Best I had see what I owns back yon. Mayhap some of my serfs have chose the spot to live. Best I had see."

So he walked the greater part of the mile toward the bay, slowly and with caution. Watching at every crook and bend, but there were no moccasin tracks in the sand at all. Only the ancient trend of the trail itself to show that men had ever gone that way. Soon he could see the shine of the bay, off between the open trees.

For back from the wooded shore was another deserted camp. To the north was young growth: cedars and sassafras and sprouting pine as high as his head; deserted by man, the farms were going back to nature. The shoreline was low; the beach was littered with those uncut "diamonds." Caught by the sun, some showed their colors there: green and blue, pale amber, while others were as white as milk. Clams lay among the stones, the tide half ebb. McJack put his pack and adze and bear cub down. Gathered perhaps a dozen of the stones, choosing carefully for color and size.

"I know not what they be," he told Saint Pat. 'Mayhap they be of worth, and do they be I have more wealth than any king, though there be no sale in all this lonely land. But they will serve for tossing. I must not lose the skill of my hands, though there be none to see." So he juggled the stones, up and down and around. They glistened as they sped and looped. Like magic. McJack hummed a little song, there in the sunlight. Visualized an audience on a village street, or on the deck of a ship, or perhaps at an alehouse.

But the only applause was the sound of the waters of the bay, the song of the birds in the trees inshore. "Alack!" sighed Sir John. "Alack, bedamned!"

Before he went back the way he had come he looked out upon the bay again, maybe seeking a sail or a sight of the other shore. Instead, he saw a whale: a long dark spot out there. Up shore he could see a sandy, tree-grown bluff jutting into the bay, showing the pink and yellow of its eroding sands against the northern sky and the line of the bay beyond. The trees on the bluff were as yet bare of leaves; it looked rather desolate, seen from what looked like an abandoned camp below.

But that was where Wawakna lived, with his people. McJack, of course, couldn't know, looking across those two miles or more; there was no one in sight. The wigwams, set back as they were from the shore, didn't show. And no one there, as events would prove, had seen McJack.

"It's an empty world," he sighed. 'A wood, and a sea, and a highway, and none but meself to use them all. But I will search. I will not settle by the sea to watch, and starve, and grow white whiskers and be daft with the loneliness, while I wait for a ship to come. I be hungry; I must search some food, for I cannot wait again for a cat to catch another fawn. Deer tracks be plenty in the soil. And quail fly up from the bracken at times, and a hare runs off with his white tail a' bobbing. There be food, could I catch it."

He stood at the inshore edge of the camp. Looked back and around at the spots where the homes had been, marked by bareness of soil and the rain-leached ashes of long dead fires.

"I wonder why they left the land. Were it because of the curse that seems upon it? But this camp do differ from that at the pond: it seems these people have just walked away. I wonder why. I cannot know, but I will do the same — me bear cub and all."

When near the main trail he came to a sort of open glade. Indian grass grew there, yellow and shining in the sun, the new shoots not yet showing. There was a sassafras sapling beside the cross-trail, and a clump of laurel. McJack glanced casually at the grass.

Seemed to see something unusual there: a round and unblinking eye. Long ears held back. A brown form huddled in the grass.

Carefully McJack put down his cub, and then his pack. Adze held loosely in his hand he walked stealthily to a spot behind the rabbit. Perhaps the creature was watching Saint Pat where he sat in the pathway, sniffing at the pack which contained the hide of his mother. He needn't have sniffed; he could have smelled the thing with ease. Perhaps the rabbit smelled it too; he twitched his splitted nose. Sat still and waited. And he waited a bit too long.

"Praise to the saints, and the dumbness of the beast that he sat so still — I have got me a feast! But first I must open me pack to get me flint and steel, thanking the man who no longer needs it. And I will spread me robe upon this bush, for the airing. Judged by its stink that robe be about to rot!"

And then he tinkered with his flint and steel and tinder, there in the midday sun. This shone with a lazy warmth. Saint Pat backed off and sat in the trail when the first flame showed. Sat still and watched, not daring to come closer. Sniffed at the scent of it and felt an inborn fear. McJack grinned as he skinned the rabbit and wished he had some water to wash away the blood. But he wiped his hands on the grass instead. Sat cross-legged on the ground to attend to his cooking, the rabbit propped over the fire on a stick. He hummed a little ditty, forgetting for the moment his fears.

Up in that camp on the bluff Wawakna sat by his wigwam in the sun. There were perhaps a score of the houses set roughly in a circle among the trees. Here and there, in the open, some little fires were burning; one had a pot on its coals. Nearby, two women were pounding corn. Another came from an inland spring with water in an earthen bowl. Two others were dressing a deerskin. A man was stringing a brand new bow; another smoothed an arrow shaft with a stone. Two babies hung from an open branch in their cradleboards. Lagunaka, the magician, sat just inside his wigwam; one could see his back but not what he was doing.

Wawakna, the chief, took the eagle feather from his plaited, graying hair and used its quill to scratch his scalp; then he yawned and smiled lazily at one of his silent thoughts, and reached for his pipe. His wife came out of the wigwam and scolded him for using so much tobacco. Wawakna grinned at his woman and requested a coal from the fire. All seemed well with his little world; the winter was gone; the early spring sun was shining; he knew that the women were at work in the field, back in the woods where the soil was more fertile, getting ready to plant again. Why should he worry? The spirits had been reasonably kind. There was no sickness among his people, and no more than a natural hunger. So Wawakna went on with his smoking.

Back in one of the fields, Minyanata was working with some other women. Digging the soil with tools of stone. Clearing last year's rubbish away. Preparing to plant, in a month or so, the corn and beans and squash and tobacco. But she felt disinclined to toil. Perhaps her thoughts were more of romance than of work. Perhaps, out of the woods from far away, would some day come a man so tall and straight and bravely kind that she would choose him for a mate. The red-wing, over on the meadow there, as he swung on last year's reed, was calling. That she knew, though she couldn't hear him. Sweet and clear the red-wing sang: "Come over he-re! Come over he-re!" In any tongue that was what he sounded like, the red-wing. His love call in the springtime.

Minyanata, the fairest maiden in the land, tall for her age and slender and lithe, was slyly working away from the others. Edging toward the little trail. Carrying last year's stalks to the edge of the forest.

Suddenly the girl wasn't working. Instead, she was running down the trail toward the main one. She would go for a walk. Listen to the red-wing. Watch the squirrels in the tree tops. She had small fear of her father's wrath, for the chief was inclined to spoil her. At least that was what the other women thought. Perhaps she presumed on her social position as the daughter of the chief. "If nobody worked any more than she," grumbled the women, "the whole band would starve, come winter!" They hoped that when she married, her husband would be stern.

Minyanata knew what they would say, but she laughed as she ran along. Coming to the main trail, she paused. Took a moment to consider. Should she go north or south? She had no particular errand but, because of the tales the others would tell, perhaps to her father or even to Lagunaka, she had best invent one. She would placate Lagunaka; she would go toward the south, for down that way grew a pungent shrub that the man would need for his springtime brew, to help with his magic.

But she wouldn't go too far to the south; in these later years none of her people went very far, for down that way, down where the bay and ocean met, in and near the Camp by the Pond, the Curse still lay upon the land. This was a strange and fearsome thing which came — or so it had been deduced from the signs they had seen — when white men came to the land in unseen ships. And the people died and lay where they fell, and on the beach and through the woods the Gray Thing walked to this very day!

Some of the men of her camp, daring briefly to go down, had seen the Gray Thing from afar. It was shaped like a man, but Lagunaka declared it was a devil. He had made magic against it but had only succeeded in keeping it down near that other camp. Had held it to its woods and beaches there. Some day, when his magic was very strong, he had hopes of killing the Gray Thing. Meanwhile the people must stay away. Both the chief and the magician has said so.

So Minyanata would only go to where that cross-trail led down to the bay. Even that was further than the other women dared to go, and she felt a thrill from being so brave. Perhaps she doubted Lagunaka's powers of both magic and deduction for she reasoned in her youthful conceit that the magician had never proved much of either.

But, although more practical than some others and inclined to form her own opinions, she had no intention of daring any further. Down near that side trail she loitered a little. Gathered a bit of that pungent shrub along with some brew-berries — to placate

Lagunaka should the women carry tales. Of her mother she had little fear; she wouldn't do worse than scold her.

Suddenly the girl raised her head. Startled, she looked quickly around. Sniffed at the air; was she catching the smell of smoke? She frowned and slowly turned her head in half a circle, breathing deeply through her nostrils. Yes; she surely could smell it, though faintly, from somewhere in the direction of the bay. Perhaps from along the cross-trail there. She must investigate the matter, though with caution. None of her people were supposed to be down there, unless the men had come down to scout. To see if the Curse were still on the land. If, down at the pond the cedars still hung from the oaks, or if the strange Gray Thing were walking.

But in that case they wouldn't build a fire; the Gray Thing might smell it and come. Unless, of course, Lagunaka himself should make a fire, for his magic. But the magician, she was very sure, was still in the camp on the bluff. So this present responsibility was in a way her own, and it made her pulse beat strongly, partly from curiosity but mostly from fear: it was just possible that the Gray Thing had ventured father north. Perhaps *it* had built the fire, to counteract Lagunaka's. Perhaps, even, this smell of smoke was only the breath of the Thing!

Minyanata moved down to that cross-trail, and stopped. She trembled a little. Even took a half-running step or two toward home. Then stood and listened intently, although poised on her toes for flight. Her eyes searched down the cross-trail; she thought she saw a wisp of smoke, but wasn't certain. Then she bent forward, to listen.

For down there someone — or something — was singing. The voice was that of a man. Not loud, but deep, and the tongue was strange; she couldn't understand it at all. It must be a devil song for sure! The Gray Thing was making its own magic, perhaps against her people, not daring to come closer for fear of Lagunaka's charms!

Minyanata trembled as she stood and listened. Took another step toward home, then clamped her white teeth together. Her fear was great, but her curiosity was very strong. If she ran away and went back home it would torment her. In the nights she would hear it and fear it, not knowing what it could be. Not knowing if — Lagunaka's charms failing to keep it away — the Gray Thing would come to the camp on the bluff as it had done by the pond, there where the red people all had died, along with the three white men: the ones who must have come in some unseen ship, for her people had found the bodies there, along with the red ones, and had seen no ship come to shore. But there on the trail this voice went on:

> *Ho-ho, we sail the seas!*
> *Ho-ho, we walk the leas!*
> *Ho-ho, and away we go*
> *A' searchin' for a maiden!*
> *Ho-ho, we find that same!*

Ho-ho, we find a dame!
Ho-ho, and away we go
Still searchin' for a maiden!

And the only words the girl could understand were the "ho-hos" for her own men sang them in their dances. Minyanata backed away from the cross-trail, then clenched her fists as if she stifled her fears with her fingers. She cautiously stole toward the song and the smell of the smoke. Taking cover behind a laurel as she went, or a tree or a pathside thicket. Stealing from one to the other. Determined to see, even if it killed her. Then she crouched behind some laurel.

Out there beyond the little fire, beside a sassafras tree and a laurel bush, the sun shining down on the back of his head — he facing the east — sat what looked to the girl like a man. Not the Gray Thing at all, as she had feared. Perhaps she breathed more easily then, although her eyes grew wide with wonder. For on the laurel bush was the great skin of a bear; in the pathway sat a tiny cub; and over the fire was a rabbit. But the man himself was the wondrous thing, for such a man she had never seen. His shirt was brown; on his head was a strange hat. But it wasn't his appearance as greatly as what he was doing — was he making his magic with those stones from the beach? Was he laying a charm or a curse, the while he chanted?

"Ho-ho, and away we go
A' searchin' for a maiden!
Ho-ho, we sail the seas!"

For while he sang his hands moved quick as light. Sitting there, he tossed the stones into the air and seemed to chase them up and down and then around. Back over his shoulder now and then, and the westering sun caught the glint of them there, and the colors, and the speed. Surely no man could be so swift with his hands and so sure with his sight. This thing was magic. The white man's magic, perhaps, or else why did he sing that song with none to hear, and display his skill with none to see? And then, when the song seemed done, the man bent his body a little aside, and the stones rained down and vanished. They went into the side of the belly of the man! Minyanata saw them do it. Even heard the clicking sound they made, striking themselves together.

And next the man did another wondrous thing: this was the way he arose to his feet. First he placed his hands on the ground before him, then with no apparent effort his body came up, inverted, and his legs and feet came over his body to the ground, and the man — if he was a man at all — stood erect on his feet, like any other.

Then with his right hand he took from the ground a strange thing on a crooked stick; with his left he grasped the sassafras tree near the top, and with one blow of the that thing on a stick cleft the tree at its trunk! Tossed the little tree aside as if such a deed were a trifle.

McJack was breathing deeply and his eyes looked hard at the laurel. "Saint Pat," he whispered to the cub, "did my eyes tell true there was a face beyond yon bush?! I glimpsed the same as I came to me feet! But mayhap I were wrong; we will go and see."

But he found no sign nor footprint in the trail. He followed the path to the main one, watching sharply. In a softer spot was a footprint. It pointed northward. The print of the toes was deeper, as if made while running.

McJack's pulse was pounding a little: "Sure, it would not be a man, full-growed. May-hap a lad — or a maiden. It could be a maiden, by the look of it." He scratched his head, perplexed. "Sure, man or maiden, it will be able to tell its tale. I wonder what that tale will tell. Mayhap it will say there be a lunatic at large! Mayhap it will bring the whole tribe down. Mayhap they will pin me to a tree with a shaft! Or mayhap they would be friends? I scarce can tell the best to do — to stay and wait, or flee to the woods. One thing I will do: I will eat me roasted hare. If I die it shall not be of hunger." And he grinned rather wryly as he thought things over. Wondered while he ate if his hidden audience had been a maiden.

Minyanata had come quite close to home before she slowed her pace, and she'd been thinking things over as she ran: it would not do to rush into camp and create a panic. She had learned her fear of panic from her father.

Wawakna was sitting before his wigwam. Minyanata approached quietly but the old chief frowned. Already he knew that she had played truant from the field; he pretended to be stern, aware that the other women were watching — curious, perhaps a bit jealous.

So Wawakna gestured for the girl to stand before him: "My daughter, my ears have heard that you have again run away from work. The women are angry. They have told the tale to Lagunaka. What have you to say?" And, although from where the women watched he looked so stern, a tiny smile showed in his eyes and mouth. Perhaps a bit of admiration, too, and pride.

"My father, I have strange news. Send me into the wigwam, and then come."

Wawakna caught the cue. "You will," sternly and more loudly, "go into the wigwam. I will come later."

These wiles concluded, and hiding his awakened curiosity, the chief sat for a few minutes and then followed his daughter. Two of the other women nodded: "She'll catch it now," was the implication.

But in the wigwam all remained quiet, listen though they would. No loud voice nor wailing. Then Wawakna came out and quietly crossed the camp to where three other men were sitting. He spoke in a low tone and one of the men went off to fetch others. The women watched and whispered. This wasn't what they'd expected at all. A group of young men came in from the hunt; they too seemed curious. Half an hour later each trail that came into camp had a sentry hidden beside it. In the Lodge House, larger than the wigwams, a private council was being held. There were seven of the older men, including Lagunaka. Minyanata stayed in her wigwam, thinking things over. A girlfriend went in to visit, but Minyanata wouldn't tell the secret. Her father had told her not to, fearing panic.

In the Lodge House, Wawakna was speaking. First came a long preamble, as was the custom. This concerned the glories of the red man's past, and he told of the tales they had heard when visitors came down in the summers. How in the land of the Algonquians, where Powhatan ruled, the white men had already come to the shore in great winged ships. Had built houses there and taken the Indian farms for their own.

"We had thought, at first, that the tales were but whispers on the wind. Whispers caught by the ears of men and passed along. We had not been sure, for we know that whispers grow to shouts: small tales grow large and carry far, as eaglets grow to be eagles and scale the sky."

"And then one day so many winters gone" — he held up eight fingers — "we saw from here a great ship leave the land, there by the end of it, where the east wind is broken and the sea lies calm behind the land. But that time the men from the ship did our people no harm; they took water from the stream and sailed away, while our people by the pond hid in the woods and watched.

"But what has been can be again: three winters past another must have come, but mist was on the waters and we could not see. Then came the snows; the trails were filled, and there was a quarrel between our people and those at the pond. But when the snows were gone, and the quarrel was done, we found that all of the people there had died, and three white men from the ship. A curse had fallen on the land down there.

"So we called a council of all the other camps, and it was decreed that the people be buried, their wigwams burned, and that cedars be hung about the camp by thongs. These, sweeping in the wind, would clear away the curse, and when that was done — and not before — the cedars would fall to the ground. Until that time no man should set his foot upon the soil."

"And more than that, the Gray Thing began to walk in the woods and on the shore. Our young men, scouting from afar, could see the Thing. Two seasons or more it had walked alone. Lagunaka declares it is an evil devil, so we have kept away."

Lagunaka nodded and shook his rattle, and looked very wise, while he scratched his own ribs for a flea bite. This done he drew the sign of the turtle in the sand.

The chief walked back and forth before the other men: "This day I have learned that another white man has come to the land. He seems alone, yet we cannot know. He is a strange man, such a one as we have never seen. He has short hair upon his face and he sits before his fire and sings. His voice is strong, and while he sings he does strange things with stones, like the round ones that lie upon the shore. He makes the stones fly in the air in streams as swift as water as it shines in the sun. They flow back and forth and up and down, and around, while he makes the magic with his hands. We do not know if this magic be good or bad. But when he is done, by that same magic power, the stones fly back into his body, and they are gone."

"He has slain the great bear, for its skin is on a bush beside him. He has put his spell upon the cub of the bear, and it sits silent while he sings. His weapon is a mighty thing upon a crooked stick.

"And when he rises from the ground he rises first upon his hands, and his feet come over his body before they touch the ground, and he stands as do our people. But then — we know not why — but with that thing upon the crooked stick he strikes off a tree as large as the leg of a man, with one blow of his hand! He is a man of magic and of might.

"Brothers, if his magic prove good, and if he have no ill-will against our people and be free from the curse, perhaps we have little to fear. Perhaps we could take him as a friend." Wawakna paused and looked gravely about him. "These are my thoughts. They may not be wise ones. What will be yours? Has any here ever heard of such a man?"

Wawakna sat down. There was a sober silence. Then one and another spoke briefly. The gist of their thought was that, if the white man were alone, while they were many, he could be overpowered if he proved unfriendly.

One, however, propounded the thought that the mere fact of the stranger's aloneness was a bad sign. Before, in the tales they had heard, there had been many men. They had come in a ship. And, by contrast, if this man came alone and had no ship, he must have come by some powerful magic and with evil aims.

Perhaps it was from this thought that Lagunaka took his cue. In his considered opinion there was only one way to tell. Perhaps he had concluded that his own prestige might be sadly deflated if compared with the powers of the stranger. So he, Lagunaka, proclaimed thus:

"If this man be shot through the belly with an arrow, and received no harm, it is a good sign; he will be a friend. Otherwise his show of magic power would be pretended. If he die it will but prove that he deserves to die; we should cast him into the sea lest the curse be brought again to our people. I have spoken."

The council adjourned and went out of the Lodge House. Wawakna glanced off toward the west. "The sun is still a long run high. Our men will form a line upon the trail, the older ones behind. These last shall stop and stand guard a small shout distance from the trail that leads to the bay. Two men shall go down that small trail to scout the stranger's camp. They are to scout, and not to fight. Perhaps the man is not there; he may have moved. He may be a friend; to do him harm may bring us evil. We must be sure.

"The other men will go down the main trail, by twos. The two on the far end shall go down to the Camp of the Curse and see what they see and return here by sunset."

Those arrangements were quickly made; but when the party was ready to go it was seen that Lagunaka, armed with his bow and arrows and a small ax of stone, was the third from the last in the line. According to his reasoning, which seemed very logical, if the stranger were still encamped along the trail Lagunaka himself would probably be the man chosen by fate — and his own mathematics — to put the rival magician to the test of the arrow. Lagunaka's ethics held very few scruples, or so it would seem. If he'd had the time he'd have made a brew to assist his secret intentions.

Chapter 3

John McJack, not wishing to make contact in the dark, had moved his camp half a mile to the south and well away from the trails. He would have been reassured and somewhat amused had he known what a fuss he had raised with his neighbors.

At sunset he sat in a thicket and thought about the white beard of the man he had buried; ruefully he felt his own chin and jaw. "Sure," he informed Saint Pat, "this stubble itches like the devil in a pork brine. In the morn I will sharp me adze and shave them; I will at that. Do I meet with a maiden I would not be bristled like a pig."

Which, in a roundabout way, was how it came that at the camp up on the bluff the story spread that there were two men in the woods, and that one wore a hat and a beard while the other had neither. That both had done magic but only the first had sung a song.

This was because McJack, after a painful and clumsy shave, had gone down to the beach to fetch clams in his hat, having found no better food. And there was another factor, too. Seems that in the camp was a youth named Wamuta. Although stricken by Minyanata's charms he'd found small favor, perhaps because his previous deeds were small. But, reasoned Wamuta, if he could prove that he feared neither man nor devil by killing or capturing the lone man in the woods, perhaps the girl would change her mind. As simple as that it had seemed to him, at the beginning of his valorous dream.

To fire his imagination and to make his project seem greater he knew the details of the scouts' report. How, off a little from the trail, led there by their noses, they had found the bear with the hole in its skull. He had also heard that the cedars had fallen, and that perhaps the curse was lifted. This last part Wamuta doubted, for he had talked with Lagunaka, while keeping his own plan secret.

Thus it was that Sir John McJack, coming up on his beach toward the cover of his woods, carrying the clams in his hat with the same hand that held the adze, had seen a stealthy movement back among the trees. The bank was low at that spot, so low that from the beach he could almost see the level of the ground. Almost but not quite; a man, lying flat, would be hidden.

But McJack was watchful, his pulses suddenly throbbing. With his one free hand he was juggling a couple of the stones. These seemed to chase themselves around a little circle. Perhaps they befuddled the youth on the bank. For when he sped his arrow the range was too long; it lacked full force; it was badly aimed and McJack had seen it coming. His free hand moved quickly; he grabbed the thing by its feathered tail as it was going past him. He held it out toward the man on the bank and kept on walking toward him. Had Wamuta known how McJack was feeling then, he probably wouldn't have run away.

But he was already leaving. He seemed to have forgotten the direction of his own camp, or perhaps deep in his heart was the heroic purpose of leading this terrible man away. At any rate, he ran, and didn't get back to his camp until nightfall. Too late to do anything but talk. But his story was quickly spread, with very little shrinkage. There must have been two men in the woods, if one wore a beard and a hat and the other had neither. That much was clear. As to their purpose, perhaps they planned to lay the white man's curse upon this camp, as on the one at the pond. So Lagunaka in his wigwam spent half the night making pow-wow, while the people worried and talked and the sentinels watched the trails.

But Minyanata, although she said little, had her own line of thought. Some of her deductions seemed logical, too. One man had a beard, the other had none. Well, Minyanata shrugged a shapely shoulder. She had seen the men of her tribe pull out their own whiskers, each scattered hair at a time. Not so very painful, for there weren't so many hairs. So-o, if a red man in his own crude way could get rid of his beard, would not the white man have a way of his own to do it? He would, to be sure, she decided.

Minyanata was nearing the mating age; for quite a while she'd had some thoughts. And McJack had aroused her interest and curiosity as well as her fears. He appealed to her sense of romance. Was this strange man not bold and strong? Had he not slain a mother bear? Was he not kind, that he had befriended the cub? And the song he had sung in that strange tongue — did it not thrill her now that reason had abated her fears and memory had begun to build an airy dream about the deep cadences of his voice?

She could not know the song had been a ribald ditty; she thought it mysterious and grand. Minyanata had those dreams and thoughts of her own, so personal that she kept them secret. And a plan began to form in her mind. It made her smile; there was a little dimple at the corner of her mouth. Her eyes, as she smiled, looked far away.

Now as to McJack. When a young man tries to shave himself with an adze and to some painful extent succeeds, he too has personal and private thoughts based on the theory that he might meet a maiden. It was spring. McJack was young and strong; in the past he had been fickle too, regardless of reason and season. He had taken women, as well as the world, as he found them. But that had been in other times and places. When jewels were as many as the "diamonds" on the beach, and when a man can simply reach down and take them, they have less value than when they are rare. When rare they must be sought. Or bought. Or perhaps they must be fought for.

And, too, Sir John was lonely. Lonely and poorly fed. The muchness of clams and snails made his belly wriggle. It had rained, also. Grown reckless he had tried to make a fire but his tinder was wet. It was an hour before sundown and his mental world looked gloomy. He was not as cocky as he had pretended, for if the first man he met would shoot him with an arrow — well, things looked rather bad. He sat beside his thicket while the woods grew dark, and it began again to rain. He crawled into his canvas hut, cuddling the bear cub. Thankful for the company. Thankful, too, for the rain which would probably keep the red men at home, and for the canvas which kept him dry, for when great comforts are lacking the small ones gain value. That was the way he tried to reason, but he couldn't be happy at all.

Next morning the sun was shining. McJack was still hunger but his spirits were brighter. He found where in the night a weasel had discarded the carcass of a rabbit after sucking its blood. Afraid to build a fire, he ate part of it raw. Acorns he had learned to leave alone; their food value didn't pay for the pain the caused. Shooting pains, like when an arrow...

"I have me an arrow!" he said aloud. "Mayhap I can make a bow for to shoot it. Mayhap" — and then he turned and looked toward the bay — "Saint Pat and Saint Peter! When that injun was running away he had naught in his hands whatever!"

So he went down and found the bow and three arrows where Wamuta, the frightened and inefficient archer, had thrown them when he ran. He called on the saints to bless the poor injun and went back to his camp to practice. After an hour or so he announced to the cub, "Sure, I be getting the trick of it now. And best I'd stop shootin' at me hat; it's full of holes."

So he sat down in the warmth of the sun, Saint Pat cuddled against him. McJack hadn't intended to fall asleep, but both he and the cub took a little nap.

Next, Sir John jumped wide awake. The cub opened his eyes more slowly. McJack looked toward the north and listened. For, off there, someone was singing. The sound was faint at times, then on a breeze it came stronger. Weird but sweet, in a woman's voice. Wild and high, the words meant nothing. McJack made the sign of the cross.

"Saints help us!" he whispered. "It's a great pixie or an elf — it could not be a banshee in the open light of day! McJack, ye should see what this singing means. Ye should, at that."

He left his tent and robe where they were but his hands were encumbered with too many weapons and he slipped the handle of his adze in his belt. The three spare arrows he thrust through the holes in his hat, pointing fore and aft, and his appearance was at least unique when he came to the cross-trail in an open spot some fifty feet from the voice.

Minyanata, standing there in the trail, her voice already trembling with her fright, thought those arrows were sticking through the head of the man. Perhaps this was a third man — there had been three at the camp by the pond — or was this a man at all?

Her wild song died to a sudden gurgle; she turned and ran down the trail. Just before she disappeared she turned and looked over her shoulder. McJack caught that glimpse of her frightened face, then she was gone. He took off his hat and scratched his head, mightily perplexed.

"Sure," he breathed in audible relief, "it was no pixie at all. It was a lissome lass of flesh and blood. But mayhap she were but a winsome bait, and some of her men be nigh!"

So for caution's sake he looked sharply about, fearing to be encircled. His hands trembled a bit from excitement. Wamuta's archery had made him wary. This might be another attempt. But the woods were empty and quiet, and when he turned the girl was standing again in the trail. Perhaps a hundred feet away. She stood there watching. Turned a bit sideways, poised for flight.

'Lady!" he whispered. "It's a wondrous sight ye be, all slim and supple there, your hair shining in that spot of the sun, black as a raven! And even from here the stars of the night be shining in yer eyes, they do at that."

Forgetting his suspicions he started walking toward her. Forgetting everything but her. But Minyanata held up her hand, palm outward, meaning he should stop. In that last glance as she had fled she'd seen McJack remove his hat; some doubts were removed with it, but not all. Now that she was really embarked on her adventure, she was terribly afraid. But within limits she was also determined. She made unintelligible signs and came a bit closer. Still in the sun, she showed the throbbing of the veins in her throat. Her graceful but frightened poise and high-held head.

He had never seen anything like her. The simple dress of her people became her well. Around her throat was a necklace of small "diamonds." A red-tinted feather was thrust in her hair.

Compared with McJack she was extremely well dressed. His shirt and knee breeches were torn and splotched. His beard showed dark just a little. But he had forgotten such matters; he smiled at the girl and held out his hand. Walked slowly toward her. "Me lady, will ye not talk with me? Will ye not come close and be a friend?" And his own voice shook a little.

A few steps more and she stopped him; there was something imperious in the way that she did it. Then she spoke; her voice trembled with her fright, and that was all McJack understood. "It's a queenish manner ye have, to be sure, but ye speak like naught I did ever hear except the jumble of waters beyond the mill. If ye will not let me come to ye, ye should come to me, I will not harm ye."

She was by then some twenty feet away and he beckoned. She shook her head. Her gaze she kept on his face, watchful. Then she knelt on one knee, and somewhat blindly because she still watched McJack, drew a rude circle of small circles in the sand.

"Aye," agreed Johnny. "Ye means tents, or whatever. Go ye on, tell me some more."

She smiled and drew a shoreline before the tents, and outside of that there were lines that rippled.

"Sure, they be waves on the water, your town be close to the sea." McJack nodded his understanding. The girl seemed pleased, she was losing much of her fright. She stood. Pointed toward the north along the line of the main trail, then made a sweeping gesture toward the bay up there. She pointed to McJack and made walking signs with her hands.

McJack nodded again. She kept on smiling. He noted her dimple and the whiteness of her teeth. The girl looked lovely to Sir John McJack.

"And now," said he, "ye be charting me a course to be sure. It seems inviting and do it slay me I will go! Will ye lead me the way?"

But she stopped him again. She was not so sure in her mind as to the wisdom of what she was doing. Perhaps it would be well to prepare her people for this great event, lest a panic be born of sudden fright. Besides, she did not trust Lagunaka — he was a better archer than Wamuta would ever be. Minyanata knew he was jealous, too. Minyanata was daring, but diplomatic. And wily — she proved that fact to Sir John McJack.

Suddenly her eyes had been focused down the trail, to beyond where he stood. She made a startled gesture and opened her mouth as if she would scream. McJack whirled about. Glanced sharply back along the trail and among the trees. His nervous fingers slid along the handle of the adze. But the trees and the trail were the same as before; there was no one there.

Puzzled, but relieved, he turned to look at the girl. But she had gone. He was alone except for little Saint Pat, who came out of hiding and sniffed at where she'd stood.

"It's half a mind I have to do that same," confided McJack. He chuckled, then laughed aloud. "It's a crafty wench I be trifling with the now. And let me tell ye, Sir John, best ye had quiet down yer nerves, ye have a journey ahead. Some folks to meet. Best ye had start lest some other man shall spit ye on a shaft."

He shrugged his shoulders and went back for his possessions.

Two hours later the night had come down and McJack was lost in the woods. Finally he got back to the main trail up somewhere near the camp, and saw a stealthy movement there. Heard cat-owl calls in the dark. Wished to the saints he had waited until morning. Had renewed his suspicion that the girl had used her siren song to lead him astray. Those cat-owl calls first here, then there, sounded weird in the dark. Would they be the keenind of the Indian banshee — did the red men have them here? A stealthy form just crossed the trail up yon. Another cat-owl called.

Fearing to linger along the trail, McJack went off through the woods toward where he surmised was the bay, though he couldn't be certain. But the thought persisted that the red man's town was somewhere to the north. Aside from being lost he felt almost starved and to aggravate the condition he imagined he caught the smell of smoke and of food cooking. But the woods were dense; there were thickets in between; he could see no light of a fire at all. Heard no other sounds than those of the natural night, and the frequent cat-owls.

Then suddenly he sensed that these had stopped. Crouched down in the dark, he listened; no more of these quavering sounds at all. "Was injuns that made them!" he concluded. "The dirty rapscallions! But what means the deadly silence now? Be they sneaking up to spit me on a spear?"

That was a rather disconcerting thought and McJack involuntarily arose from his crouch. Felt the point of something touch his rib. Struck blindly with his adze in the dark and clipped off the end of a drooping branch of deadwood.

"Sure," he muttered, "it's no wonner that the man on the shore went daft what with being alone so long! McJack ye must take yerself by the hand the now and still yer fear. These injuns know not where ye be, else they would come. Mayhap they all would shoot me with a shaft. Mayhap would ye walk into the camp, they'd treat ye kindly. Could ye but first meet with that lissome lass, but best ye wait until the morn. The moon be westering a bit the now. I see a lighter spot out yon as if the wood were open."

Up in the camp, where the trees were more widely spaced and the light less shaded, the people were waiting. There was an air of tenseness and of fear. They were expecting a new man from a new world, such a man as but two of them had ever seen. A man, perhaps two men, for the one might bring the other, to whom were accredited great deeds of magic.

They reasoned: Why should not our people be afraid? Do they not remember what happened at the camp by the pond, where through the years those cleansing cedars had hung beside their brothers' graves?

Minyanata had partially confided with her father and had succeeded in convincing the chief of the friendly intentions of the man from the other world, and, against Lagunaka's advice, the sentinels had been instructed to allow him, or them, to pass. They were to give warning with the cat-owl calls. Then the sentinels had come to the edges of camp, to watch.

But one, at least, had failed to be watchful, and had lost McJack's location. So they waited, and McJack waited. Matters were decidedly muddled. McJack was growing impatient and his hunger was urgent.

Minyanata, too, was impatient. Her scheme was too slowly unfolding. She had given directions as well as she could, but the stranger had failed to come.

McJack's impatience gave way to desperation. He did not like hiding in the dark.

Aside from creating a constant and growing fear, it got him nowhere. He tried to reason matters out: She had come, at first, because he sang his ditty. Then, the second time, she herself had been the one to sing. Why had she done it? It had been a decided sign of interest, and a kindly interest at that. Perhaps most of the others would be kindly, too, in spite of what Wamuta had tried to do. He didn't, of course, know about Lagunaka.

'I will sing that song!" decided Johnny McJack. "I will do just that!" "It's wearied I be of this loitering in the dark, cuddling me fears to me breast and all. Puttering around like a ghost amongst tombstones, so. But best I'd get out in the clear, some place where the moon shall shine."

So he groped his way to where he'd seen that lighter spot and came out on the lower end of the bluff. There he found a pathway. Below and as far as he could see was moonlight on the water. Nothing more. Nothing but the mystery and the beauty of it. Nothing but its loneliness. Beside him was that shadowed wood. The trail ran along the edge of the bluff and yet he could see no light from the camp at all. Breathing deeply he took his pack and hung it on a branch. Readied himself for action in case his song failed to serve.

Then he sang. He put full power of his lungs into the song. The girl there in the camp might recognize the ditty as the one he had sung before. At least she would know its meaning. McJack was advertising his presence and position to the whole of the camp. Theoretically, he had burned his bridges behind him. There could be no retreat and no more hiding in the woods.

> "Ho-ho! We sail the seas!
> Ho-ho! We walk the leas!
> Ho-ho, and away we go
> A'searchin' for a maiden!"

And he was doing just that. Reaching out into the speckled dark with the very fingers of song, hoping to find that maiden; that she would be the first to come and find him there in the path on the bluff, beside the sheen of the moonlit bay. But the girl must come, if she should come at all, from up there in the dark.

McJack stopped and listened. He forgot his bear cub. Forgot the man he had buried. Forgot his own shipwreck and his mates. But he remembered his adze and clutched it while he waited. At first, except for the little lap of the waves on the shore, there was nothing but silence in all the land. He bent a bit forward to listen more; the stillness hurt his expectant ears. He shrugged. Made a grimace of dismay. Most likely he had failed. The people there, knowing his location, could easily surround him, for they knew the woods and McJack did not. They would be many and he was alone.

And then, from off toward the north, back a little from the line of the bay he heard her voice. Wild it was and high and clear. Strange words in strange cadences winging through the night. Plaintive, appealing and mystifying. Fascinating in their weirdness.

But hopeful to McJack, for he knew she was coming. He hoped she'd be coming alone. The voice was moving in the direction of the bay as the girl came out from the camp to the trail. Then it came down the bay-line on the edge of the bluff. McJack couldn't see her as yet.

He walked a little way forward and sang again. Then, after a moment, he could see her. At first she was shadowy and like a waith; then she stood clear in the light of the moon. Lithe and young and an angel of hope for Sir John McJack. And then they met. Neither spoke but both of them smiled. She took his hand. Made an eloquent gesture with the other. "Come," it seemed to say, "I will lead you to my father and my people."

And with his adze and his bow and his arrow-pierced hat, ragged and tattered though he was, with the souls of them both thrilling there in the night, Minyanata led him. Although they, for the moment, had the world to themselves, neither could speak to the other.

Chapter 4

On the seaward side of the camp was a fire. The chief and two of his men stood before it. One of these was Lagunaka, but he wore no trappings of his trade, he being at a loss as to the proprieties. He looked the same as the other men — puzzled, anxious and a little afraid. Wamuta, the inefficient archer, was well in the background, lest the stranger remember unkindly.

Most of the men stood in a sort of half circle. The women and children held the shaded background. The whole band was present, for the sentinels had come running when McJack had begun to sing.

Minyanata led McJack to the chief. "My father, I have brought the strange man to our camp. He is a friend and a man of great deeds. His heart beats as does that of our people."

Wawakna bowed gravely. The dark eyes and the blue ones met. McJack was smiling.

Wawakna made a speech of which McJack knew not a word, but he smiled again, and bowed. He found, somewhat to his discomfiture, that he still was holding the hand of the girl, perhaps for the moral support. But he made a very courteous bow and smile and let go of her hand, turned to the chief and offered his own.

Wawakna looked disturbed. Hesitantly he held out his hand, wondering perhaps what the new man would do with it: McJack, with his hat under his arm, with his adze and his bow and arrows. The indians crowded closer.

"Yer honor," quoth McJack, "it's pleased I am to meet ye. I know not the words that ye speak, but senses the meaning. "It is a fine town ye have and a fine people. Sure, it's the finest I've seen in all the land! And I give ye great and admiring thanks to the young lady that brought me here." He bowed to Minyanata and smiled. There was a murmur among the people. McJack looked about him, at the blurred figures among the trees. The murmur had expressed astonishment. Friendly curiosity. McJack was doing better than he knew.

Wawakna took his daughter's hand, placed it in that of John McJack and the latter, without even knowing it, became a partially married man! It was all as simple as that, but McJack still didn't know.

By gestures Wawakna invited him to be seated on a corn husk mat. The chief and his greater men sat on the ground; they were doing their guest the honors. McJack, wondering what it was all about, was agreeably surprised. "Sir John," thought he, "it's a great man ye be and all."

He had laid his warlike gear upon the ground beside him and the adze was appraised with awe, although none ventured at first to touch it.

Minyanata brought him food still warm from the fire — some sort of stew in an earthen bowl. McJack feasted and soon felt better and the red people waited and watched. Minyanata stood near just beyond her father. This was a great event for her. A very unusual romance. McJack could see the shine of her eyes, and those veins in her throat were throbbing again. He could see plainly because one of the women had placed light-wood on the fire. There was a continuous murmur of whispers in the background. McJack listened and watched trying to catch some sort of cue.

"This world be good for the now," he thought. "It's a strange world, but a kindly one. I wonder what I'm to do now?" While he meditated he'd unthinkingly tossed a couple of stones with the one hand. The indians eagerly watched. Perhaps Lagunaka's eyes showed more than curiosity, something not so kindly. He, with the other men, had been sitting silent. McJack looked for Wamuta but couldn't find him — that archer of the erring aim still stayed in the dark. Then McJack was suddenly aware that he was doing something of great interest; even the chief was watching those stones. "Sure," he told them, with another smile, "should ye like the tossing, it's me that can please ye."

So he emptied his pouch, placing the stones beside him and began to toss. First two, then four, then six. They glistened and gleamed in the light of the fire. Eight — best he'd hold them at eight, there in the firelight. In the light of day he could do a dozen. McJack sat on his mat and those stones rose and fell and circled and looped, red and green and blue and flashes of white. McJack sensed the wonder of his audience and thanked the saints for his skill. As he slowly arose the stones rose with him and the hearts of the people were made light with their wonder, though the heart of Lagunaka was dark and fearful.

McJack was doing his best, but he knew he couldn't finish rightly. When he got to his feet the mouth of his pouch had closed and he couldn't reopen it in the middle of his juggline act. Doubting that he could catch all of the stones in his hands, he had to try something else. So, carelessly, he let them rain down to the ground. They fell before where Lagunaka sat. Within his easy reach.

The man stared darkly but did not move. There was a moment of tense silence: McJack could feel it, though he thought that he was laying a challenge at the feet of a rival never entered his mind. He did not know Lagunaka from any other man, but the people knew. They sensed the challenge. McJack, with a bow and smile, gathered the stones and put them away, while the people waited. "Sure," he told them next, "it's glad I be that my tricks can please ye. And ye need not fear. It's naught that can bring ye harm. Ye cannot know the words I speak, but there be something in a hand-clasp ye will mayhap understand."

So, starting with the chief and the men, who had risen, McJack went the rounds, shaking hands with each and every one. With Lagunaka, too, wondering the while at the red man's frown. Wamuta he missed — that young man was hiding behind a tree. An unsuccessful attempt at assassination may throw a wrench into the machinery of the social amenities, to be sure.

Then McJack saw that one of the men had cut his thumb with the edge of the adze. The trickle of blood was viewed with amazement. That was indeed a terrible tool! The indian laughed and sucked his thumb and McJack gave him a pat on the shoulder. One of the men had gotten McJack's bow and recognized it. They all seemed amused. McJack looked for Minyanata; she stood nearby with her mother. He flashed the two of them a smile.

Next, again seated in the place of honor beside the chief, McJack was formally inducted into the tribe as a brother. There were unexplained speeches and gestures. McJack, amused and a little bored, watched and listened, reading a few of the gestures. This was a strange and incomprehensible world, so different from the one he had left.

The difference was vividly brought to mind when the ceremonial pipe was lit. The chief solemnly puffed it. The smoke drifted to McJack in little whirls; it suggested the odor of incense. That made him think of a priest and a church and chanting and images and people on their knees, back somewhere in a very different past. The white man's world, whose past was still the present in that other land. Where men and maidens were wedded by the priest; where mass was said for the souls of the departed dead. Where children were christened...

McJack suddenly came to and saw that Wawakna was offering him the pipe. He tried it and choked and gasped and wheezed. Felt rather ridiculous when the red men smiled. The red men who, turn by turn, puffed at the pipe and passed it along. Even Lagunaka, although he frowned. Then the chief made a gesture to his wife.

Smiling, she placed Minyanata's hand in his and motioned that they follow. Bewildered, holding her hand again, he led with the girl to one of the wigwams on the south side of the camp. The flap was already open and on the ground in the centre was a tiny fire, just enough for a little light. McJack and Minyanata went inside. Her mother let the door flap fall and went away. It was as simple as that. For once in his life McJack was briefly speechless. The meaning of things had dawned on his mind.

Then: "By the saints in glory, and what have I done?" He, Sir John McJack, standing there with his bride beside the little fire. Beside the new clothing made of skins hanging there on a pole. Beside himself, too, for the moment. His amazement was mixed with a strange repentance. Not for his own sake but for that of his bride. The bride whose trembling he could feel when he put his arm about her. "Tell me," he said in a husky voice, "be this your own will or that of them that sent us here?" She looked up, shy and puzzled.

"Ye cannot know my words at all. It's a fine fettle I have found me in! What be your name?" He pointed to her and finally made her understand. "Minyanata."

"Sure, ye say it plain and nice to hear. It's the single thing that's clear to me. Me, McJack... them other wenches! But this be different. With them it was just a passing play, and they were gone and so was I. But that was THEN. In these late days I have felt the fear of the wrath of god with the tossing on the waters and the wanderings in the wood.

"Would seem ye're given to me as wife and ye be heathen. It's against the law. What shall I do, the now?" Minyanata's face was thoughtful. She was trying to understand. "Aye, for all your beauty and your lure, it's against the law! Ye've never been christened. There be no priest to do that same. Such being so, mayhap we can best the devil about the bush! Mayhap we can, at that!"

McJack raised the flap and looked out into the dark. Then he took two of the skin blankets and laid them ready. "It's quiet. Mayhap the people sleep. Yanata, me lady, would ye strip the clothes from off yer wonderful self and wrap this skin about ye?" By signs he made her understand. The fire was burning low. A little later, wrapped in the skins, he leading the girl by the hand, they stole out of the camp and down to the bluff. On down to the beach. The moon hung just above the water there in the west. Its silvered path was long and wide and it softly glistened on the sea. All else seemed dark. Behind them was the graveled bluff and the forest. Behind them, too, were the days that were done. Before them was that pathway to the moon. The moon, there where the clouds were showing, at the rim of the world, silvered and shaded.

McJack pointed there. She nodded. Her eyes were wondering wide. She vaguely decided that this was some strange ceremony of the white man. Something that pertained to marriage.

Minyanata was willing. McJack could read it in her eyes. "May the saints in glory look upon us and smile!" was his fervent plea. "It's no irreverence I means to priest nor pope nor church, I have none of these at all. I have naught but yon moon, and the widen sea, and a woman for to wife. Old moon, I would not have her be a heathen; she has never been christened nor baptized. And so, old moon, would ye act as me priest and give yer blessing to this that I'm to do?"

He took the blanket from off the girl and laid it down with his own. She stood there, a golden woman in the night, on silvered sands. In the night that was chill. And he baptized her in the bay, with no irreverence to anything in heaven or in hell or in the mystic land between.

They came out. The girl shivered. He threw a blanket about her, the other on himself. And there, facing the moon as it dipped to the darkening sea, of his own free will and choice he took unto himself a woman, for his wife. Solemnly and sincerely, having "felt the fear of the wrath of god."

As they climbed the bluff, the moon, which had been their priest, went down in the sea behind them. And before them, from the rim of the bluff, there in the dark that came when the moon was gone, dim forms glided back to their wigwams. The ways of the white man were strange indeed. Both he and they were puzzled.

Before the dawn came an April shower; softly it sounded on the wigwam walls. "It's the blessing of the saints coming gentle down," said the bridegroom, half in slumber. 'Manitou," she murmured, "has been very good to me." But neither knew what the other said. And then they slept a little, while the mills of their differing gods ground slowly on, and blended their grists.

That first morning of McJack's wedded life had its problems and its thrills. One of these last was when in the light of day he really saw his woman; she hadn't awakened. Physical feminine perfection. As to color, this might have been made by mixing gold and old copper and cream. This contrasted with the black hair and McJack was pleased. A bit fearful for the future perhaps, but for the time he was pleased.

Minyanata awoke and blushed and covered herself with the deerskin. McJack pulled its upper part down and bent to kiss her. This was a strange thing for a man to do but Minyanata liked it. She giggled and McJack broke out in song.

> "I ha' got a sweet colleen, for me own, for me own,
> Do ye know just what I mean without bein' shown,
> But it's time she was a' dressin',
> May the saints give down their blessin'..."

His poetical inspiration ran out on him then and he laughed. Minyanata giggled some more.

Outside, heads popped out of the other wigwams. Eyes asked questions each of another's. But none could answer. This new man from the mystery world was unpredictable indeed. Unpredictable but friendly; the band of red people were released from their fears. Wawakna had assured them there was no danger of another curse. But Lagunaka pretended to have grave doubts. He'd have to think it over.

That day was social in most of its aspects. McJack was still, or again, the center of interest. By signs the people tried to ask where he had come from and how he had gotten ashore. Wawakna, gesturing as with a paddle, asked if he had come in a canoe. "Not I," replied McJack. "Never did I ride in a canoe at all. Ye should come with me to yonder shore. I will show ye my craft." And the indians were amazed at the magnitude of the wreckage. They made the mast and spars into a raft and towed them up to the bluff. For cargo they had the ropes and rigging, for passengers some of the children.

One day McJack made a swing on an oaken limb beside Wawakna's wigwam. He made it for the boys but often the chief took over. He would swing and smoke and smoke and swing in regal splendor. Gravely. And all the while he pondered on the things he saw. On his daughter and her man. The courteous and kindly way he treated her. The laughing light that was in his eyes. And in hers, too, for Minyanata was happy. The spirits had indeed been good to her beyond all that she might have expected. That her man was of another race mattered not to the girl at all.

Right from the beginning, without the understanding of a single one of his words though these were many, she had sought above all things to please him. To keep her wigwam spick and span, for he hated an excess of dirt. Indian women were like the whites: some were good housekeepers and some were not. Minyanata strove to be best in all things, to hold her man. As time went on she caught some of her husband's words and spoke them and her eyes would light with pleasure when he showed he understood.

Polygamy among her people was neither uncommon nor unlawful and the women concerned didn't seem to mind. But Minyanata would never be that way. Not unless, as with some others, her spirit should be broken and her lovelight die. But the idea slowly seeped into McJack's observant mind that he'd best not try polygamy, or even an outside interest.

Just then, at least, he felt no call nor need to wander away. He was strangely contented. The life he was living was better than the one he had lived before. It had, for the time, something of a sense of security. A freedom from the worse elements of the white man's world. Here was no press-gang. No piracy nor petty thievery. No political nor religious persecutions. A man's opinions were his own and he dared express them freely.

McJack was interested in the things he found to do. He was amused by some of the habits of the people, rather aggravated by others. These last perhaps he'd slowly change. But kindly. Tolerant. Biding his time.

And Wawakna, sitting in his swing and smoking, watched and wondered. Sometimes he smiled gravely. Slowly he began to understand. To cooperate, at least passively. To side with McJack in his notions and decisions. To depend on his judgment in many matters. This didn't please Lagunaka at all. And the magician, too, like Sir John McJack, decided to bide his time.

Chapter 5

Two years had passed, as had three ships. The month was May, the woods and meadows were beginning to green. Out on the bay, there where it and the ocean met, and beyond the shoals, was a school of whales. Two ships, before that day, had been bound toward the south, most likely to Jamestown. These had stayed far out; the red people had only seen their sails. But the third, bound northward, came closer. Perhaps two miles at sea she had held her course, and then McJack and his people saw her outline change. She came bow-on for the bay. "I wonder why?" queried John McJack. "Will she come to the land, and all? Or do she come so close to look at the whales?" This seemed the answer, for she put about and resumed her former course. "The men be curious about the whales," he concluded. "I feared she would come to shore. Next, I feared she wouldn't. I would like right well to learn the news, and meet some people of my kind; but I be right well pleased with my world as it be, here with the injuns. I fears, did the white men come to stay, they would make unwanted change, for their ways be rough and ruthless. I have lived in that world, and I know. What the white man wants, he takes, can he get it."

But at the moment it never entered his mind that the whites might *want* the whales. Each spring those great creatures would come to the bay — had done it as long as the red man's legends told, for in all of that time there had been none to molest them. Except for the storms which might cast a weakened whale upon a shoal, they had born and suckled their young in peace.

As had Minyanata, in the meantime, there in the camp. Her daughter had been born in March, while the rowdy winds howled over the bay. While they shivered and shook the walls of her wigwam. While she had crouched on her knees at the birthing-stakes, and the midwives tended. While McJack, unmindful of the wind, walked up and down among the trees and fretted, and sent his prayer of pleading to the saints, and all.

Lagunaka, had he been asked, would have made good pow-wow to ease the pain and assure good health to both mother and child. But McJack hadn't asked and Lagunaka was again offended, in spite of which both Minyanata and her baby got along very well — for which McJack was mightily pleased.

Saint Pat, retrieved from the woods the day after his master's wedding, was a good-sized nuisance around the camp, a favorite with the children but not with Lagunaka. He, in a bad temper, had kicked Saint Pat; the latter, in an unsaintly mood, had bitten the magician through the heel and the medicine man made medicine for the healing of his wound, and limped for a week or more.

Lagunaka wasn't happy. Seemed that since the white man came his own prestige had dwindled. McJack could draw a crowd at any time by his tumbling and juggling, his backflips and handsprings and cartwheels and his walking on his hands. He might have set himself up in the magician's trade and have put Lagunaka out of business. But he claimed no magic and unlike Lagunaka, who kept his pretended secrets to himself, McJack was training some of the boys. Teaching all of the people to speak his own brand of English, too.

"Sure," he had reasoned, "I could take small praise did the lot of them teach me to talk, but if I, alone as I be, could teach the lot of them, I might be proud to mayhap serve them well. For some day the whites will come. They will not always sail on past. Then, do these red men know the white man's tongue, mayhap they'll be less easy fooled. So the while I'm here I shall both teach and learn. I will mayhap know more than many a great one, over yon. And I feels these folks be somewhat in my care, even as I have been in theirs. For had I been forced to live alone and grow long whiskers, and be daft with the loneness and watching the sea, I might, as did that other one, but die of joy at the sight of a man." And then McJack felt of his own whiskers and went to his wigwam and his barber. There, Minyanata heated a long stone and singed off her husband's beard, with some satisfaction and a stink of burning hair. Not so close a shave as McJack had gotten with his adze, to be sure, but much less painful. And the adze was not as sharp as it used to be, what with work and lacking a grindstone. Minyanata, while she worked, gave her customer the local news. Bits of gossip about the neighbors. Told how smart her daughter was for her age, how in a week or two she would likely walk, and that before very long she would have to be weaned because the mother's milk was getting scarce, and Yanata could already chew her food, and how proud he should be of his daughter. And McJack, he grinned and agreed, but he couldn't tell his wife where that ship was going, although she inquired.

As for other foreign news, that was brought by visiting families, some of whom would come from the inland, even from as far as the hill country and beyond the Great River.* These, as usual, brought small quantities of flint and other material not native to the district, for arrowheads and knives. They told, too, of steel and iron points for the arrows, traded by the whites at Jamestown. Of the incipient quarrels between the reds and the whites. Of how, at first, the whites would have starved but for the red man's corn. The red people, down on Virginia shore, were not satisfied with their visitors. They feared they would, in time, try to crowd the red men out. In places they had already done it — King Powhattan had called a council and some of the chiefs advised war.

And there was a tale about a white man named Smith and Powhattan's daughter; how she had saved the white man's life. How, after that, Pocohontas had married a white man and sailed across the sea.

These were bits of the news which came that year from the south. And there was a rumor that, far in the north, more white men had come. No definite news, just a rumor. The whites had brought their women there in the winter. Bad time to come, the winter. What had happened the visitors didn't know. Perhaps it was just an untruthful yarn; the Naragansett indians were known to be liars.

And another tale from up in the inland, where the Huron people lived: How a man named Champlain had helped the Hurons in a little war against the Five Nations. How the Five Nations had sworn vengeance against all of the French, and how those French-men were trying to placate the Five Nations and make them forget.

McJack had listened and got the gist of the news as best he could, and didn't greatly doubt the stories. Although he only knew vaguely where he was, he had sensed the white man's westward trend, for he'd seen the germs of its starting. Had heard the tales of the great new world beyond the seas. Was sure that the whites were coming. How long would it be before they came to the cape? He didn't know. As yet he had no way of learning.

Meanwhile he was working on a boat. A dug-out boat from a great cedar log, up along the little creek. The indians had started to burn and chip it, but McJack and Nan-quemoke, an indian of his own age, had taken over with the adze. This was the only steel tool in the land — the boat would be the largest ever seen on the cape and the finest. Naturally they would berth it in the creek because this was always calm, and the best fish-ing was just outside. It would serve for deep-sea fishing, too, although as a rule this wasn't necessary. Instead of going to the fish, the fish would come to them. Like the eels which could be thrown out on the shore by hand. Or the striped bass and other fish; these were driven upstream to a trap. The herring, caught by thousands in the spring, served mostly for fertilizer: a fish to a hill of beans or corn or squash or tobacco. These tricks had been

*Delaware River

new to John McJack.

McJack, who in those two years had become a man of some importance, had learned a lot of other things. His greatest asset was his inborn political acumen and kindly good humor, although as yet there'd been no call for real leadership. However, he sat next to the chief at the councils, and had succeeded in quenching a few quarrels by counteracting the influence of that "trouble-makin', bubble boilin' varmint" Lagunaka. McJack would grin when the sorcerer scowled. "McJack," he would tell himself, "if ye would live to be Lord of the Land, ye should keep watch of that critter. Ye be growing too great in favor here; the man be jealous." And he was wary with the fellow while the social and economic life went on. A simple life, full of what might have been called hardships. But shelter, such as the wigwams were, food and fuel and family would keep the race going.

It seemed that none of the Lenape had any great ambitions beyond what they had achieved. They were passively content. Lacking as a clan any great warlike trend, hoping to merely go on as their fathers had done, they had reached by their own efforts the probable height of their culture. Thus it had been for centuries.

Once they had attained a degree of efficiency that would enable them to exist, their progress stopped. Around their little fires they boasted of their little deeds and thought them great. Such individuals of their race as had been ambitious, like Powhattan, the man of his day, had been greedy for power and not for progress. Greedy for prestige and the power to tax, with little thought of the development of the power to produce.

Had they been able, as had some other crude but strong peoples of other times, to conquer some race or regime of a higher culture, they might have made history repeat itself by stealing that culture for their own. But they did not, and had not. There had been no higher culture there to steal. On the cape, as far as anyone can tell, they were the Original Humans, and this would apply to much of the seaboard.

Amongst them were many men of many minds, revolving and reviewing their current thoughts, but not one had gotten around to the making of a wheel. They knew that things would roll: as a stone down a hillside, as a log on the ground. As a child or a beast at play, as a year with its seasons. They knew that spring would roll around again after the winter was gone, but they had never made use of a wheel.

And spring had come again to the land. The trees that were dead knew life again. Off to the east and north the meadows that had been black with mud and fallen grasses, before and after the ice which has sheathed them in the time of cold, the ice which rose and fell with the tides and crackled with its breaking, those level meadows, eroded with the little streams between which the muskrat houses showed, were greening again with verdure.

These were the meadows. The ice had long gone from the bay. The breeding whales were there again, that day on the second year after the ship had sailed so close to shore. And that was the day when Saint Pat, large for his age and feeling an urge, went out in the woods for a walk. He often did that, in a casual way, but this was different. There was that impelling urge, and in this mind of Saint Pat it was nothing vague. He thought he'd do something about it.

The whaler, she came in slowly, with the breeze, but against the tide. The air at first was clear and McJack could guess she was lightly laden, even from as far as the bluff and before she had come into the bay. Then, ignoring the whales that were closer in, she went about. Settled to a starboard tack and went out to the sea again. McJack couldn't be sure, but he thought she lowered a boat. Then she was brought head to the wind and seemed to lay there. But a mist came drifting in from sea and he lost her. That had been about noon.

The same breeze held and the tide had changed to flood. The vessel did not show again until three hours later. She came very slowly. McJack wondered why. With the flooding tide and the breeze so fair she should make sight fast, at that. She came into the bay, sluggish; McJack thought she steered badly. She seemed trying to hug the shore but had some trouble. There was an off-shore eddy there.

At the camp was great excitement, but McJack tried to keep it subdued. Tried, too, to keep the people back from sight. Wawakna was worried. The chief had been more or less worried for a long time; he had nursed weird forebodings about ships. So had McJack. He knew more about ships and the men who manned them than could Wawakna. His pulses were jumping a little; would the seamen come to the land?

At least he could now see why she came so slowly: she was towing a whale as well as a boat; had evidently been waiting for the turn of the tide. There was, when she came closer, a leadsman in her prow; the tide had risen a quarter. At the bluff by the camp the beach was narrow, but down beyond the deserted camp where Wamuta had tried his archery, it was wide and had little slope. There, too, the wooded bank was low, same as at the abandoned campsite, which lay between the ship and the bluff. The ship came on nearer the campsite, edging shoreward.

Finally, and still below the campsite, she cast anchor. The whaleboat, with eight men, carried another light anchor ashore, and the men clambered out. First thing some of them did was to pick up some of those "diamonds." They seemed momentarily interested, but then two of the men went down the beach and the others entered the woods. They all carried guns. They were a long way off but the people on the bluff could hear them shouting back to the ship. Very faintly. McJack could still see the two men who had gone down the beach.

Then there was the faint report of a gun, smothered a little by the woods. Another. The echoes repeated them. More shouting and for a time it was still. The indians were frightened, but a quick count showed that all were present or accounted for. None of their men were down in that part where the boat had landed, although some man from another camp might have wandered there. Curiosity overcoming fright, some of the indians wanted to go down to the shore, but McJack advised Wawakna to forbid it. Repeated his demand to keep the people out of sight. They were so eager to see, had maybe concluded that perhaps the white men weren't so bad after all; was not Sir John a white man?

This ship, McJack figured, was neither a freighter nor a colonizer. He remembered that time, now two years gone, when that other ship had come in close to look at the whales. Put two and two together; added them to the conclusion that, over yon where seamen met, they had told their tale to the whalers. McJack shrugged his shoulders. What the white men wanted they would probably take. Before, there had been nothing on the cape to lure them there. Then they had learned of the whales.

It was perhaps an hour before the shore party returned to the ship, taking the beach anchor with them. Then came the sound of the bow windlass. "They be heaving in the iron," muttered McJack. "Mayhap they will leave. McJack, would ye have them go or have them stay? Ye cannot tell. Ye do not know the which ye be, an injun or a white. Aye, but the ship be coming closer. Comes up-shore with the tide. They have found that place displeasin'."

Faintly he could hear the shouting but couldn't understand it. However, he surmised the intentions; the men, while on shore, had discovered the deserted camp. There the ground was already cleared beneath the trees; there was wood and fresh water handy. The beach was flat and the bank was low, little more than two feet above the top of the tides, and the trees grew quite close to the bank.

"Sure," decided McJack, "they will be landing there. We have got some neighbors, that we have! Saint Pat preserve us; make them good ones and the kindly. But I have doubts. I know the sort of men they most like will be, for I have met the whaling crews afore. Rough men and ready. But I think this crew be not so large for the task they have to do. That gives for the doubting!"

But McJack didn't say what those doubtings were. Wawakna was worried enough. McJack could note that fact as the chief stood there in the westering sun, the dusk close at hand. The ship was anchored further off the shore for the night. The men, using a tackle hitched to a tree, hauled the dead whale as close as they could to the shore. It looked pitifully enormous.

"Sure, this thing we call life be strange and wondrous," mused McJack. "As late as this morn the whale could have towed the ship, and now a few small men can drag it where they will. As the tide comes in they'll take it to the top, and at the ebb there'll lay the fish all high and dry and ready for the cutting.'"

It then grew dark. All of the men had returned to the ship, but on the top of the tide they did as McJack had predicted. The listeners could tell by the distant sounds. By the shouts, and all; it was too dark to see. The whale lay there in the dark, the first of many.

The dawn came in with a creak and clatter and a shouted curse. With the sounds of axes in the wood. The white man's dawn on the wilderness shore.

The mists were not yet lifted. The sun was still behind the woods and sea. The silent dignity of the Coming of the Day where for eons past she had come alone, on soundless feet, to lift the eyelids of her sleeping world with bird song and her kindly light — all that was gone.

Great melting pots, axes, immense knives on long handles, all of the equipment was taken ashore. Smoke began to rise from the once deserted camp. Not that of little breakfast fires, smoke from fires so high and hot that they made possible the passing of a whale through the bunghole of a barrel.

On "Whale Beach," there where the "diamonds" lay. Before and upon what had once been a campsite. There where in ages past the Original People had toiled and lived and loved and begot their young. On that one spot their phase of life was done and gone; another phase was born.

Chapter 6

O n the evening of that day when the whalers came the chief held a council, this time in the dusk and without a fire. In fact, no fires which would show a smoke were permitted in the camp. At the council the chief presided, but McJack's were the thoughts he used.

"Sure," McJack had explained, "It's best that we find them than that they find us, for have they no other evil thoughts, they must not know of the women here. They must not know of the camp at all, as they would did some injun straggle down. So when we find them we want more men than we have the now, but get this thought in the minds of your people — it's peaceful we must be! Mayhap the whites will be peaceful, too, but first they must prove it.

"Wawakna, send ye some runners to the camps in the inland, the two which they can reach tonight. Let their men come here in the morn, but none shall go to the ship alone. They must come here." It would seem that with the best of friendly intentions McJack was not trusting anyone too far, either red or white. Especially Lagunaka. He, McJack feared, would have ideas of his own; he had already gone to his wigwam to boil a brew. To make some magic. At intervals through the night they could hear his rattle. Wawakna had placed sentinels about the camp and nobody slept very soundly.

With mid-morning the men from the indian inland camps began to arrive. Reinforcements to keep the peace, but some looked rather warlike. Faces smeared with paint and clay. Carrying bows and small stone hatchets. When all had come they, with McJack, totaled some sixty men. Three times as many as seemed to be on the ship.

Faintly on the breeze they could hear the whalers working, especially the sound of their axes. McJack looked his reinforcements over. Grinned a little: "Sure, the look of them would mayhap fright a child, but with the men on the ship I have some doubts. Mayhap they be a scurvy crew, but alone in the land as they be the now, they will hold together. Most be bold men else they'd not be here. Ye must use yer wits, Sir John McJack, ye must make ye a plan, and all."

He explained that plan to Wawakna and his head men: "We will wait until two hours afore the dark, for if anything goes wrong the men of the ship will not dare go in the woods at night." He glanced about the camp, at the red people gathered. Bewildered. Most of them frightened. But many, he knew, were curious. Some, emboldened by that curiosity, might steal down to the men on the shore.

"On the other hand, did but a few go down, they would think us weak and fearful, the which we be, at that! So I aim to make each side afraid of the other. It's no great trust I'd put in red or white did one have all the advantage. So I plans it thus:

"We will not go down to where we heard the guns, for they were beyond the camp, downshore; the men will not be there now. First we will go to the overgrown farmlands this side of the camp, where we can both see and hide. For I have a trick in the mind of me, to tell what the whites be thinking." And McJack grinned as he further explained. Wawakna made sure that the head men understood. McJack kept an eye on Lagunaka; a sorcerer friend from an inland camp had joined him, and the two were making pow-wow. They kept it up until late afternoon, when the force was ready to go. First they went by the main trail to the one that led to the whaling camp. Then along that until within a quarter of a mile. Here McJack had Wawakna lead the men in a circle toward the north and west; they came out into the new growth, among the thickets and cedars and sas-safras. McJack and Nanquemoke crept forward to look, leaving Wawakna and the other chiefs in charge. The sounds of the whalers could plainly be heard. Of axes and the creak of tackle and the curses and shouts. The new growth went clear to the edge of the camp, on the upshore side.

From the covert McJack saw the men and the layout of the camp. But an incidental thing caught his quick attention: the hide of a bear stretched over a barrel. McJack gritted his teeth together. "Saint Pat!" whispered Nanquemoke. The red man looked angry. McJack put a hand on his arm, and nodded and frowned. Shrugged a shoulder; this was no time to grieve for his pet. Besides, he couldn't reasonably blame the white men. Saint Pat, accustomed as he was to people, would have walked right up to the whalers. Mayhap expecting a titbit. The white men wouldn't have known; they'd have thought him wild and have shot him on sight.

Perhaps, even had they know, they'd have done the same. Might do the same to an indian, too. But McJack had his doubts; he thought the whalers were wiser than that, and on that thought he had based his maneuvers. From there in the bush he studied the camp. There wasn't even a sentry. All of the men were working. Their guns were stacked against a tree above where the kettles boiled, to be out of the way.

Offshore lay the ship; the sinking sun touched her topmast there. But McJack didn't like what he saw: four men on the foredeck, just aft of what he knew to be a tarpaulin-covered cannon. They were emptying ballast water from some barrels; this belched and bubbled from the bilge and cascaded down from the scuppers.

McJack frowned: "My trick will not work so well until they come ashore. Did the men but think to fire that piece with shrapnel, even if they aimed it at the sky, every injun on shore would run like a rabbit! So we must wait. Mayhap, Ah-h!" And there was great satisfaction in his voice.

The saints and all must have been with McJack, for "Avast!" yelled the master from the shore. "Make haste; we need the casks. We have but an hour afore the dark, and ye linger there! Bring what casks ye have emptied." And McJack, watching from the bush, saw the men make ready to obey. He chuckled softly. Looked more closely around the whaling camp.

At the top of the tide lay the whale, head to the bay. Long strips of blubber had been pulled down; these simmered in the pots and filled the air with a greasy stench. Six men on the tackle, its shore end hitched to an oak, were hauling down another; two men were cutting it loose with spade-like tools. Right beside them and the whale lay one of the boats. The men on the line hauled languidly. They seemed tired; this was hard work and slow. The master cursed and demanded speed, while he helped some others tend the fires and used a great dipper to fill a cask. The new oil stank and stewed. There other men were cutting wood.

"It's fuel enough for the time," declared the master. "Lay aside your axes and help with the haul-line. Could we catch a half score of injuns it would lighten our task. Bill, make haste to the shore with the casks." He yelled this last across the water.

McJack noted the scowl on Nanquemoke's face. Thanks to McJack the indian knew what the master had said about the lightening of the white men's' toil. "Aye, it would tell why he has so small a crew: he planned to slave the Injuns to the toil. Seems that has been done afore. That would be bad, but this be a scurvy crew, at that, and not so clever.

"See, Nanquemoke, where they have stacked their guns? Can ye and your men but lure the whites to yon side of camp, away from the weapons, we from the bush can come between. Mayhap the master spoke but idle words about slavin your people; we cannot tell until we test. Between peace and strife the man must have the choosing if our trick is to work well at all. Can ye control your men?"

Nanquemoke nodded, and the two of them crept back through the growth to the others, after seeing that the boat was coming to shore. McJack nodded his satisfaction. Grinned a little and thrilled a little and went on with the details of his plan.

He had Wawakna count out ten of his most dependable men, just the number that the master had wished for, with Nanquemoke to lead them. Unarmed, they were to circle the whalers' camp and from the south come out in the open. Once seen by the whites they were to stand still. Pretend to be curious and afraid, and McJack knew they could do the latter. They were already afraid, with the exception of Nanquemoke. McJack got them aside in a little group. He knew the whites couldn't hear him.

"Now, me friends, ye should still yer fears and hold yer courage fast; there be small chance ye will come to harm. So ye will come into the open on your side of camp, away from the guns. We will be close to this side, here in the bush, and do the whites show but a sign of harm, we will come between them and their weapons." He paused and made the sign of the cross, silently asking a blessing from the saints. "Will ye do this thing for the sake of your people? Do any man be too great a coward to go he should let a brave one take his place afore ye start, and show his people that he be a coward. That would be bad; the tale would long be told. A brave name would be changed to a craven one. The squaw of such a man must hide her head in shame; his children could not boast at all, for their father would take the name of a rabbit or a mouse. But, if ye go, and do your part, your names and your deed will be told in the councils. The chiefs and the people will point ye thus, as a true man and a brave."

And McJack pointed to each in turn, calling his name. The indians nodded; they would go. Nanquemoke led them away among the cedars. Out among the whalers the master raised his voice again for speed. The men on the line complained they were too few, and tired. They'd been at the task since the dawn, and by then the sun was sinking.

McJack, listening, had the chiefs move their men in closer, to where all could see the camp: the men on the line, those at the fires and pots and casks. The muskets stacked by the tree. The long strip of blubber had at last come loose; the men with the cutters laid the tools in the boat and came up on the shore. Stood for a moment to look on the bay to where the sun was half gone down. Just the half of a disk on the horizon there, amongst little clouds. But these men turned quickly; a man had let out a shout. And McJack knew why he had done it.

On the other side of camp, there in the gloom among the trees, stood ten timid and unarmed men. Stout fellows they, but huddled and gaping and with the exception of Nanquemoke, not pretending at all. Shaking in their moccasins and ready to run.

"Hell's bells!" exclaimed the master exultantly. "There be the help we needed! Look ye sharp, men; make pretense to be friendly. Smile. Hold out your empty hands. We be two to their one; do we work this right we can catch them! We will work our way amongst them, and when so placed, we be two to one, I'll give the sign. But do the fools no crippling harm, for a wounded man can't work so well. We'll shackle the brutes to the stripping line, and they'll work, or wiggle beneath the lash! Move in, but slow and easy. Come around and amongst them. And smile!"

So, spreading and slowly widening their line, the white men carefully walked across

the camp. Some made signs of friendship as best they could. A few seemed reluctant, but the master must be obeyed. The circle closed around the trembling red men. Nanquemoke watched the camp over the shoulder of the master.

McJack, just ready to give the sign, could hear Nanquemoke, in Lenape, talking to his men, even as he took the master's outstretched hand, trying to encourage them. The master thought Nanquemoke was speaking to him and nodded as he watched how his own men were deploying. Gave orders to them while pretending to speak to Nanquemoke: "As quick as ye can get ye two whites to one red. Then grab the fool by the throat!"

He was looking straight into Nanquemoke's eyes, and thus his back was turned toward the camp and McJack; the other whites were too intent to watch the woods at all. But, by accident, one let his eyes glance off toward the camp. He gave out a shout of dismay. "Look beyond ye!" he yelled to the master, and the latter dropped Nanquemoke's hand and whirled. His mouth fell open but he couldn't speak. For there, between his crew and their guns and the pots and the ship and the whale — and between all that pertained to their own white world — stood fifty red men and one white. A white man wearing indian garb and a short dark beard, and with an adze in his hand. The reds were armed with bows and shafts. Their arrows were fitted and ready. The master still stood gaping. Then... "Damm, man! Hold them injuns away! Don't let them shoot!" His voice sounded hoarse and strangled.

McJack's smile was crooked and somewhat cruel. He bade the chiefs hold their men where they were and slowly walked forward. Nanquemoke and his men had quietly stepped aside out of the line of arrows. They moved around and quickly, to where their own people stood. Proud as peacocks, though so lately afraid. "Don't let them shoot!" repeated the whaler.

McJack stood before him, lightly swinging his adze. The eyes of the master followed it, fearful. The score of whalers were crowded closed and there was more stark terror in that small group than they'd ever known before. This thing had come without warning; they had been caught in the act of their treachery. McJack knew it; most of the indians knew it, though some of the inland men hadn't understood the master's words. "God help us now!" croaked one of the men.

"D'ye think he would?" inquired McJack. "What with yer hands so soon took down from the throats of them ye thought ye had, for the slaving at the line? What with false smiles so soon wiped off yer foxy faces? Scum and scattle, that ye be! The foxes would be ashamed to know I said it! So ye had thought to use the lash on these men here? How think ye would like that lash yourselves? Ye have well earned it!"

Ye cannot do that!" yelled the master. McJack looked at him with contempt. "I could, but mayhap I'll not. It would gain me nothing but a sense of shame when I'd had the time to think upon it. So, ye should think this over: We on the land would have been friends, but ye would not. Ye but pretended. Ye thought ye dealt with dumb red folk who had none to make their plans. But listen hard: I be Sir John McJack, the Lord of this

Land where I Lives the While! These be my people; they cared for me when I could not. Between them and yourselves stands none but me; their fingers be itching on the shafts. What would ye have?"

He glanced around and read the faces. The men from the inland camps were beginning to gang together. Lagunaka was speaking to them, though Wawakna tried to stop him.

McJack was frightened, then. Perhaps his trick had worked too well; he had no taste for murder. At any moment, the indians might loose their arrows. He had held them a bit too long. Presumed too greatly on his frail authority, unbacked as it was with intimate acquaintance with the inland men. Lagunaka was explaining what the whalers had intended to do.

McJack's voice was urgent to the whites: "Quick. Walk quiet to your boats! Get out to yer ship, from the range of the shafts! Do it now while I try to quell this thing afore it starts. Once loosed there'd be no stopping!"

Lagunaka protested, and McJack knocked the indian to the ground. The others grunted and backed away, but Wawakna and the other chiefs took hold and calmed the incipient rebellion. Lagunaka, half stunned, still sat on the ground. But McJack knew he'd never forget.

By then it was dusk, and the whites were halfway to their boats, trying not to hurry. Unable, though, to resist looking back. McJack made a noise like a whistling arrow and chuckled softly when some of them ducked. Twenty feet behind the whites the indians followed. They had gotten over their fright and some felt a warlike urge again. These were the ones McJack feared. "Nanquemoke," speaking back over his shoulder, "do ye keep watch of Lagunaka. Let him loose no shaft nor cast a hatchet!"

He saw the whalers eye their guns as they walked past them, just before they reached their boats. They walked, too, right over their own axes, there on the ground. Right past their own long knives; one of these lay on the frame of the grindstone.

"Make no move to touch them," warned McJack. "It would quick be the death of ye all. But when ye be in your boats I will give ye your guns — did the red people have them they'd do more harm than good. Hold high your hands, ye scum and scattle, lest I change me mind and turn the injuns loose! Their shafts be dipped in the brew!" McJack was still grinning as he watched the men climb clumsily into their boats, their hands held high. He grinned, was afraid to laugh, while he handed the guns aboard, for he choked each muzzle by ramming it into the soil. "Do ye fire these things they will blow your dammed heads off, as well ye know. Them as will row shall take up the oars; the rest keep reaching for the clouds. When we are gone ye can come to the shore and get your gear: your pots and casks and such. Ye have more need of them than we. Now! Ye on the oars! Dip! Pull! Ye are off on yer voyage! Hi-yo! Hi-yi!" he shouted.

He felt exultant, but he yelled too quickly, for a yell is contagious. Some of the indians took up the cry. "Hi-yo! Hi-ii!" they yelled and fitted their arrows. McJack saw Nanquemoke knock the magician's aim upward; the arrow was lost in the dark of the sky.

Another young buck, not daring to disobey McJack but unable to control his impulse, let fly an arrow at one of the casks. *Thump!* It struck the barrel. McJack pointed and more arrows flashed. The red men began to yell like mad. *Thump! Thump!* The arrows struck the cask. "Hi-yi!" yelled McJack. "Go ye to it! Ye may spit yer spite upon the cask without doing any harm! "Hi-yo! Hi-yi!"

He made the sign of a circle and the reds went into a war dance. Grabbed the axes and knives and swung them in the air. And when the boats were out of range some aimed their arrows there. The white men dodged and yelled and cursed in the boats. The master yelled for haste at the oars. He pointed toward the deck, but the boats went around to the seaward side to reach it. Fearful that an arrow might reach that far.

McJack sat down on a cask and laughed. Suffered a reflex action from the tension of his nerves. Watched the indians yelling there, and thought he had solved the problem. Then he looked out at the ship and jumped to his feet. In the half-dark there he could see what the whalers were doing: they were bringing the little cannon to bear. "Stop!" McJack yelled to the red men. "Quit with yer yawling and yowling. Git! Wawakna, Menotac, Manumump, Nanquemoke, make these injuns run and hide! Git behind a tree! Off in the bush!" He jumped up and down with excitement. Waved his arms toward the woods. "Git out or git riddled!" he yelled. And by the time the cannon boomed across the water and echoed down the coast and from the inland cedars, McJack stood safe behind a tree and every red man had vanished, although not before Lagunaka had snatched the bearskin from the barrel. The hide of Saint Pat, and McJack hadn't seen the theft.

His laugh was high strung as he heard the thud of the slugs on the trees and casks and saw spatters of sand when they struck the shore. He trembled a little. Almost his plan had failed him, even when he thought he had gained success, for he'd forgotten about the cannon. It boomed again and more slugs came whining in. One struck a tree quite close to McJack and stuck fast. In the little light there was by then the thing gleamed dully. He was curious and before the next blast, went over and got it. Flipped it from hand to hand, for the thing was hot. "Hah! The man would save his iron; he has used the stones from the beach for bullets. He would slay the red people with their own pebbles! He be crafty as well as cruel, but not enough." And McJack chuckled again, quite pleased with his own shrewdness.

In a few moments it was dark. McJack shouted for his indians and the chiefs answered from back in the woods. He and Nanquemoke and a few of the others were waiting there. No one had been hurt and McJack chuckled: "I will lay a wager that some be a league in the woods now, they were that frightened by the cannon." Out on the ship a hub-bub seemed to be going on. Shouts and curses. McJack hailed the men: "Ahoy, ye scum and' scattle!"

"Ahoy, ye white bastard!" was the reply.

"Spit and spivel!" McJack's laugh was taunting, filled with his mirth of triumph, though perhaps a bit unthoughtful of its long-range results. "But ye have done no harm with yer flying stones, else I might not play ye quite so fair. Do ye come again or should some others come they should come in peace. Play fair your game and do your own toiling with the whales."

"Who be ye?" The vice was surly, but the master was curious; he would have a report to make.

"I told ye afore, I be Sir John McJack. By the grace of the saints and the will of the people, I be the Lord of the Land."

"From whence do ye come?"

"From me town in the woods, a bit back from the shore."

"How come ye here? We thought there were no whites in the land."

"Sure, kind sir, the land be broad. We came in a ship."

"Where be it now? How come ye have no guns at all?"

Evidently the man was skeptical.

"What with the shafts so poisoned that a cut will kill, we have no need of guns at all," lied Sir John McJack. "I only tell these things, ye scum and scattle, that I mind me manners, not wishing to be rude, and all." And his laugh was taunting.

"Ye lie!"

"Do it give ye a shock to hear a man lie, yerself as be so filled with truth? Now listen to me; I have talked with ye enough. Do ye come to the shore and get your gear, I will warrant ye safe. But get it and begone. Do ye come again ye should mind yer manners; the injuns would not like the toil. Do ye try your tricks I will have ye lashed until your stinkin' bones be bare!"

"May ye burn in hell and..."

"Tell what ye think to yer scurvy crew; see if they think ye be shrewd as the devil himself, and small lot better!" And with that McJack took the grindstone and dragged it well back among the trees. More of the indians came out from where they'd been lurking. But most, McJack figured again, were a league in the inland.

When the dawn was come the whale lay there upon the beach, black and gray and red and white. It stank and the gulls were feeding on it. The casks and gear were gone, as was the ship. On the shore were marks of heavy boots and of the prows of boats.

And later, along the waterfronts, beyond the leagues of the salted sea, tall tales were told of "Sir John McJack, Lord of the Land Where He Lived the While."

And the tales gained a little in the telling. For instance: McJack's indians, there on the bay shore, were very different from those on the ocean side of the land. At least six inches taller, they were correspondingly savage. The poison of their arrows was so powerful that just a scratch was fatal. These were killer indians and if Sir John didn't hold them in check, no white man would be safe. There had been other red men there — the whalers had found their deserted camp — but McJack's men had either killed them or driven them away, being so stealthy and subtle that one hundred of them could rise up from the ground without warning.

The east-shore indians never went to the bay shores for fear of Sir John and his hordes. And McJack, because according to his own lights, dealt fairly and kept his word, never went across to the eastern shore. And there were hints that he owned a pirate ship and buried his treasure on the cape.

Such, in spots, was the fame of Sir John McJack. A fame which served in very good stead for a couple of years, for though a few whalers ranged the more northern coast, none at all came into the bay.

But the whales were still there, in the springtimes. McJack could see them from the bluff. So could the few ships that happened to pass a mile or more at sea. Those masters would write in their logbooks, then: "Whales in the Bay by the Cape," with day and date.

Chapter 7

The axes and knives taken from the whalers had been divided between the three camps, being so few the people took turns in the use of them. They proved much better than the tools of stone, and the red people would wonder what other marvels the white men possessed, and how they, the red people, could get them. Thus, curiosity and cupidity were already aroused.

And there had been one fatality: Wenowen, a man of Menotac's camp, becoming too familiar before getting acquainted with an eighteen-inch knife, had cut an artery in his shoulder. Then, though the medicine man pranced and sang his song of healing, though the squaw sat crouched and prayed to the Manitou for mercy and the life of her man, the indian bled to death in an hour.

Before the body stiffened they pulled his knees up toward his chin, folded his arms about them as if he were sitting at ease, and after much pow-wow to fright off the devils, the man was buried, sitting in the sand, with his arrows, his pipe and an earthen bowl. With a deerskin about him to keep his soul warm, the while it lingered there. It was an unlucky accident but it proved educational. Wenowen became, in his humble way, a sacrifice to the science of cutlery. The people learned from his fate to be more careful.

As for the axes, the human mind gets sundry notions, especially where and when the mental fields are both fertile and fallow concerning the dignity of deeds as they may be apportioned among the sexes. According to the teachings of McJack, the axe is a superior tool; a squaw, being inferior to her man, should not be allowed to use it. This was gravely decided, in common council. McJack grinned to himself when the law was passed, and he set the example at his wood pile. He would smile when he saw the other men working, too. Taking turns with the axes, upholding the dignity of their manhood. Their wood piles grew greater than ever before, but later, dignity running low and the novelty fading, the women were allowed, at first as a favor, to use the tools. But a man could still do so without losing caste and so McJack smiled as he watched. But, playing his politics in a practical way, he continued to cut his own wood, while Minyanata did her own tasks and tended their daughter.

Still young and comely though slightly stouter, "Lady McJack" was very happy with her husband and child. Little Yanata was healthy and handsome and mischievous. Perhaps this last was the Irish in her, the diminishing strain come down from her sire. She was able by then to toddle alone, to visit Wawakna and climb all over her granddad. To wrap the plaits of his graying hair about his throat and pretend to choke him, while grandmother giggled and petted and scolded. All of this, of course, inside the wigwam, for such a show of affection was not for the public. There was that matter of traditional and paternal dignity, which McJack openly flouted. He carried the squealing child around on his head, or turned her a flip-flop. But once, a bit too early, he tried to teach juggling, and Yanata bumped her head with a juggle stone. He was proud as a peacock of the lass he'd begotten. Sir John McJack. Sometimes a busy man. Sometimes a crafty man. Once in a while a careless man, too.

Like on that winter's day, after the breeze had blown away the night fog, when he and Wawakna and Nanquemoke went hunting. Down near the coastline but above where the cross still marked the castaway's grave, and between the grave and where the upshore meadows were. There the trees and thickets were very dense, a covert for the deer. There were oaks and maples and locusts, and in the marshes, the cedars. Cat-briar and laurel and huck and prim. Nearer the shore were bayberry bushes. Amongst all of these a man couldn't see very far, neither inland nor seaward. When he went there he must walk in the game trails. These twisted and turned, some plain and some fainter, and a man must be fast with his arrow else the deer would be gone.

Nanquemoke was the best archer in all of the camps, much better than McJack. The two had practiced together and the fact was proved, so it was small wonder that, the day they were hunting in the thickets and a deer showed for an instant, that Nanquemoke killed it. Not instantly, of course; the deer had run crashing through the growth and stumbled and blatted. Got to its feet and staggered on and blatted again when Nanquemoke cut its throat.

McJack didn't like to hear those sounds; he somehow felt guilty after killing a deer. "Sure, it has done nothing against me," he had explained. "And it be a beautiful thing, and all. Aye, I know; the gods made it to be food for man, but seems a shame. Before it's killed, while I know it be afoot, there be a thrill and thumping of the blood, but..." McJack would smile and shrug his shoulders. He did it that day among the thickets and trees, and while the others dressed the deer he walked out toward the shore. Perhaps this was a quarter of a mile away, though more by those twisting and turning paths. Because of the growth, even though it was winter, he seldom could see more than a few yards before him.

He went carelessly; there was no longer any need to hunt. Just rambling down to the shore to look at the ocean. There wouldn't be anything there; there seldom was, especially in winter. Springtime there might be a whale or a school of porpoise, but in the winter these would be as scarce as ships.

And McJack wasn't thinking about ships at all, nor of the men who sailed them, even when he came quite near the shore and could hear the unseen little waves. For the surf was light; there had been three days of offshore breeze and the night just past had been entirely calm. Calm with a winter night fog. But McJack had forgotten these, while he watched his footing on the twisting paths because of the cat-briars. As he went he whistled. Careless. He came to a bayberry thicket. Started to walk around it, out to the upper beach. "Halt!" said a hoarse and startled voice. "Be ye Sir John McJack?" And McJack was startled, too, so much so that he nearly dropped his weapon. Between him and the shore stood a man with a musket. On the beach was a boat and five other men. Beyond, perhaps an eighth of a mile from shore, was a ship standing high on a shoal. A rather small ship with two stubby masts and sails furled on its spars.

"Be ye McJack?" the man repeated, his excitement showing in his voice but holding his musket ready. McJack at first was too surprised for words, especially that the man should know his name. Over the sentry's shoulder he could see the other men grabbing some guns from the boat. McJack grabbed at his own self-control.

"Sure, I reckons I be," he told the man softly. Then he made his voice stern and louder: "Ye men on the beach stand where ye be!" Come no nearer the bush lest ye be drilled with a shower of shafts!"

McJack, both startled and scared, was throwing a wonderful bluff, but the men stopped running. "Hold where ye stand and tell me who ye be. Do ye fire one shot my men will swarm the beach and slay ye all!"

Then, to the sentry: "We will go down to your shipmates where they stand. They have, I can see, a wise man to lead them. And ye yerself, should stop the shaking in yer shoes," with one of his crooked and bewhiskered smiles. There were crinkles, too, at the corners of his eyes, as he and the sentry walked down to the others.

But, inside of himself, McJack was quaking. For all that he knew these men might be as dangerous as the whalers had been. But, caught by surprise and alone as he was, he had to take the chance. Learn the minds of the men if he could. "Saints pray for me now!" he pleaded while he walked. Smiling that crooked smile of his, seeming so sure of himself.

And that was how he became acquainted with young Master Mundell and his crew, of the good ship *Melrose*, returning from Jamestown to England mostly in ballast but stranded on a shoal in the fog and calm of the night before — perhaps because Mundell, hardly older than McJack, lacked full knowledge of the coast and perhaps of navigation. The bow of his ship stood high but the stern was afloat. Her deck pitched toward the stern, for the flood of the tide had just started. Later that stern would lift.

"Fast forward in the sand," Mundell unnecessarily explained. "She came bow on with the flood, but slow. Just drifted, the night so calm we had no steer-way. Aside from that we were lost in the fog. We cleared the land down yonder* half a league at sea, at dusk. It looked then like the open sea. Next, the wind failed and the fog came down. This coast was strange to me. We thought we were still in the open, else we'd have anchored."

McJack felt sorry for the man. Glad to talk to someone, too: some decent white men. But there wasn't much time for casual conversation; offshore a squall seemed brewing. High winds from the east would break the ship; they all knew it. To make Mundell feel less at blame, McJack said: "At times there seems an inshore current here, and mayhap ye drifted with it. Ye could not know. Have ye tried to free her?"

"Aye, we carried an anchor to the shoal above: the one that's bare, now the tide is down. Wound on the capstan, but the anchor dragged; the sand would not hold it."

McJack considered a moment, looking out and up from the shore. There was that shoal where the anchor would not hold; it was really all one shoal, the north end being high. The sand was a yard above the water: an ebb-tide island there; at flood the water would be half-knee deep, in a calm. This McJack knew. And on that flood the stern of the ship would float, though her bow stay deep in the sand. McJack frowned; he had him a thought. He forgot about the many men who were supposed to be in the bush, and remembered the score or more on the bluff. Or there would be a score could he find them all. He turned to Mundell. The crew stood listening, now and then glancing at the bush. Maybe some were suspicious that McJack was playing a trick. "Have ye weight in the forehold?" asked McJack.

"Not much; we had ballast but moved it aft."

"Light her some more, can ye do it. On the flood, should a line lead from stern to yonder shoal, mayhap she could be twisted loose, should this calm but hold the while."

"But the anchor will not hold," objected Mundell. "We tried it, and it failed. Nor will it hold astern, out in deep water. The iron but drags; the ship stays still." The master's voice seemed hopeless. He further explained: "We have no line to reach beyond the shoal up there."

McJack grinned: "But, Master Mundell, where one iron will fail mayhap four score of feet will hold, what with the anchor helping. As for the line, mayhap we can lend ye a length. We... hold ye with the gun!" He shouted this last, for one of the men had cocked his piece.

The declared excitedly: "But I saw an injun in the bush!"

And what if ye did? It's the injun's own bush; he have a right to be in it! Be a red man

* Cape Henlopen

a thing to be shot on sight?"

He turned toward shore and shouted: "Wawakna, ye and Nanquemoke should come to me. The rest shall stay in the covert."

So the two red men walked quietly across the sand, and Mundell remarked: "Fine looking men, both, the young and the old. Each treads the strand as if he were a king!"

"Aye, the old one be a small king of a sort, and his have ruled this land since first they came. He be the chief of one of me clans. Wawakna, Nanquemoke, I would have ye meet with Master Mundell; these men be part of the crew of his ship." And McJack laughed as he pointed to the ship. There were seven men in the bow. Mundell waved reassurance and turned questioningly to McJack, who watched the incoming tide.

"This flood will serve three hours afore dark," said McJack. "It will be a moon-tide and it should be high. Do this calm hold, though in the east there be that threat of storm, mayhap we can help. Meanwhilst, take again the iron to you high shoal, and make it ready." And in a lower tone, "ye should treat the injuns gentle, does one be curious and come down. I..."

"But ye said..."

"Aye," and McJack's eyes really twinkled, "now that I know what temper ye have and how ye are, and that ye mean no harm could ye do it, the which ye will not even try do ye be wise, I will tell ye this: When first ye saw me I was all alone. My wits as well as me men were elsewhere. I did not know your ship was on the shore. The men ye feared were not in the bush at all, and ye might have done me murder at the time, had ye so choosed."

Both Mundell and McJack laughed then. "But, suppose I had done ye harm?" asked Mundell.

"Aye, in such a case, when Wawakna was told the news, and your ship so stuck in the sand, and all, even did ye take to cover there and hold the injuns off with guns, they would camp in the bush and wait for the sea to break your ship and cast ye on the shore. So, ye see, ye were wise to have more kindly thoughts." The two men laughed again. The crew wondered why; there seemed so little cause for mirth.

McJack sobered and spoke to Nanquemoke: "Ye shall stay here on the shore. Do any men from the other camps come down, ye shall bid them wait, to do the white men no harm at all. They be not like the whaling crew. They be our friends, and stand in need of their red brothers' help. Wawakna and I will go to the camp to make ready."

But after he and the chief had started away he had an afterthought and came back to Mundell: "Ye should, while the sea be low, cut stakes and mark the edge of yon high shoal. On flood it will be a foot of water there; did one but step into the deep he'd freeze or founder. As it is there'll be some wetted feet"

Mundell nodded, and McJack and the chief went away. "Sir John" would have liked to stay and talk with the men; there must be white man's news to hear. But Master Mundell would not be in the mood. Too busy getting his gear adjusted, and all. Too worried about his ship to give his mind to gossip.

And McJack had another reason for going himself to the camp: Lagunaka. The medicine man might insist on delay, the while he made pow-wow. Or he might appeal to the cupidity of the people, telling how helpless the white men would be to protect the treasures they carried in the ship. Or how one white man was the same as another: Mundell no better than the whaler had been.

However, although most of the other men were there or within easy reach, Lagunaka was not; he had gone some other place. Perhaps he was hunting. Or maybe he'd gone to meet his sorcerer friend in Menotac's camp. McJack didn't care which: "It's mayhap just as well; he will not hinder. Though the varmint will be sad to miss the show, it's well we can spare his bother."

Then from the bluff he looked at the sky and at the rising tide in the bay; he couldn't of course see the ship. "It will take some time to make ready: to carry the men to the shoal in boats, and all. Can I but make them do the task there'll be some shivering feet down yon."

Down yon, two hours later and nearing the top of the tide, the ship still sat with her bow in the sand; her stern had lifted. From the stern-bitts and the capstan — this last through a snatch-block on the stern — two lines ran out to the higher shoal, the capstan's hitched to the anchor. Grasping the other line, shin-deep in water and shivering while they waited, and wondering, too, were twenty red men and half as many women. And six of the sailors, to lend their experience and make the line draw steady. Deep water between them and the shore. Deep water aft of the ship.

Out there were the ship's two boats, lines looping slackly to her bow. Waiting, once the ship was free, to warp her out to safety. A little east wind began to blow. The winter sky looked squally. McJack waded on the shoal, lining up his man and woman power. Mundell with a crewman worked the capstan; its line grew more taut on its anchor. The other line, too, took up part of its loop as the people laid back; dug their feet in the sand with the strain on the line. Slowly, as evenly as McJack could direct them.

At first there was no movement of the ship at all. "Hold hard that line!" shouted McJack. "Do not surge; a surge be followed by a slack. Even and steady does it... Now!" For the line gave a little. "Walk ye slowly back as the ship gives! Her stern moves now! Her bow comes twisting from the sand! Hi-yi-hi-yay! She moves!"

And the sailors and the red people took up that common cry: "Hi-yay-yi-yi!" The two whites on the far end of the line forgot to watch the safety stakes and backed clear off of the shoal. Floundered clear to their necks and clambered out and cursed and laughed and shivered and waited for the boats to take them back to the ship, and the red people to the shore, while the wind from the east blew in squally gusts, and the little waves grew larger.

Master Mundell had two reasons for taking his craft to the harbor behind the cape instead of heading straight to sea. First was the weather: it threatened a storm and the wind was wrong. That first reason was caution; the second was courtesy. He wanted a chance to thank McJack and his people, so he had him bring Wawakna and spend the night on the ship. And McJack had two reasons for sending the others home: he wanted them to dry their clothes lest some catch cold, and he wanted the women away from the sailors lest they catch something else.

So that evening, in the ship's cabin, McJack learned what he could of the white man's news. Of Jamestown with its trade and trouble with the indians there, what with the rum and all. Of Plymouth with its starvation and cold and its fat young graveyard, and of the people's religion: fanatic, strict and unbending. Filled with zeal but lacking charity. With faith in god, and in witches, too.

He learned of England, where James the First still reigned as a despot, forbidding prayer to the saints, and all. Learned that the king's soldiers were over-riding Ireland and chasing the catholics into the bogs. That a priest could be shot did he stay more than an hour on the isle. That the English had confiscated nearly all of the Irish shipping and that such as were still free had been forced into piracy. Dodging the king's warships but preying on his commerce, for the sake of their own maintenance and the good of the homeland. For they would slip into some hidden creek at night, in Kerry or in County Cork, and leave their loot for the people there.

And the listener chuckled as he heard the blood tales of one "Sir John McJack," he who ruled the Capelands and the reds. Strange tales, and only slightly true.

"Sure," he concluded, "the white man's world be in a hell of a mess, the now; best I had stay where I be. I could not leave my lady here, and I could not keep her over yon. Not her nor the child. So I will still be Sir John McJack, and stay here with me people."

The idea pleased both his vanity and his judgment; so far as he was concerned he had small regret when the *Melrose* sailed. In a small sort of way he had profited largely: he had gained the men's friendship by lending the many helping hands. He had gotten some things as a small reward: some carpenter tools and such odds and ends as the ship could spare, though these were few. Two sailmaker's needles with curving points and eyes that would take a sinew thread. Some twine and steel fish hooks and other odd trifles. But the best was a razor, with its hone. Now Minyanata could discard her singe-stone.

But, though McJack was pleased with the razor, he had gotten another worry. A story that Mundell had told him, but couldn't prove. Something he had heard on the waterfront, before he had sailed from home. It concerned what some whalers were planning to do and worried McJack immensely.

"Hounds!" he whispered to himself. "Saints grant they do not bring the hounds! For a man cannot hide from a hound at all!"

Chapter 8

There was plenty for McJack to ponder after the *Melrose* was gone. The *Melrose*. He would wonder how far she'd gone and how she'd fared, out there in the open sea. In the nights he would wonder about the tale that the master had told him, that bit of waterside gossip — he fretted at the thought.

Mundell's ship missed the *Phoenix* by some seventy leagues; he never knew that the eastbound ship was even there. The *Phoenix*, bound for Jamestown. The weather had so far been good. Her master and men thought that luck was with them. So did some of the women, a score or more of whom were bound for a new world and a new life. For matrimony. For mating with whom they could, having little choice; they would go to the highest bidder. Fate having denied them their men at home, they went to the new world to find them. In spite of their fears of the sea, of their uncertainty as to what sort of man or monster that each might draw, some had felt bound to take the chance.

A few, though, had been press-ganged for the profit of their passage. For the good of the colony and the incidental welfare of the throne. Among these was Mellissa Mallore. She hadn't wanted to come at all, and she'd been seasick most of the voyage. She was vengeful and unhappy. She was also, when not seasick, a buxom and vigorous wench. But, "Hell's bells!" she groaned as the ship rode a swell. "Does the sea get worse I will die!"

And, Mellissa, it will get worse, for a storm bears down from the north of east. Your ship lies in its pathway, though you be so near your journey's end. Though you are almost in sight of the coast.

The winds reached the cape just before the dawn, and awakened Sir John McJack; he heard them in the treetops. He listened for rain but couldn't hear it. Then he snuggled down beside Minyanata. Little Yanata was sleeping. The dark of the night was turning to gray.

And when the cloud-racked dawn was fully come, so was the fury of the rainless wind. The bay, out beyond the shelter of the shore, was whipped to whitecaps. These raced with the low-hung clouds above; the flailing treetops seemed to whip these latter on. McJack and Wawakna and Nanquemoke were watching from the bluff.

"It will be bad on yon side of the cape," shouted McJack. "It will be breaking on the shoals and pounding the shore somethin' dreadful! Would the rain but hold I have half a mind to go and see."

But Wawakna, wise in the ways of the weather, shook his graying head: "Rain will come. Soon. Me, I have pains in me bones." But Nanquemoke was young and had no pains; he would go with McJack. Wawakna would sit by his fire and listen. With the eyes of his mind he could see it all, then; already the chief had seen many storms. "Rain will come," he insisted.

But the other two went down; on the trail the wind was not so bad. Above, the treetops twirled and twisted; at times the clouds seemed to hang so low that the branches beat their bottoms. The half-shelter of trees reached on down beyond the camp at the pond, but coming near the beach they felt the brunt of the wind. The sea joined its roar to that of the gale, and the rain began. Instead of falling it seemed to fly. Pelting and pounding. McJack and Nanquemoke, at the edge of the forest, sought shelter behind trees, peering around the trunks.

The sea seemed coming to meet them, in great green combers house-top high, losing their crests in the gale. Breaking in thunder over the shoals. Adding their salted spray to the rain. The welter of waves came after and climbed far beyond their normal beach; in spots they swirled among the trunks of trees. Twirled through a thicket. Piled ridges of sand on the inland. Threw clams and conchs and sea snails into the fringes of the forest. The white salt of the spume caught in the crevices of the bark of the trees, which twisted and threatened to fall. Dripped and ran from the faces of the men who watched; despite the rain they tasted the salt of the spume.

They crouched there and watched. Perhaps McJack prayed to his saints and his god. And Nanquemoke thought of the might of the gods, of the strength of the Spirit of Storm. Neither, as yet, had seen the ship.

But what thought the people aboard the *Phoenix*? Her masts jerked and strained and her cordage whistled. She pitched and rolled; the seas swarmed over. The hull of the ship groaned. So did the people there, and Mellissa Mallore. Some prayed. Some cursed.

Huddled beneath the poop deck, clinging fast. Or down in the stinking, swaying hold beneath the battened hatches.

Nanquemoke was first to see the ship — in a lull of the rain he pointed. It was up-coast, and out, phantom-like in the rain. Half a mile out from where the dune lands and the meadows began, and the tide streams. Off from where the dunes in common times held back the sea. Heading, they knew, for a shoal. Deep water between the shoal and shore.

McJack made motions that they go down to the dunes, but they found no dunes. The pounding waves had broken through and washed the little hills away, inshore into the meadows. Sand from the dunes. Sand from the sea. Sand and pebbles and clams and conchs, and fish too weak to fight against the storm. Fish that were strangled by the sand they breathed. Fish that were fashioned by the hand of god to live in the sea and prosper.

And the feeble hands of men had fashioned the *Phoenix*, and men still strove to steer her in the sea. Strove hard to bring her around the point of the cape and find the harbor there. Instead, the ship came down on the shoal. Her masts and spars could be seen to fall. They angled for a swaying moment there, and then went down.

McJack gasped when he saw it. He called on his saints but they couldn't help. Not when the sea was having its wanton way with even the fishes. The hull raised high and then turned over.

Then, after a little, the wreckage came wallowing in parts of the housing. Masts and yards and tangled lines. Casks and planks and a broken and capsized boat. They went over where the dunes had been, on out into the meadows. Half-seen corpses on the crests of waves; these would float grotesquely, then they'd dive. Dead men diving, over what had been the land. Over what would be the land again, when the storm was done.

In the midst of the welter rode another boat. Tossed on the waves and riding low it was still upright. This went over the meadows, too, twisting and turning. It seemed heading for the fastlands. McJack pointed, and shouted to his friend: "Nanquemoke, the sea has had its will. The men be dead. We cannot help, but yon goes a boat which we well can use, can we get it. It bears toward yon shore, but do this wind go down all of this water will cast back to the sea again, and the boat will go with it. The boat, and mayhap the dead men, and the gear."

McJack held his hand to his throat; with his shouting in the wind it was aching. They watched the boat; it held on toward the trees on the fastland. Seemed caught in an eddy. Swirled round and round and went nowhere. Seemed almost to be waiting, while McJack and Nanquemoke ran back through the woods.

They came out near the boat. A spar was caught in the whirlpool, too, and the first time they waded to reach the craft the timber drove them back. They stood for a moment and shivered; felt the tug of the whirl on their legs. Waited for the spar to pass. "It would crack our ribs like bird bones!" McJack tried to tell his friend, but the wind blew the words away.

The spar went past, and they nodded. The boat was coming around again. There was something in the stern; they could see it. Something in a tarpaulin there. The boat was half filled and the water sloshed around it, whatever it was. But at the moment McJack wasn't even curious; his thought was centered on the boat.

At last they reached it and lugged it to the shore. Leaned on the gunwales and panted. McJack shivered again with the cold. "We have got us a boat!" he confided to the whistling wind. Then he waded back and felt the tarpaulin. He looked at Nanquemoke with widened eyes.

"It be a man!" the motion of his mouth told the indian. But when they dragged him ashore and into the lee of a thicket, the man proved a woman. Gray skirts and white stockings and iron-buckled shoes for immediate visual proof. The face, at first, told them little; it was contorted and blue and livid; her hair straggled down across it.

"But she be dead," declared McJack. "She be most nigh drowned, or smothered with the tarp. Mayhap we can help her live. We will try, at that."

So they turned her face downward and McJack lifted her body, at the waist. Lifted and lowered, as if he were pumping. Forcing water from the woman's lungs. At last she gasped and strangled. More water came, and froth. She groaned and her chest tried to heave. McJack turned her over and worked her arms.

While they'd been busy the wind had slipped the boat offshore a little, and Nanquemoke went to get it. Above the wind McJack heard him shout. The indian beckoned. And from the water in the boat they dragged out a man. Drowned. The head of the woman had lain on the chest of the man.

McJack figured that he had wrapped the tarp about the woman's head to keep out the spume and spray. They'd gotten into the boat before it had been torn loose from its chocks. The man had been drowned by the spume and spray in trying to save the woman.

And so it was that Mellissa Mallore came onto the cape to live for a while, the one white woman there. Mellissa Mallore, a man's woman at heart. Press-ganged for the profit of her passage to the brave new world. That man in the boat must have valued her once. Even as late as that morning, while on the ship, there had been a little hope. He had fended for her as well as he could. Never would know that he had achieved success.

McJack and Nanquemoke had fended for her, too. And back in camp the women helped, fighting pneumonia. Minyanata and her mother, Nanquemoke's woman, and others. For Mellissa was sick for a longish while in a little wigwam there in the camp. Wrapped in furs to keep her warm. Fed on good gruels to preserve her strength. Depending after that on the strength and the will to live.

Lagunaka was again offended. Before McJack came to the bluff the medicine man would have been the first one called. He would have rattled and pranced and danced around. He'd have worn a mask to fright off the devils. He'd have sung a song.

But nobody called him. He protested to the chief. Wawakna was shrewd in his way and explained that the medicine of the red people would not work with white men. It was especially futile with the white women. Lagunaka was mollified for the time, but not flattered. He went off by himself and made a brew, and when Mellissa got better he tried to take credit.

Sir John smiled, as did the chief. Lagunaka didn't like those smiles, and he blamed McJack. In the magician's own way and in his own good time, perhaps he'd get even. McJack had failed to observe the ethics of professional courtesy, a rudeness which Lagunaka could neither overlook nor condone.

He was so hot and bothered that he committed a breach of his own people's etiquette: he spoke to Minyanata about the matter, but Lady McJack only smiled. Nothing, she contended, could shake her faith in the great man she'd married. He was a great and brave and good and kindly man. And handsome, especially since he'd gotten the razor and was able to shave his face. He had great wisdom, too, and was crafty or bold as occasion required. Could give good council to her father, the chief.

But, argued the wily Lagunaka, why was the white brother so interested in this strange white woman? Did he hope, when she should have recovered, to take her into his wigwam? Where, in that case, would Minyanata be?

The thought made her frown; she was a bit perplexed. Mellissa in her ravings had said some strange sayings; she spoke the same idiom as did McJack. Her skin was whiter than his own. As she slowly got better her face grew smooth and comely. Her arms and legs grew rounder. Her eyes were deep blue, the same as Minyanata's man's. Once in a while, just then of late, they'd hold a twinkle in them. Or maybe a look of shrewd calculation, especially when she saw McJack. Was the woman figuring for the future? Lagunaka had at least accomplished something, and Minyanata conferred upon the matter with both the gods and the saints. After that she felt better, but she couldn't ignore this Mellissa Mallore. Yet there was a comforting thought: perhaps some of the other men would want the white woman. Panquenack, for instance; he had no woman of his own. He was young, and very tall and strong: a fine-looking man. And Minyanata had seen him watching Mellissa even from the first. He hadn't as yet asked the chief for the woman; perhaps he was waiting and watching her health. If Mellissa grew strong again, and able to work, perhaps Panquenack would take her.

Chapter 9

One day that winter McJack was sitting in Wawakna's wigwam and staring at the fire. Suddenly: "Wawakna, come spring I would like a pair of live skunks."

The chief looked perplexed. McJack laughed and explained what Wawakna already knew: "There be no critter in the wood that would brave the stink of a skunk, lest it be starving. Nor mayhap would a hound, yet of that I be not so sure. Ye would not know, for ye have never seen a hound; mayhap a hound would have less sense than a beast in the wild. But it's a thought worth trying, in case the whalers bring the dogs."

The chief looked worried; McJack tried to reassure him. Perhaps the tale that Mundell had told was just an idle one; last spring the whalers hadn't come to the bay. Perhaps they thought it safer to go some other place. McJack chuckled, remembering the trick he had played before. Wawakna nodded and lighted his pipe. Little Yanata came in for a visit, and so, that was in the dead of winter, they let the thought lie.

But McJack didn't forget. He planned, among other things, to go up into the inland as soon as the weather would let him. He mentioned this to his wife, along in early March. The winds were howling over the white-capped bay and over the bluff. The walls of the wigwam trembled.

"Minyanata go wid ye?" she inquired, looking up sharply as if taken by surprise.

"Not now, me lady; I be thinking of going far, to be sure."

She looked frightened: "Where ye go?" She was sitting on a stool and making a deerskin dress for her daughter, using the sailmaker's needle. "Where ye go?" she repeated. He still did not reply: he was looking at the fire. Slyly she reached out and pricked his leg with the needle. "Where ye go?" Her eyes were laughing but there was fear in them, too.

McJack had jumped with the feel of the needle: "Sure, and I will go to the mayor of the town, and I will tell him ye be cruel to me, that ye punch me full of holes! I will, at that! And the mayor will say: 'Put the woman in the pillory, and give her a licking.'"

She pretended fright: "What be pillory?"

"It's a board on a post, with a hole in it. And the hole goes about the neck of who be in it. And nothing can ye do but stand and stay an wait until those that put ye there do choose to let ye loose." He chuckled.

"Ye make pillory for me?" Her head bent over her work she glanced up slyly.

"Please of Blarney! For why should I do it?"

"Ye make pillory. When ye get bad thought about go away, Minyanata go to mayor. Minyanata say: 'Put my man in pillory!' Mayor say: 'Sure, and I will at that!' and my man stay home!"

Then he drew her to him, remembering mayhap the lonely days before he met her. She laughed, for the sudden fear had left her. "Me, I like pillory, at that."

She resumed her sewing but remained curious. She persisted: "Where ye go?"

He regarded her gravely: "Minyanata, can ye keep shut your mouth if I talk with ye plain?"

She nodded, deeply interested. McJack pushed a fagot further into the little fire: "It's like this: there be things likely to happen soon. Things not so good, and all. We be too close to the whaling beach, and so it's likely the men will come again. If they do they will be many, too many for me and your people. So, should it come wise for us to move, it would be just as wise to know the where to go.

"Me thought, me lady, was to spy out a spot for to move. Mayhap in the Menticos, or the Muskees. Where we would be far from the whaling. Nanquemoke and me will go to find the spot. Your father will stay here; he knows why we go. Wawakna, he be growing old; he be worried, too."

She nodded gravely. She had noted those facts of late.

* * * * *

McJack and Nanquemoke had been gone a full ten days. They had taken to the Great Highway about the middle of March. The whales had not yet come into the bay, for the weather was wild and the waves ran high. Over the shoals, out there, those long waves rolled and threw their spray. They, the shoals, when the winds were high, were bad for whales and ships alike.

On the shore at the whaling beach the great white bones were scattered, at storm-tide levels. Ghastly things half buried in the sand: the ribs, the great and grinning skull. There was nothing left for the gulls to eat, but one would sometimes perch on the end of a rib or walk about on the whitened skull, as if waiting.

The month of March was nearly spent. The winds grew less; some days the seas were fairly calm. McJack sensed but could not see the fact; he was far inshore, up-country, but homeward bound. He and Nanquemoke on the Indian Trail. For some forty miles they had spied out the land. Along the creeks. The river. And on the river, between Muskee and Manumuakin, they thought they'd found the spot they sought: an abandoned camp-site, the farmlands a bit overgrown. Their wigwams could be sheltered by a dense growth of cedars, with running water. So they had taken the homeward trail: that path so trodden in the soil.

"My people," remarked Nanquemoke as if reminiscent, "make this. Much time. Much people."

And that set McJack to thinking, too: With the eyes of his mind he must have seen that age-old march through the wooded lands. Men who were dead two thousand years had been the first to mark it there. And through the centuries other men had come, to pack the soil. Exploring? Fleeing? Both fleeing and pursuing? McJack couldn't know; but with those men had gone their women, else the race would have died. Many had died; perhaps some sat in their sandhills there, beside the trail, having failed their goal. Often there were sandhills beside the trail, among the thickets and the trees. From Wahatquenack, the river, on down to the cape. The way the two men were walking.

Perhaps three leagues from home they met Panquenack; the tall red man running. He brought tidings of a ship they had seen on the sea. On the ocean side where, closer in, the land calmed the winds and the waters.

"We should haste down and see," decided Sir John McJack, proud that Wawakna had sent him the news.

The wind held strong all day. The ship had tried, against wind and tide, to beat into a little harbor there, but failed. After that she had held offshore but in the lee of the land. Sailing up and down, Wawakna explained to McJack. He nodded and asked: "Wawakna, did ye get the small beasties? Ye did? It's mayhap good. We cannot be sure."

But another scout had come running. Two more ships were beating in against the wind, far out on the sea.

"Three ships!" There will be the many men! And do they bring the dogs. Wawakna, best ye had send word to the chiefs of the other camps; I must talk with them. Now, I will go down to the shore, and see the ships. They will do nothing this night but wear it through, for the wind still holds from the west."

Down at the shore he found his prediction verified: the three small ships were wearing out the weather.

Back at the bluff, McJack found that Menotac and Manumump had arrived for the council. He explained: "It be like this: the whaling here be good when the seas be calm. The beach on the bay be good for the drying, with wood and water. The men on the ships have made up their minds to see that they stay. They have the guns and the men."

He then waxed dramatic: "But they may bring the hounds, the like of which ye never did see, the sound of which ye never did hear at all. "It's a sound to fright the bravest man, do he hear it in the wood!" And in a quarter-hour he had the chiefs so frightened of a hound that he was sure they would obey his order to keep their men away. Hold them to their own camps or to the north. That had been in the evening. The winds were calming.

With the first of the next dawn McJack and Nanquemoke had gone down to the lee of the camp, where the skunks were in a basket. McJack carried several pairs of new moccasins, dangling from a thong. Others of the camp, some of whom had not slept well, followed. Very curious and more or less amused. McJack grinned. Chucked the moccasins into the basket, and nothing happened. The skunks looked sleepy. The white streaks on their backs showed dimly in the dusk.

Nanquemoke poked them with an arrow. McJack quite suddenly choked. Nanquemoke gurgled in his throat, and everybody ran to windward. To the lee, among the trees and on the breeze that had taken the place of the gale, the ungentle odor wafted. The oxidized essence of offended skunk was ever amazing.

McJack found it persistent, too, when he wore those moccasins, even after he and Nanquemoke had waded along the beach to the whaling camp, to wet out a possible trail. Then they tramped all over the ground; this was a test case: would a hound follow the trail of a skunk? McJack didn't know; he was just experimenting, forgetting that a skunk's foot scent wouldn't resemble its spray. Wishing, too, that he'd chosen some other plan, for the persistent stink made him faint in his belly. But, soon after, he looked down toward the point, and forgot such trifles.

Down there, above the line of stunted growth, a topsail showed. It seemed to sail on the tops of the trees, toward the entrance of the bay.

"Best we had wade in the water again, afore she rounds in sight," suggested McJack. "Up yon on shore be a little point, where we can see, and be hid. And now, Saints Mary and Monica and Moses, do Moses be a saint at all, would ye bless the skunks and curse the hounds, the now!"

This while they were wading past the overgrown farmlands north of the camp. The little point was an eighth of a mile away. From there, hidden in the bush, one could see far down the beach and into the seaward edge of camp. The first of the ships had shown her hull; she swung to starboard to round the point of the cape. Then she came bow-on, wind on her quarter. There were no whales at all in sight, the calm among the shoals too new. Perhaps tomorrow they'd be there. Always, sooner or later, they had been.

The crew had scrambled aloft to take in sail. Voices could be heard; McJack saw the splash of the anchor. There were shouts and rattlings of gear; the men were lowering a boat, although McJack couldn't see it. The deep bay of a hound came across the water;

Nanquemoke looked frightened.

"It'll be bad; saints help us now!" pleaded McJack. "First will the dogs and the men with guns be put ashore, to track and trail and see that none hide in the bush as we did afore."

The ship had found her setting; she lay bow out, quartering, and the boat was manned over the starboard rail. In the bow of it, when it cleared, stood two of the dogs, forefeet braced on the bends. Etched clear and bold and fiercely strong against the morning skyline.

There where they watched, McJack and Nanquemoke were tense, crouched in the bush. Those were not the first hounds that the indian had ever seen. But McJack said, "Aye, they be bad! I have seen such dogs afore. They be big and swift and trained to be fierce. I minds them well; I've seen them tear a man apart. They will trail stag or man or wolf. But I wonder...?" And he grinned a little.

The boat grounded. The dogs leaped ashore, on leash, each held by a man, one of whom was gigantic; the other was average. Then the men with the muskets stamped about on the beach. The land felt good to their feet perhaps, but they kept sharp watch on the woodline. Let the dogs lead the way to the upper shore.

McJack, tense with his curiosity, could see the big man point to the ground. Tracks. New tracks. Men had been there, on moccasined feet; the men knew it but the dogs did not. They shook their heads until their ears were flapping. The hounds seemed displeased and puzzled. The big man swore.

"The saints be praised!" breathed Sir John McJack. "The saints and the skunkies! Give praise where praise be due; the stink of the skunks has served us well!"

They could hear the men shouting, especially the big man. "The tracks show plain, but they be old," he shouted back to the ship. "There be no scent to follow."

"Such be yer thought, me overgrown friend," gloated John McJack. "There be scent a'plenty; did ye put yer own nose to the ground ye could smell it. But ye would be as duddered as yer dogs." And he chuckled his satisfaction.

Down in the camp the big man was talking again: "We will beat about in the bush; has anything been there the hounds will find the trail. We'll hold them on the leash until we see." He laughed, and McJack didn't like the sound at all.

"That man be brutish as the rest," he muttered. "Best we had go; the hounds will mayhap circle here. They be casting about in the bush the now, but they be fooled."

The deep baying of the beasts had broken into the morning. It echoed in and through the woods and brought chills to the spine of McJack. Then he listened closely: "It's the trail tongue, and not the chase. Mayhap it'll lead..."

"We not been there," declared Nanquemoke, and McJack heaved a sigh of relief. "It's right ye be. It's somewhat else — mayhap a buck. I think it be; they've loosed the dogs and they bear away!"

Then came such sounds as had never been heard in the land: the baying of hounds on the chase. Deep toned and steady. Echoing. Catching on the cedars in the swamps and ringing again through the wooded stillness. Sinister and savage and strange. Growing fainter; the chase was heading toward the ocean shore. The high and wooded ground was only three miles wide right there, then would be the meadows and the mud. And many little tide streams. There the hounds might lose the trail.

McJack and Nanquemoke listened, then turned toward the bay. The second ship had moored, the third was coming in. More boats went ashore. More boats, men and guns.

"It do be bad!" declared McJack. "It most sure do! The hounds, the deer, I had not thought of that, the more fool me! Aside from keeping the injuns away, they have brought men and hounds to hunt the deer, to feed the men who work on the whales. And deer be none too plenty as of now. The signs be bad; no red man may walk in this wood at all; the hounds would find him. And ye, Sir John McJack, kephaw! Ye was so wise that other time! Ye said, ye did: 'Bring men of yer own; the injuns do not like the toil!' And now, they'll like the hounds even less than the toil; they will at that."

And conditions kept on being bad. The calm weather held; the whales came into the bay again. The whaling camp was busy; from the bluff above one could see them. The lights of the fires showed all through the nights, the men working. When the wind was fair one could hear them.

During the daytime the hounds ranged through the woods, following the deer. Their barking and baying rang for miles. Once they came quite near the bluff, but turned and bore away. Often the people could hear the guns. Frightened, the indians kept close at home; McJack advised it too. The other camps were further away, toward the north and the eastern shore. They seldom heard the hounds, and then but faintly. It was April; there were many little showers.

The farm work lagged; the women, hearing the chase, would flee in terror to the camp. McJack asked the men to take over the task but had small success. They too were afraid; and Lagunaka, always jealous of McJack, made more trouble for him. Covertly, but McJack felt sure. Lagunaka cooked his roots and herbs and declared the time had come for war. McJack knew that would be fatal, as did most of the others. Lagunaka, though, had convinced a few. He demanded a council.

McJack patiently explained: "It be like this: we must wait the men out, and take care for the peace while we're waiting. They have the dogs and the guns and more men than we. They have more dogs than we hear: there be six in the camp. They hunt but the two at the time. The men be catching plenty whales; the ships be settling with the heft of the oil. And mayhap the whales will leave the bay, do we wait but two weeks the men will be gone. There be no advantage in a losing fight, so I ask for peace."

But the crafty Lagunaka had other ideas. One was that Sir John go down and talk with the men. He, McJack, was one of them, was he not the white man's brother by the kin of his blood, the red man's by act of adoption? Perhaps, if McJack went down, the white men would give him gifts.

McJack grinned and chuckled, reading Lagunaka's thoughts. He explained that, although he could be friends with some white men, as with those of the *Melrose*, with others he could not, unless he sided with them.

"Sure," said he, "it's less the color of the skin than of the mind and heart. White folks do differ at the heart, same as do injuns." He smiled shrewdly at Lagunaka. "Sure, I could go down, but I would never come back. Even though they did me no other harm the whites would hold me there. That master would not be fooled another time at all. We have so little that they need now, most likely they'll let us be. So I say to wait — it will not be long. It's the whales they be seeking, not injuns."

Lagunaka was silenced but not convinced. His jealousy still rankled. The sorcerer in Menotac's camp was a friend of his; the two got along quite well. Sometimes they visited and conferred. Seriously. As seriously as they believed in their own powers of magic, little though they'd done to prove them.

The days wore on as things grew worse. The schools of fish were coming in, but few of the Lenape men would catch them. They feared to leave their women in the camp. Game food was running low; with those hounds in the woods the men feared to hunt. Those deep-throated bays sent chills through their bones. The ships were loading their casks of oil. The work was not bothered by the little showers, for the fires were protected by tarpaulin tents.

In the woods the course of the chase began to change. At first the deer had held down toward the cape and toward the eastern shore. They reached the streams and meadows there and often lost the dogs. In the nights they would come to the high land again, but were only briefly safe.

Then day by day it changed. The deer that were still alive ran more to the north, in the rear of the bluff but closer. The people heard them plainly then, the dogs and guns. They had fear and terror in their hearts, and hate began to grow. Hate for the men who, day after day, were stealing their clothing and their food. The high land, even there, was only four miles wide, and the sounds came clearly, often.

None of the whites had come to the camp; perhaps they didn't know it was there, especially as the people kept back from the beach, under orders from Wawakna. Watched by McJack and Nanquemoke to see that none disobeyed. One day these three were listening to the chase, and the chief had spoken.

McJack agreed: "Aye, ye be right; the deer be moving. Did the men but stay a month there'd be no deer at all near the Point. The dogs are forcing them toward the other camps, further to the north, between us and the sea. It's bad, to be sure; but we can do nothing to save the deer. The men be salting the meat to serve the voyage home. Have ye seen Lagunaka today?"

The chief had not, nor had Nanquemoke. No one knew where Lagunaka had gone. Wamuta, too, was missing. And neither came back, that day nor the next.

The whales had decided to leave the bay by then; there were no living ones in sight.

Offshore near the whaling camp the ships lay deep in the water. Strewn on the beach was the wreckage of their catch, grim and ghastly and stinking in the warming sun. The casks seemed near all filled. Perhaps one more day and the men and the dogs and the ships would be gone. The people on the bluff were more cheerful at the thought. McJack whistled a tune and sang a little song, in a little voice. He did a bit of the tossing of the stones. It rained a little.

Mellissa, who was well enough to walk about, hurried to her wigwam. McJack grinned when he saw her go. "She has fear of the damp though she fear not the devil," he told himself. "Do I but read that wench right she could take great pleasure in a bed, but not in sick-bed, and not alone. Mellissy, ye will, as ye grow weller, grow worser the while! Ye will not keep fast in mind the man who saved ye from the sea, and died a saving.

"I have seen the looks the young bucks give; should Mellissy get well they will want her. Do she take one man she'll be safer. She will, at that. But the bucks be red. White women cannot take the red so easy as can men. Mellissy be white... and the only other whites be them on the ships. But Mellissy would not take the dare! They have not seen a woman for weeks and weeks; they would wear the wench to death. They would at that; may the saints help Mellissy!"

But McJack had other things to think of. Affairs between the whites and the reds were nearing a climax. He hoped that this would pass, for the living whales were gone. Those ships had nothing to cause them to linger there. They should be leaving.

He had been watching while he meditated on Mellissa, but one thing he failed to see was the face of his wife. Minyanata, while McJack was watching Mellissa and thinking his thoughts, was looking at her husband and thinking hers, and Lagunaka's. She had watched Mellissa go into her wigwam and had frowned a little, standing there in the rain.

She wasn't afraid of the rain, for the weather was mild. It was so warm that the crops should be planted, but they weren't. Her people had too greatly feared the hounds and the hunters. The hunters who were stealing the deer. The whalers who mayhap would leave tomorrow. She'd speak to the gods about it.

Chapter 10

Lagunaka, the man with the bright idea, had acted upon it: he and Wamuta and Kenowac, his sorcerer friend. For he had gone on a visit, to confer and to confab. Seriously, and with both good and bad intentions. The good intent was to stop the whites from killing the deer; the bad, to discredit the council of McJack.

But Wamuta's heart failed him, so Lagunaka and Kenowac took over and made a brew. Of herbs and roots and the guts of an owl. Of some urine and some bedbugs and some worms. Then, very solemnly, Lagunaka dipped a piece of deerskin into the pot, while he made incantation.

So the pot simmered on the coals and the magicians chanted their prayers. Imploring and earnest, there in the night. Calling good devils to cast out the bad. To put the scent of the brew in the nostrils of the dogs, that they follow the deer no more. That the souls of the worms should eat out their innards and that all of the hounds might die.

And lastly, and this was important, that the chanters themselves be empowered by the brew: their arms be strong, their eyes clear and their spirits bold. The two of them, Lagunaka and Kenowac, implored that their bright idea become a glowing deed.

Really, that brew should have done it! And to some extent it did. Menotac, the chief of the other camp, overhearing the chant, frowned — he endorsed the council of Sir John McJack. Without Menotac's knowledge, on that last day while McJack watched from the bluff and saw the whalers make ready to leave, taking their gear to the ships, Lagunaka and Kenowac acted.

It was a gray sort of day, with threat of rain and with little wind. One of those days when sound sends far and a man feels uneasy and doesn't know why. McJack should have felt cheerful, watching the gear being taken aboard, but he felt foreboding in spite of himself. Perhaps he was psychic, at that.

At Kenowac's camp, in the afternoon, the sound of the chase could be heard. This chase would be the last; it was far down toward the cape, coming closer. The people in the camp heard faintly, at first. As it grew plainer, it stopped. They wondered why.

Lagunaka and Kenowac had heard more plainly, there in the woods while waiting. And the brew had made their arms so strong, their eyes and aims so true, that they could not fail. And later, when they returned to camp, they were very proud men. They had done a great deed. They carried in triumph the scalps of the hounds. Two scalps, with ears attached, gray-haired and gristly and limp. Menotac disapproved; this was an ill-done deed. Opinions differed between truculence and fear. Menotac pondered. He should send the news to Sir John McJack; he would do so in the morning.

But Menotac couldn't sleep because of his worry, so an hour before dawn he sent out two of his men. One was to go straight to McJack with the news. The other to stand watch near the trail that led to the camp of the whalers. He, too, would report to the wise white brother; and that was how it came that the latter knew, but didn't know in time. He who sat in the early light watching the doings on the ships below. He who was already puzzled.

"Sure," he had told Wawakna, "there be fewer men at work than went ashore in the boats. The pots and the weighty gear be all aboard; I do not like the looks of things! I wonder what they be doing?"

Then, as if in answer, the first of Menotac's messengers came. He brought the news about the dogs.

"Damn!" exclaimed Sir John. "It was that bubble-boiling varmint I was fearing all the while! Wawakna, rouse out the men to stand ready; I know not what will come, but I be fearful. Many men who should be on the beach are gone some other place. Many men, it were so dark I could not see the dogs nor guns, mayhap they took them, too. Do they come to us we must be readied best we can. Rouse out the camp, but silent.

"Send Nanquemoke to me; set sentinels on the trails. I will still watch the ships. It's not so clear I can see them now, for the clouds be bearing down."

There was confusion in the camp. In spite of orders for silence, a small babble arose, especially among the women and children. This hushed a little when Menotac's other messenger came, the one who had watched the whaling camp trail. More than a score of men from the ships had gone toward Menotac's camp. With guns and four dogs. But none had come toward the camp on the bluff.

"Saints help the people there!" implored McJack. "The saints and god and mayhap we can do a little. But we cannot fight against the guns. Wawakna, what think ye now?"

And he looked overhead at the weather.

They held a quick council, then, and decided to go toward Menotac's camp to see what should happen. To help if they could, although the chance seemed small. But some of the men insisted on a war dance, to make them brave.

McJack frowned rather derisively. But: "Then ye can hold the dance while on the way. Did ye do it here ye would betray us with yer racket. Panquenack, could ye run to Menotac's camp and keep the watch, while these others dance?"

Panquenack nodded, flattered to be chosen. He set off before the others, and McJack waited in the camp to watch the whalers on the beach. Nearly all of these soon went aboard and McJack was reassured. None would be likely to come to the bluff, and he could join his own men. "Nit-witted fools!" he grumbled. "Dancing and shouting and prancing and wasting the time to make them brave, and mayhap running like rabbits at the sound of a gun!"

McJack tried to calm the women before he went, and Minyanata simply said: "Saints save ye now, and make ye brave, and I will pray to the spirit goods." And McJack felt a choking sensation in his throat as he trotted away, looking now and then at the lowering clouds, for he had a thought in his mind. About the uselessness of muskets should the powder-pans be wetted.

It seemed an ominous silence there in the woods, immediately after the dance, while the twenty men trotted down the trail. No rain came. The little wind could not be felt there on the ground. No birds sang nor even chirped; squirrels scampered but were silent. The moccasined feet made a sifting sound, and each man could hear himself breathing. Feel his own fears. Hold his own doubts, for nothing like this had ever happened before. But what *had* happened?

Nobody knew. "But," thought McJack, "we must go and see. Mayhap we can do nothing when we get there. Aye, we be now half a mile from the camp."

And then, as if to emphasize their nearness, and perhaps their lateness, there came the sound of gunfire. Faint and scattered shots, they seemed smothered by distance and the woods.

McJack had Wawakna stop the men to listen. No more gunfire; the woods were as still as before. Each red man listened; some were quaking with their fears. The false courage stimulated by the dance was quickly slipping away. McJack tried to reassure them: "Ye should not fear too great, nor yet too small. We must go on. Panquenack will warn us before we run into harm. We must go and see."

McJack had often been to Menotac's camp, and knew the lay of the land. Near the spot, in the direction from which they were coming, there were thickets and trees to within a hundred yards. Same to the north. Eastward were the farmlands. South, where the diagonal trail came into the camp, it was open a gunshot away. Then the denser growth.

They had almost reached the camp when Panquenack met them, stealing out of the thickets. The big indian was shaking with both fear and wrath; the eyes of him were blazing even though his hands trembled: "White men shoot our people! White men burn wigwams! White man's beasts run through the camp! Many of our people die! Menotac die! Lagunaka die!"

"Hold!" demanded McJack. "That be enough. Where be the white men now?"

"They make ready to go. They steal the furs. Panquenack do as Sir John tell: I hide near the camp and watch. The white men will go the way they come, by the trail that leads to the Great One." He made a motion toward the south and west. McJack nodded. Looked at the indians crowded there on the trail. He knew they were frightened; he couldn't blame them; he himself was frightened. And badly.

"Do ye all hold firm and still, while we go to look. Mayhap we can do nothing, but we must see." And he raised his eyes toward the clouds again; they hung just above the treetops, dense and gray and silent. Nanquemoke sniffed the motionless air: "Smoke!" he declared. "Bad smoke."

The scent grew stronger, and when they came to where they could see the camp, the wigwams were overturned and some of them were burning, smoldering and stinking of hide and of hair. No white men were in sight; some of the reds lay there on the ground where they had fallen. Some men, some women, and from where he stood McJack could see three children. All lying very still. And, too, there on the ground where Menotac's wigwam had stood, lay one of the hounds, an arrow through its side, the feathers pointing slantwise toward the clouds. The clouds which would not loose the promised rain.

There was not a moving thing in sight. Not a sound except, suddenly, and down in the woods where the trail went back to the whaling camp, the booming laugh of the big man. McJack gritted his teeth in silent rage. Felt the handle of his adze. Felt, too, the lust for vengeance. Saw that his red men felt it. Sensed that to a great extent it overcame their fears. They were silent and grim, looking first to their chief and then to McJack. Wawakna made a sign that McJack take charge. The latter nodded.

"Nanquemoke," in a voice that was strangely slow, "lead us down to the trail where the men will go. Far ahead of them, do we hasten. We will run while they will walk; mayhap there will be time. We will find some fallen tree aside the trail, and pray for rain. I have me a plan, but it has to rain!"

And Nanquemoke led off through the woods, bearing south toward that diagonal trail. They followed a game path where they could dodge between the thickets when they must.

When they paused all were panting, but not in distress. Even Wawakna, though ageing, was holding up well. There was a look of black fury in his eyes; perhaps that sustained him. He pointed toward where he knew the trail to be, then, as McJack was doing, looked up at the clouds. McJack prayed to his saints for rain; perhaps Wawakna appealed to the spirit gods. But it wouldn't rain.

Nanquemoke swung to the left and led them out to where he knew the whalers must

pass. Beside the trail, and parallel, lay a great pine. Between the pine and the trail were cat-briars, low to the ground and tangled, climbing up and over the fallen tree.

"It's good," said McJack, and Wawakna nodded. The men arranged themselves behind the fallen log, their hearts thumping and their eyes alight. Glancing up at the clouds, or to the gods, then turning their gaze to the trail. McJack watched them: "Sure, their temper has frightened their fears away," he thought. "They be brave men when they're mad!"

Then, from back along the trail, came that booming voice of the big man, the one with the dogs. McJack could see his indians crouched down low, fitting their arrows to the strings. The whites were not yet in sight. Maybe a minute, two minutes, or three. McJack compared the arrows with the guns. Looked again at the clouds.

"Wawakna," he whispered, "we cannot take the risk from here. The rain will come if we wait — it drops a bit the now. We should go back in the woods and down a way, to gain the time for the rain to come. There we will wait."

So they found another spot, a half-mile down, behind the waist-high prim and bramble, all of the men on one side lest an arrow should go astray. On that other side was a brambled wall higher than a man. On the right were the hidden red men. Waiting. Wawakna, Nanquemoke, Panquenack and the seventeen others. Thinking their thoughts as they waited. Puzzled, perhaps, by the ways of the white men. Comparing one with another. McJack was a white man, and the kindly Master Mundell. So were the whalers white men, and they had done murder. Murder as the price for a pair of hounds. Lagunaka lay back in Menotac's camp beside his broken brew pot.

And the rain, at long last, was coming. In pattering drops at first, just as they heard the whalers, but before they could see them. And then the floods from the heavens. The blinding and drenching and pouring rain that had held so long above them.

"The saints be good!" exulted John McJack, and he felt the wetted handle of his adze. He was on the far end of the line; he had chosen that spot because, just before him, was an open space where he could step out on the trail.

There was no thunder but the rain itself roared. It dimmed the forest and the trail. In itself it was fearsome, yet McJack exulted. Felt that primitive urge for vengeance in his veins. His indians felt it, too, crouching there, with just that thought of vengeance in their minds. Waiting, while the rain kept pummeling down. Thudded on their backs. Splashed and ran off their faces, fading the paint and the daubs of clay. But it took none of the fire from their eyes, that fire that was born of their fury.

By looking over the brambles and up the trail, McJack saw the whalers. Up there they were coming. Heads bent, eyes on the ground before them, avoiding the rain that might blind them. First was the big man, with two of the dogs. There must be two dogs back in the camp, with arrows in them; there had been four when they'd started, there in the dawn. Now, coming back, the two dogs came first, and their leash was taut, fastened to the big man's belt.

On his back was a bundle of furs, stolen from the raided camp: bed clothes and blankets of the people. There were several such packs in that line of men; McJack could see them dimly. So could the indians. They knew what toil those furs had cost, and what they meant when the nights were cold.

The whites held their guns carelessly, making no attempt to protect the powder in the pans. That would have been futile, anyway, although perhaps they thought it unimportant, feeling so sure of themselves. Having taught the reds such a lesson. Having forgotten, it seemed, one "Sir John McJack."

The dogs and the men came on. Behind the big man was the master of the ship, the one they had met before. Dimly, through the rain, they all could see. The hounds appeared awed, cowed by the downpour. Tails hung low and heads bent down, straining at the leash. They were very close. In fact, they were passing.

McJack stepped out on the trail, in between the dogs and the men, who in the rain seemed not to see him. Then he gave a yell through the thunder of the downpour: "Hi-yi! I be John McJack!" And his arrow went into the big man. The indians rose and loosed their shafts, and yelled. "Hi-yi-hi-yi!" A white man screamed.

"Hells be...!" But the master did not finish; with an arrow through his throat he wobbled and swayed and clawed at the thing. The dogs, fastened as they were, ran back into the crowd and tangled. Tangled with feet, and with guns and with bundles of furs, there in the trail that was walled by the briars. Where men scrambled and screamed and fought and cursed. Perhaps, some of them prayed.

For the arrows kept pounding in, there through the rain. Few missed, the range so short. Men with arrows in their ribs tried to run, sometimes in little circles, screaming. Some tried at first to fire their guns; there was not even the faintest flash. A few tried to use them as clubs, wading into the briars, and being caught. Close targets then; the indians could have speared them.

And on the trail at the head of it all stood John McJack. His adze flashed. Twisted as it struck, to tear loose the skin from a skull. To be ready when another should try to come, trying to pass where he couldn't.

In a very few minutes it was done. The indians came whooping out into the trail, their stone hatchets swinging. Their devils turned loose to wreak vengeance. McJack, at first, couldn't check them. He was white-faced and splattered with blood. Exultant, and yet with a sickness in him.

The indians grabbed the sheath knives from the whites and began to scalp them. Some were not dead, and their faces contorted with the tearing of the scalp. From beneath the pile, there at the front, a man's foot moved strongly. Moved as if it tried to get free. Out from under the blood that was pouring on him. The blood and the rain.

McJack and Nanquemoke dragged the man out by that protruding foot. Nearly dead from fright he was otherwise unhurt. Nanquemoke raised his hatchet. McJack grabbed his hand: "Hold! Do not do it! I have need of the man; if he be scared any more, he will die of his fright. I have a need for him: there must be one to tell this tale!"

Then he took stock of his own men; one had a broken arm where a whaler had thrown a musket. That seemed the extent of their damage. The whalers lay sprawled or piled in the trail; some were hanging on the briars, but most lay there in the trail, with their dogs, their blood soon pinked by the rain. But none moved greatly.

"Give me the scalps," demanded McJack. They could hear him better for the rain had slackened. Soon, almost as quickly as it had come, it went down to a drizzle. Just that drip and the drizzle, the clouds hanging low. "Give me the scalps!" he repeated.

But the first man refused. That scalp was the sign of his personal triumph.

"Give it me!" McJack spoke harshly and extended his hand. "I have need for it." And for a reason he couldn't explain the indian gave it over. So did the others. Reluctant and puzzled, but they did it. Understanding when McJack explained: "Sure, this task be not done at all. We cannot waste time for the boast and brag. We must see that the ships do begone from there, lest they send more men for the searching. Drag out that man, the one who was master. And when ye have done it ye shall slice off his ears!" And the red men were again perplexed.

He took all of the scalps and thrust an arrow through them. Then, next to the point, went the ears of the master.

"Here," to the trembling white man, "ye shall take this. Take the scalps and the ears on the arrow. Walk ye in front, and go down to the ships. Tell them the things ye have seen this day, but do not forget to stress why we did it. Make haste! If ye can run ye shall do it; yer haste may save yer worthless hide!"

And so they went. The white man in the lead with the scalps and the arrow. Pricked with another arrow when he slowed. Slopping through the puddles and sobbing as he ran. Followed by McJack and the red men, who carried the guns, even though they didn't know how to shoot them. Down to the shore near the ships, where a breeze had commenced to blow. The clouds were breaking away.

Rather unwisely, there were two boats waiting on the beach, rainwater deep in their bilges. Two men in each, since the rain had stopped, were bailing. Offshore, glistening a little in the wet, lay the ships — the men in the boats were facing them as they bailed. "They should be back," declared one. "I be glad that they went, and not I. But them as went chose their own course. They went for the furs, and the dogs, and some wanted women."

Came a yell from the nearest ship: "Avast, on shore! Look beyond ye! Injuns!"

The men in the boats whirled about, and at first stared stupidly. Then one tried to rally and reached for a musket.

"I would not do it," advised McJack. "Instead, ye should listen. I've brought ye a messenger; he will tell his own tale. He bears the scalps of yer men and the ears of the master, with me very fine advice that ye profit by the same!" He turned to the man with the arrow and scalps. "Here, ye shaking and shivering twelp, take your token to the men on the ships, lest they not believe. And tell the tale in full. We have your guns and yer knives. Do ye come ashore now the ships will rot where they lay!"

The messenger almost tumbled aboard. Amid a stunned silence the boats reached the ship. Men there were gathered on the deck; they let out a roar and a curse. These held bewilderment and rage.

"Did ye pray to the saints," shouted John McJack, "it would be more seemly. And best ye not fire that cannon there, lest the slugs come back and slay ye. Ye have none too many men as it is. It's Sir John McJack as tells ye."

And, strangely enough, the cannon wasn't fired. Some unholy fear of that man on the shore forbade it. A boat went from one ship to another, dividing the crews; most of the marauders had been from the one that was now missing a master, a master who was missing his ears. Back there on the trail. Where the raindrops dripped down for none to feel. There where, in the sunlit days to come, the buzzards would soar, and settle.

McJack watched the ships grimly. So did the indians, although they were still excited. As the sails were set and began to fill, McJack turned to the red men, and with a sort of diabolic grin, made a sign like a circle.

And then, there where they could still be seen from the ships, the red men danced. A dance of triumph. McJack stood and watched, and remembered the ones who would dance no more, in Menotac's camp. But the men on the ships could see their own guns, flourished by the red men, in that weird circle on the shore. Could still see Sir John McJack standing a little apart. Growing small and dim across the water, hidden by distance and the trees.

* * * * *

When McJack stopped the dance and led the indians back to Menotac's camp, it was late afternoon. The sun had come out from behind the clouds, and the people had come from their hiding in the bush. Wailing, there in the wreckage of their homes. Some were wounded or torn by the dogs. Lagunaka and Kenowac, their bright idea exploded, were stark and still near their broken brew pot. Menotac, still clutching his bow, lay sprawled. His widow sat on the ground and wailed grief. Over there was another. There were dead women, too, and children.

"May the saints look down in pity here!" implored McJack. "It were so needless, to be sure!"

Later. Across the big, wide ocean. At the Boar and the Anchor pub. There where the seamen spun their yarns. Where men told tales of a widening world. Over the ale pots and before the fireplace, over which was an arrow. "He be the most terrible man as ever I see!" declared one. "He bewitched of the devil. He do appear from nowhere, and make his injuns come out of the ground. It sets the blood curdling to see him. And I have seen him myself!"

"I, too, have seen him," declared another. "This Sir John McJack. He do be a pleasant man, and a kindly one. His injuns be peaceful, too, to those who come in peace. Our ship lay helpless on their shore, and they stood to the knees, in the winter sea, to free her."

Conflicting tales of one Sir John McJack, across the thousand leagues of the sea.

And at the camp on the bluff there were conflicts, too, but mild ones. Of opinion, of policy, of affection. Some were elated and exalted with pride. Some grieved for their dead. Others nursed the wounded, for Menotac's people had been brought to the bluff to join with Wawakna's band.

Lagunaka and Kenowac were gone; so was much of the peoples' faith in them. They listened more kindly to John McJack. The people admired him. He was a great warrior. A leader who knew how to fight. Around many a fire the tale was told, the story of the Battle in the Rain. And McJack would chuckle; at times he was proud, at others humble. And then he'd be fearful, and he'd work out a plan. And he would watch Mellissa, Mellissa who herself was none too strong but helped the women with the nursing. Perhaps she remembered her own great recent need.

And being useful seemed to help Mellissa. The fears of McJack for her social and sexual status were lulled a little, she being so busy. Besides, she wasn't as yet so strong. Not yet could she feel the full tide of her wantings. Mellissa, the one white woman among the red. With McJack the only white man. McJack who, as soon as the crisis was over, had begun to plan again.

"Sure," he announced to the council, there under the budding trees, "we have much to do to be readied for the days to come. For one: the boat we left on the meadows, she be a quarter league from the water now. The little crick be filled with sand. She's beyond the reach of common tides. Best we'd go down with a score of men and heft her to the sea. And best we had search for oars and tools."

Chapter 11

It was getting into the month of May. Because of the disturbances and the toil with the wounded, the farm work had lagged. The harvest would not be heavy. But there were plans in the minds of McJack and the chief: "Sure, the cape will not be safe, come spring again. Do I know the minds of the whaling men, they will not give up — it's too good to be passed up. Their world be waiting for the oil; there be a profit in it.

"What the white men want they go far to fetch; they be not easy daunted. They wanted the whales, and the deer, and they took them. So the signs be not good for the winter, nor the spring. Come harvest, we will gather what we have; then let us move to the inland. There be that place on Wahatquenack that looks very good. There be dense cedars along a brook to break the winter wind. There be farmlands, too, though some are overgrown. We think it's best that we move, Wawakna and Nanquemoke and me."

He read disapproval in some of the faces, there in the first of the councils; but, with the craft that was in him, he did not insist. Instead, during the summer, he let the thought sink in. Some of the men visited the spot, and found it good. Opposing opinion dwindled. Sir John smiled as he saw his will working.

And in the fall, with their belongings and their meager crops, they left the bluff and went to the river, and none too soon. For with the spring came a company of many men, and they ranged the woods of the cape in search of McJack and his red men. But Manumump's camp, too, had moved far to the north, and the capelands for miles were empty. Just the barren soils of the campsites, the untilled farms. The unseen dead, sitting there in their sandhills. Waiting. Lagunaka and Kenowac and Menotac, and myriads more. What the men did find, on a certain trail where the briars grew high, were whitened bones.

And the whalers kept watch as they worked lest the killers should come from the ground again, although for miles the hounds ranged over the land but found no scent of a man at all. For the people had gone away. Some went by boat and the few canoes; some walked the trail with their burdens. These last, after fording Muskee, walked south of west to the river. They came before sundown, on an October day, before the first of the fronts. And all were weary.

The sun was in the northwest, diagonally up the river. It was very calm; the water was almost still. Only the little whirlings of the flooding tide. Across were the meadows, green-gray with tall grasses: the reeds and the rice where the red-wings were feeding. And the plover and the ducks and the geese. The rail-birds and the marsh hens. There was high land beyond; they could see the trees, the first of the colors of autumn. The promise of deer.

Running from east into the river was the little brook, in the midst of dense cedars. Above, a little tide-bay for the mooring of their craft. Inshore, the overgrowing farmlands.

On the site were oaks and chestnuts and maples. Due east were the pinelands. Along Muskee, not so far away, were more maples and the swamp-growth. Meadows like doormats just before them. Down near the campsite the curlews were calling. White cranes flew across the river, in the last of the sunlight. Striped bass were feeding near the shore, just beyond where the boats were moored.

That night the people slept in the open, too tired to build their wigwams. Each family chose its homesite and, there with their scanty personal goods, lay on the ground in their blankets of skins. The night was a little chill. A late moon came from there in the forest.

McJack, waking in the night, looked all about him. Raised on his elbow. The light filtered down with its shades and its shadows. Minyanata and her child lay beside him. Next, a little way inland from the river, slept Wawakna and his wife. Beyond lay Nanquemoke and his wife and child. Here and there were the others; some lay in the shadows; these showed but dimly. On others the moonlight was falling full.

Across on the meadows the wild-fowl were talking. Wawakna snored a little. He stirred, and broke wind in his sleep, but didn't awaken. From up the stream came the call of a loon; its lunatic laugh. It sounded like personal ridicule, as if making fun. McJack grinned, there in the gloom. He lay in the shadow.

"Ye can laugh, ye long-necked feathered fool!" he muttered. "Ye cannot daunt us with yer midnight mirth, to be sure. Come night again ye'll see a village here, do ye care to look."

The moon shone clear on the water. McJack could see it, across near the edge of the meadows. The river, sliding along so smoothly, made a little murmur as it ran.

Then he heard another sound, a very little sound. Mellissa had made it. She who had lain a little way off, alone. She was sitting on her blanket, there in the moonlight. She wore the indian garb of skins, for her own clothes were long since ruined. But, there in the clear of the light, she wasn't an indian at all. Her light hair shone a little. The white of her face showed pale. He couldn't see the blue of her eyes; yet, as he leaned on his elbow, head raised a little, he knew she was watching him. All of the others seemed sleeping.

Mellissa made that little sound again. It wasn't speech. It wasn't a song. Just a low hum. If one were awake he could hear it. If asleep he'd never notice. McJack grinned in his hidden amusement.

He felt sorry for Mellissa. She was out of her element, yet she hadn't complained at all; she had no other place to go. She and McJack were the only two-of-a-kind in the village, and the rest of their kind were elsewhere. Mellissa would have gone to them; McJack wouldn't.

Mellissa made her signal sound again; McJack didn't respond, although the blood in his veins raced a little. Mellissa's face was fair. Her limbs were round and smooth again, since health had come back to her. And with that health had come her problems. Her wantings. She, in that other world of hers, had never wanted for very long. She hadn't had to. Did she take what she could get she needn't abstain, even here. In the night, along the river, there among the sleeping redskins.

But Panquenack, the tall one, wasn't asleep. He was a fine-looking buck, almost brown, clear down to his naked waist. Mellissa had noted him often. He, with no family to care for, had lain a little apart. Wakeful. Mellissa was a disturbing woman, when she chose to be. She could tease. McJack-white, or Panquenack-red, she could tease him.

McJack saw the indian get up from the ground. Mellissa was a little outside the group. So had Panquenack been, perhaps some thirty feet away, there in the flickered moonlight. Panquenack, intent on the woman, hadn't seen McJack, who grinned, and was curious. What would Mellissa do? Surely she wouldn't dare.

Nor would Panquenack have dared had he stopped to consider. But the red blood of him was run amok with his brains, for the moment. Crouching, he went toward the woman.

McJack saw Mellissa jerk her head around, and there came the red man, crouching. His tall form stooped. His broad shoulders bare in the moonlight. Cautious but daring. His clean cut legs showed shapely and brown.

Mellissa, as Panquenack came close, could see the fire in the indian's eyes, and the clean-cut lines of the face of him. But the face was brown, so she shrank away. He reached out imploring hands, trying to touch her. To taste the feel of her face with his fingers — the white face, the brown fingers. Perhaps for the moment she forgot that McJack was watching, for she hesitated. Then she raised a hand to ward the indian away.

But Panquenack was eager. Insistent but futile. Perhaps had the two of them been alone he might have won. But Mellissa wouldn't dare to prove herself while McJack was watching, so she motioned that Panquenack should go. And when he insisted and tried to touch her again, she slapped him full in the face. The white hand on the brown face. The sound rang out in the silent night. It brought Panquenack to his senses.

Like a shadow he was gone, back to his blanket. Quickly Mellissa sank back and pretended to sleep. McJack stifled a chuckle when Wawakna got up from his deerskin. The chief came to his feet. Silently he circled about the camp, then stood and listened and watched. Looked out on the water which shone in the moonlight. Looked across where the reeds showed the line of their dark.

There seemed nothing amiss. Wawakna concluded he'd been dreaming. He came back to his bed and lay down. McJack noted, there by the moon, the graying of hair. The care he was taking of his people. And, even as he watched the chief, McJack felt sorry for Mellissa. She had her needs, and he, McJack, hadn't. Minyanata was fully capable. Any excursion outside of her realm would be in line of a luxury and not of a need. Minyanata, who didn't fully know what was going on, but who at times was doubtful. Lagunaka had planted a seed in her mind.

And Mellissa was wakeful. She frowned and was wakeful. Her worries might have been worsened long ago had it not been for McJack. Either worsened or ended, depending on Mellissa's state of mind.

Before McJack came, or even before he had become the virtual dictator of the camp, she wouldn't have had any say at all. A white woman, being brought helpless into the camp and nursed back to health, would have owed a debt to the clan. She would, willy-nilly, have been inducted into the tribal sisterhood. Some buck would have requested her as a wife, and the chief and his council would have given permission.

But McJack wouldn't allow it that way. If Mellissa took a red man she'd do it of her own choosing. If she were compelled it must be by her own compulsion. McJack had, in his covert way, laid down the law.

And so Mellissa had been free. Some of the bucks had paid her attention, but she had held them off. She had smiled. There'd been a sideways look in her eyes at times. Mellissa, within bounds, had teased and tempted. And it was only because of Sir John McJack that she hadn't been forced. Mellissa knew that, was shrewd enough to see, but not quite shrewd enough to figure why he'd done it. Was it to hold her for himself, in case something happened? In case Minyanata failed him, or if he tired of her, or if there should come a chance to get away? She would take McJack in an instant, could she get him. In spite of Minyanata. In spite of public opinion. This last she had always flouted.

As to McJack, he concluded that Mellissa would give him no bother. But he might be mistaken, at that. The Mellissas of the ages and the McJacks of the past, they both had been mistaken, at times. They come and they go, and they learn very little. Or so it sometimes would seem.

Next day was a busy one. The wigwam poles had to be cut and raised. There was corn to be pounded, which Mellissa, less an expert at tent raising, was doing. She sat on the ground with a mortar and pestle. She'd been sitting and pounding for quite a while.

The privy pits had to be dug, well back among the thickets in the upland. Mostly these thickets were of briar and laurel, but one was of poison ivy. This one they shunned, while digging the pits. They used hoes of stone and wooden shovels, for they had no steel ones.

McJack was coming back from the pits when he saw Mellissa. *Thump-thump-thump* her pestle was pounding. Mellissa pretended not to see him, intent on her corn. McJack went out of his way to pass her. He was feeling mischievous. Inclined to tease.

"Lissy," he gravely remarked, "do ye sit so much ye will broaden yer bottom, ye will at that! It be a very dangerful thing to do."

She glanced sideways. He was speaking a language she knew quite well.

"Why should ye worry at all?" she inquired. "Sure, it's no interest ye've took afore."

"It'll well-nigh ruin it," persisted McJack, his eyes twinkling. "It'll make it like a pair of pancakes, give it time."

Mellissa was suddenly feeling better; perhaps McJack was interested after all. Perhaps she'd been wise in giving that little hint last night. Wise, too, in slapping Panquenack down. Her eyes danced but she pretended to be serious.

"Do that be so, for true?" she inquired.

"Indeed it do, Lissy. Ye should be careful."

"Would ye," she inquired, "be wanting to feel it to see if the harm be done the now?"

McJack laughed. So did Mellissa.

"I be a busy man the now," he explained, "else I'd be pleased to do it. Mayhap there'd be some other one — Panquenack seems not so fit for toil the day. He sits and mopes. He be down in the dumps. Now what could be ailing the injun?"

Mellissa snorted her disdain, and took up her task again. McJack laughed and turned away. Neither noticed Minyanata, but she had seen them there. Hadn't heard the words nor their meanings. But that smoldering eyelight of hers was caused by her displeasure. She was slightly large near the waistline then. That may have affected the trend of her thoughts.

After those first few days the people were not so urgently busy. Having time to hunt and food running low, the men explored their new country. They found it pleasing. The game was plenty. The creeks and the river held the fall run of fishes; striped bass, white perch and catfish. And many of the eels were coming down, going back to the sea where they'd been born. Where the females would loose their spawn only once, then die.

The indians knew a lot about woodcraft and fishlore, but they didn't know where the eels were born. In the spring there'd be the eels, the little fry, wriggling and squirming and going upstream. In the river, the creeks, in any little waterway that led somewhere to a pond. They even climbed the beaver dams, back above the tidelines, there in the forest, urged on, compelled.

The eels didn't know why they went, any more than did the indians, but they went. Just on a visit, as it were. One year, two years or more, sliding around on the mud and the sand, and growing mature. Fulfilling the ends of their destinies, and of themselves. And when their tail-ends were far enough away from their head-ends, they'd feel an urge, an age old eternal urge to multiply their kind. Keep their kind and kin among the stream waters of the earth. Not knowing why.

They'd feel that urge that is so common to all creation. Some more than others, according to their needs. Man or mouse, or Mellissa. Or Minyanata. Or Panquenack or Sir John McJack. Not so greatly Wawakna, for he was growing old. An urge, and perhaps a fear; of some of the indians Mellissa was more than half afraid.

But she wasn't afraid of McJack. Because of her wantings she thought he couldn't harm her. So, he being sympathetic, full of the humor and the surge of things, and blinded by his masculinity and his own conceit, the two of them bantered together. Had their vulgar little side-talks. But only when they chance occurred and then but briefly. But all of it bred a difference of opinion. Mellissa thought she was making headway; he thought he was having a little fun. Minyanata was of the opinion that she didn't approve of the looks of things. So her eyes would sometimes smolder, but she kept her tongue silent. She didn't mention it to her man, and he, failing to see the trend of affairs, went on his merry way. Working, making suggestions, fishing once in a while. Laying a plan now and then, and laughing with Mellissa every so often.

Mellissa was shrewd, but she had too much conceit. She misconstrued McJack's intentions. She thought he wanted her, Mellissa, but that he didn't know how to go about it and still keep peace in the camp, for Minyanata was the daughter of the chief. But, in spite of that, and rating McJack's ethics by her own, she decided that he'd like to get clear of his wife. Why not? Who would be harmed? One of the other bucks would be glad to take Minyanata.

Mellissa's judgment was warped by her wantings. It wasn't right that a white man and a white woman should live separately there in the town, among the red people; they should be together. So, being a female pirate, she made some plans to pilfer.

McJack had gone out among the thickets of laurel and cat-briar. Not far from the thicket of ivy. The ivy looked nice to the eye; it was still pleasantly green and red, and the split fronds caught the sunlight as the tendrils climbed a tree. It wasn't so dense that one couldn't have entered, had he chosen. But, wise in the ways of the woods, no one had chosen. Not as yet.

Mellissa had seen McJack go out; he'd probably stay a while, for he hadn't hurried. She saw, too, that Minyanata was sewing. Making a small garment. Using the sailmaker's needle and the sinew thread. The needle was five inches long and sharp; but Mellissa never gave it a thought. Didn't even see it. She saw what she thought was a chance to breed trouble. And Mellissa was right, though so badly mistaken.

"Sure," she declared bluntly, "I should think ye'd be ashamed!"

Minyanata looked surprised. "For why should I be ashamed?" She thrust the needle through the deerskin again, drew taut the sinew thread. She was making a very fine seam, at that, so why should she be ashamed?

"Ye got no warrant to be living with a white man!" was Mellissa's startling statement. "Having children by him, and all. A white man should have a white woman. He should, at that!"

The sailmaker's needle had come out of the seam. The red fingers slyly slipped the white thread out of the eye of it. And in the eyes of Minyanata that smoldering light had grown to something of a flame.

But Melissa, glancing toward where McJack had gone, didn't notice. "Ye should give him over," she suggested. "Ye should take one of yer own ki... Ye-o-ow!" Mellissa let out something that was half a squall and half a scream.

McJack, coming back, saw somebody running. Two somebodies. Mellissa was leading; Minyanata was just behind. Catching up, she made another jab. Mellissa squalled again. Under that goad she put on speed. Reckless. Heedless of where she was going. McJack saw her dive into the thicket. The one where the tendrils climbed so high. Into the one where the split fronds grew.

There was murder in Minyanata's heart, but still some reason in her mind; she wouldn't go into the ivy. Instead she circled and threatened, that needle grasped tight in her fist. She screamed: 'Ye come out! I punch holes! Ye no get my man! I make fight!"

Wisely, Mellissa stayed in the thicket. The man in question came running up, as did half the others in the camp. Most of these were laughing, perhaps less surprised than was McJack. "Minyanata, what be ye doing?"

"I be fighting!" she yelled. And as proof she made a jab at Sir John. "Damm!" said he, as he caught her wrist and forced her to her knees. Then seeming exasperated, he turned his wife across a knee and spanked her hard. Minyanata twisted and turned and bit him on the leg. He yelled, and spanked the harder, and Minyanata tried to kick him in the head. She was fighting indeed, as hard, though perhaps less wisely, as she had prayed before. Back then, she had put such matters in the spirit gods' hands; now she had taken them into her own. Perhaps she wished she hadn't, for McJack's right hand was heavy. Always before it had been gentle and kind. Minyanata was unpleasantly surprised. The rest of the people were amused.

Sir John learned some things that day, some things which Wawakna had learned before. Mellissa gained education, too, in some degree; she learned that she couldn't have McJack. And the next day she was further informed, this time about the magic of poison ivy.

McJack's new hell-cat wouldn't smile, until she saw Mellissa. The white face was puffed and blotched and blistered red. The tears were running down it. Her hands were red and fumbling. Mellissa was as swollen as a person drowned.

Then Minyanata smiled; she couldn't hold fast to her fury. She apologized most humbly to her lord and master, in both word and deed. McJack grinned. Figured he had learned a thing or two. Wawakna smiled slyly. The other people snickered.

Mellissa wished she were dead, for a day or two, that she might lose those problems which she couldn't solve. But later, when her skin was white and fair again, Mellissa still had her wantings. They survived even poison ivy. The humiliation of being chased into a thicket. But, to some degree, she would have her chance to pick and choose.

That, too, had been one of the times when Sir John McJack felt sheepish. He was usually so cocksure and jaunty. Unconsciously he had become accustomed to the admiration of the people there; ridicule was a new sensation. It jarred his conceit.

But, too polite to openly guffaw at McJack, they smiled. He saw the smiles. Could hear the women giggle. For the first time since he came he felt like hunting a rathole. Clambering in. Seeking some better shelter than a wigwam wall; these were too acoustic. Mayhap that was how he suddenly came to push his latest idea: his program for better housing. His plan for the betterment of himself and his people. The skins and barks of the wigwams had served well, it was true. For centuries, none knew how many. The red people had survived the cold and heat, the wind and the rain, and those giggles which pierced when the wind would not.

"Sure," said Sir John to his lady — ordinarily he might not have consulted her first — "with the cedar at hand, and with the stones at hand, and with the time to do it, why should we not build a cabin, at that? With a door, with hinges? And mayhap a shutter to let in the light? And a fireplace for to cook and warm?"

And Lady McJack's eyes had lighted again with her old-time eagerness. After her tantrum she had determined to be a lady indeed and a better housekeeper, and all. And here was her husband planning a better house!

"It would be very nice," she declared. "Tur'ble nice, to be sure! Minyanata be tur'ble glad. She be sad she was bad, and all."

Which made Sir McJack feel a little bit better. He figured he had, in a way, both taught and been taught, and so he chuckled and shrugged his shoulders and went out to grind his axe for the chopping. To cut and fit the logs for his cabin.

As the days wore on, the heart of Minyanata was swelling with pride in her homestead, and she was swelling in other ways, too. The building of the house became a race between maternity and the winter cold. Nanquemoke and Panquenack helped Sir John to build it. Some of the others brought stones in the boat. All was done by mid-December, and the family moved in and built their little fire in the fireplace; the smoke went curling straight up toward the heavens. The outdoor heavens. A sort of miracle had been performed. Something new.

McJack noted his plan for better housing was catching the popular fancy. Others were planning to build. The people talked that the matter over around their fires. When some of the men shrugged their shoulders, wigwams had been good enough for their fathers, the women kept talking. Some very shrewd ones pretended to be cold, they'd go to Minyanata's cabin to get warm. Sometimes McJack was almost crowded out. Even twelve feet square wouldn't hold a crowd.

But Sir John chuckled. He was his old self again. He chuckled, even though from where he lived he could see Mellissa's wigwam. He felt sorry for Mellissa but daren't do much about it, although he asserted his independence and talked and chatted with her. Mellissa understood the lay of the ethical land by then, as did Minyanata who had forgiven her because — this was her logic — Sir John was such a very fine man, such a good husband, that she couldn't blame any woman for wanting him. But, this was her decision — spank or no spank — no other woman would get him!

So McJack would sit by his fireplace in his new home and chuckle when he thought things over. And Minyanata smiled in her pride of her new abode and the people smiled with, and at, her.

But a day or so after the child was born, the people frowned, and shook their heads wisely. The child was a boy born in the new house, but it died.

Minyanata had no more than the usual trouble, but the child was frail at birth. The midwives looked doubtful, even at the first. And when a day later the man-child died, there was more head shaking, especially among those who were averse to change. It was a bad sign; the red people were not made to live in houses. Wigwams were good for their fathers; the barks and skins had served through the ages and the people had lived. They did not want their children to die because they'd been born in a cabin. This was one theory.

McJack tried to explain that the cabin had nothing at all to do with it, but some were not convinced. They were very firm of mind. Others sided with McJack.

But some of his thoughts he didn't tell to the red people, nor even to his wife, especially as to how he felt about the baby. He was sorry, of course, but in a way he was relieved. He could foresee the changes that would come in the child's normal time, if not in his own. When the white men came, matters would be different. This they all knew, dimly, but McJack sort of brooded. He had great doubt as to the wisdom of bringing half-breed children into what would be a changing world. Especially men children. At times he would be very deep in thought.

"What ye think?" Minyanata might ask. And Sir John would grin and mayhap tell a lie. Then Minyanata would feel better, especially when little Yanata would climb up into her daddy's lap and after playing a while, curl up for a snooze. If Yanata had died it would have been different indeed, thought he. And he didn't smile at the thought at all, he hugged the child closer.

There was another time, though, when he grinned widely but no one saw him do it. It had been out in the open, when it was rather dark. The leaves had fallen from the trees to let the starlight show. He'd been down by the river, watching the night. The stars on the water, the dark line of woodland over yonder. Watching the place where the surface was silver, down by the bend. He'd been listening to the night sounds. To the loon, to the quacking ducks in the meadows. Just a little above had been deeper sounds; the gray geese talking in their sleep. Sir John had lately dined on goose; he was fed and contented, feeling fine.

Then he had been coming back toward his cabin. It was rather late and all was quiet in the town. Most of the people were sleeping; now and then he could hear a snore. Those tell-tale wigwam walls! Come a new winter the whole camp must have cabins.

Mellissa had a little cabin already, built a bit aside, but it was hardly more than a hut. McJack had cut and fashioned the logs down in the swamp. Nanquemoke and Pan-quenack had set it up — six by eight feet, with a tiny fireplace. But a woman living alone didn't need much space, and by McJack's suggestion and his sneaking help, they'd built the hut. Nanquemoke was a kindly man. Panquenack, more than half likely, had other reasons and other plans. He was a good man at heart and quite persistent. But Mellissa had held him away, quite distant for a while.

And then, as she'd become more accustomed to him, to his brownness of skin and bigness and strength, as her wantings increased while her fears grew the smaller, he hadn't been held so distant. Because Panquenack was quietly insistent. Because Mellissa couldn't get what she wanted.

That night when McJack came back from the river, there past the wigwams, among the trees where nothing seemed moving except a few late falling leaves, he suddenly stopped and stood, in the shadow of a tree.

Dimly he could see Mellissa's hut; the door was open. Except for just a tiny glow from her fire, Mellissa stood in the dark, above were the stars. Perhaps she had come out to look at the night. Mellissa was standing very still.

But someone was moving: from Panquenack's wigwam seemed a sort of a shadow. It went toward Mellissa quickly. It was Panquenack and McJack saw the woman start a little and seem to shrink back into the doorway. And Panquenack came on, trying again. Persistent.

The two of them seemed to whisper there. He could see the indian talk with his hands. She made as if to push him away. And then, as if her wantings had prompted and pushed her instead, she grasped his hand and drew him through the doorway. Pan-quenack had to stoop and turn sideways, but he entered. Eager. Silently Mellissa closed the little door; its buckskin hinges didn't squeak at all.

That was when McJack had grinned so widely to himself and yet he felt sympathetic. Sympathetic and doubtful, too, for he thought that he knew her.

"Sure," he decided to himself, "Panquenack will have his day, or his night, he will. But, do I know the wench the way I think I do, she will not wed him. She will not take him in the open day. Only in the nights when none shall see, to be sure. Give her a chance she would go back to the whites, and she would not have it known that she'd bedded with an injun. For the white women cannot take the red so easy as can men, and that be why I fear for the half-bred lads. They would be forced to the red again. It's why I did not grieve so great for my own at that."

And part of his prediction came true. When in the morn Panquenack came out, he came from his own wigwam. That day he seemed languid but strangely content. But in that and other daytimes there was no sign that Panquenack meant anything more to Mellissa than he had before. To the woman who lived so alone in her hut. Having her own choice to a limited degree, by the grace of the teachings of Sir John McJack.

"Mayhap," he had thought more than once, "it had been best we'd let her drown and die. But when a man can help he must do it; that be the law. However" — with a smile and a sigh — "even the saints have a task with Mellissy now, steering a course! And they, and me, and Mellissy, and her man, be the only ones as knows it. And none of us be telling."

Chapter 12

That winter was cold; the weather had more to do with pushing along McJack's housing program than anything else. The blaze in his own fireplace made the room so warm that one didn't have to huddle in a blanket at all. The same was true of Mellissa's little hut, and often she had company there, of the female kind — the wigwam women would visit the cabin woman for the warmth, and the mixed friendships grew stronger.

Mellissa, being lonely, welcomed them freely, a few at a time. And she put in a word for the housing program and set the women to teasing their men to build in spite of the theory that a house was unhealthy. The colder the weather the more the plan prospered, and some, not waiting, cut the logs for their cabins. Nanquemoke's was already done, and Wawakna's. McJack was boss builder.

They had the white man's axes with which to build the white man's houses, there along Wahatquenack, in that red world which seemed so far away from the white one.

But it couldn't have been so far away at that. Not when half-red, half-white babies were being born into their little world. Like McJack's own son, the one who had died. Like the half-breed man-child who had been born a week later to one of the women of Meno-tac's people. And like, after the winter and spring and summer had gone and October had come again, Minyanata's other baby. This one was a girl and healthy and strong. It was born one week before Mellissa's.

Mellissa Mallore. She would have kept her trysts a secret because they were just temporary, to satisfy her wantings for the time, while waiting a chance to be gone. To leave Panquenack to his own and to the things he might remember. Mellissa, who had intended to keep it all secret, pending what might happen.

But nature in a fruitful mood had published her secret abroad, to the surprise of all but Sir John McJack, who had known what might happen. Perhaps Mellissa suspected that he knew; she met him one day while gathering sticks in the woods. There where the leaves had greened the trees above and all around them.

"Johnny," she began, and she gulped as if choking, a sound that made him remember. It was the first thing Mellissa had done on that day of the shipwreck, when coming back to life again on the edge of the forest and the edge of the sea. And here it flashed, to McJack's suspicious mind, was another sign of another life. Even before she told him. In fact, he asked her: "Ye be a goin' to bear a child?" He smiled, but his voice was kind. There wasn't any ridicule in his eyes, nor poking of fun. He knew how Mellissa would hate the thought.

"How did ye know?" she asked quickly. "Has Panquenack been talking and boastin'?"

"Now, hold ye, Lissy! Ye should not vent yer spite on the injun. He be a good man, and has said never a word at all, for ye did bid him keep the faith. But, once, I saw ye with him in the night. He did not force his way to ye at all; ye drew him through the door. Do there be blame, at least a part be yours, and ye must bear it."

Her reply was desperate. "But there be other ways. There be ways to git clear, did I but know, I never was caught this way afore."

"Lissy," McJack's tone was solemn, "ye cannot do it! For one thing, there be great danger, ye will die. And it be a great sin to do. Sin against the saints and the laws of god. They'd never forgive ye! Even though ye'd cringe the years away in hell, so I've heard it told. These be the teachings, they be, at that."

The crops had been planted on the reclaimed soils. Fishing was good in the river and creeks and the tide-guts. The wild-fowl nested on the meadows and along the creeks. The game-things bore and cared for their young. The fur-things too: the bear, the cats, the racoons and squirrels, the otter and the mink. The rabbits and the skunks and the beaver.

Down in the camp a wooden town was being built. White man's houses in a red man's world.

But none of those white men came to the river. No ships, though there were canoes a-plenty, at times. Coming up, going down. Stopping over for a visit, mayhap for a day or more. Bringing news of the times and of the local people and their prospects. Of their troubles and trials which were strangely few. Just then the news was of peace and plenty, there in the land that was fruitful.

As were Minyanata and Mellissa, who had, out in the open for her little world to see, taken Panquenack for her man. He had taken down his wigwam and attached it to her cabin. It was unique, and quite strange — half-house, half-tepee. But symbolic, fitting for its people, waiting for the birth of their half-breed child. Mellissa had grown resigned and humble. Panquenack was peacock proud. The midwives were worried; they feared the evident size of the child.

Since Lagunaka's passing they had had no professional man of medicine, and had brewed their own herbs. Made their own lotions, and to a greater extent, used their own notions. So far they'd done very well.

But with Mellissa matters were different. This was her first, and she must have been thirty years old. The midwives made ready, that was in early autumn, while they waited. The weather was warm for the season; summer seemed to have come again. Mellissa lived largely in the indian half of her house, in Panquenack's wigwam. Both the back and the front could be opened. It was cooler than the cabin; the breeze blew through. As it stood a little aside from the circle, they would have the birthing there.

It began at the dawn. The mists were on the river. The wind was waiting for the sun; the two would arise together. The one from the east, the other from the west.

And after the mists blew a little ways along the shore, striped bass were feeding; when they swirled to catch the minnows they showed their fins. Sometimes even their silver and their stripes. Snipe ran bobbing along the beach, a great blue heron stood still in the shallows. The bird stood still as a tepee there, a tepee misshapen, standing on stilts.

Panquenack didn't see those things or the river; he was hastening for the midwives. Going to their wigwams to wake them instead of calling. It would be a great day for Panquenack, for that day his child would be born. Or so he hoped.

But the day brought forth no child at all, neither man-child nor maiden. Into the earth of the wigwam the two stakes had been driven. And there, crouching, grasping and pulling, Mellissa sought to become a mother. At times she'd scream and the shrill tones of it would wing through the camp and across the river. Even to the other shore, against the little breeze, the men who were fishing heard her.

And that other fisher, the heron. The striped bass were gone but the heron was there to hear. He stretched his long neck and seemed to listen. With dignified steps he waded a little away. And then, as if to flee from the agony of it, he unfolded his wings, set stance with his legs and flew, his long legs trailing. And he went far up the river, having no good cause to stay. But again and again Mellissa screamed. Panquenack, trying to be stoic, sweated out the day, and the dusk. The dark came down.

Minyanata, her own child only a week or so old, had been over to Mellissa's to see if she could help. The midwives seemed helpless. They sweated there in the heat. The little breeze which blew through the tepee couldn't stop the sweating nor still the anxiety. The midwives talked with Minyanata, they advised her not to become excited. She shouldn't be too much on her feet, at that. But about Mellissa they couldn't tell. In the old days at a time like this, which was rare indeed, in fact they couldn't recall so hard a case, but if there had been such a case in the old days...

"They do say," Minyanata told her man, "they know not what to do, for sure. The things they do, they do not help at all."

Which set Sir John a-thinking. He went down to the river and pondered about it. The news from the birthing was still very bad; Mellissa was weakening all the while. McJack pondered and scratched his head; then he hunted up Wawakna and Nanquemoke. Panquenack had gone back among the thickets to pray to the spirit gods. McJack thought he'd do what he could on his own.

To Wawakna and Nanquemoke he said: "It be like this: if Mellissy cannot bear the child she'll die. As it is she will not live the night, in spite of all that the women can do. But there be one thing we can try, at that. Just this one thing I can think on.

"Now, the women think that mayhap some devil have hold of Mellissy to hold her tight. That mayhap a pow-wow loose the holt. Let the babe be born. I think them wrong, but it gives me a thought.

"Mellissy has never seen the masks nor heard the rattles, nor the howling and prancing, such as Lagunaka did. So-o, what think ye? Would mayhap such a sight, come sudden and all, fright the babe from the woman, at that?"

Wawakna and Nanquemoke agreed that it might. In their hearts there must still have lingered some of that fantastic faith of their fathers in the old tribal customs, in the incantations and the dancing and the frightening of the devils. Lagunaka had been a bad magician; he had made bad medicine and partly destroyed their faith in him and his kind. So bad that, under the teaching of McJack, they had had no other since Lagunaka had been killed. His masks and his trappings had been left where he'd dropped them.

But the people on the Muskee had both the man and the masks and the man had faith in the things that he did. He and his people lived near the headwaters of the creek. So Nanquemoke went away on the trot, through the dark and the pines and the oaklands. He sweated as he ran.

Later, in Wawakna's camp were but the lights of the coals of the outdoor fires, and these were dying down. Bedded coals, just glowing here and there, ready to be covered for the night. The people had long since eaten, and most would have slept except for Mellissa. For they wanted to know, and their curiosity was kindly. Mellissa wasn't screaming any more.

She lay at the time on the ground. She sweated and moaned and mumbled her thoughts. The night had grown late. The little pine torches smoked and flared. The intensity of her pain increased. The midwives somehow got her to the stakes again. Half delirious she mumbled her thoughts about trying to "git clear" and being in hell, and she hadn't tried to "git clear" but she was in hell, for all of that. And very much more.

Then something caught her attention, something outside of herself. Outside of her tepee, both ends of which were open, one toward the town and the other toward the forest. Out there in the town was something she had seen.

For more torches had been lighted. They flared and smoked in the night. She could see people moving, on either side, along an open lane. Mixed and muddled. Phantom-like. Dimly, at first, she thought them the people of the town, but she didn't care.

Then, in the dim background of the scene outside, Melissa saw the THING. Something which came out of the dark and into the light, between the two lines of the people, the people who looked like phantoms. Maybe they weren't people at all, and that other THING that she had seen, IT KEPT COMING ON!

There was nothing dim about the Thing, nor in the unearthly sounds it made. In its rattles and rantings and chatter. In the arms which it moved in the dancing. Dancing slowly toward her.

The Thing kept coming; she could see it looking at her. It paid no attention to those goblins at the sides. It had the legs of a man and the head of a bear, and long feathered ears and the horns of a deer. Prongs for horns. The devil had prongs, but Mellissa hadn't known they were on his head. The head that would bend and bow and sway. Here came the devil to git her!

Mellissa screamed, leaped to her feet, whirled around and started to run, out toward the dark. And then she fell, and her child was born, and she fainted.

The people knew about the child, because it squalled. Squalled at the night when he fell to the ground. A man-child, too.

And the people knew that a miracle had been performed, there before their eyes. And some of them nodded understandingly, one to another. Mostly these were the older folk, the ones longest steeped in their tribal lore, the ones most slow to change their thinking. The old ways were the best, at that, in spite of the theories of Sir John McJack. Their fathers had known about frightening the devils, the bad devils, the ones who came into and upon the people and made them sick. Made childbirth hard. Made all the physical ills of the world.

This was why their magicians had made their masks so fearful, so unlike anything that was born of the flesh. The bad devils wouldn't understand why a bear should have horns, and feathered ears at all. The spirit gods hadn't made any beasts like that, and, lest the bad devils should get acquainted with a mask if they saw it too often, the magicians never made two masks alike — as different and as fearsome as they could.

Sir John felt rather sheepish as he watched their reactions. He'd been to great pains to teach the people the futility of all that prancing and dancing and hub-bub and all; and here, by his own suggestion, they had called on the magic when all else had failed them, and the deed had been done! The miracle performed.

"Sure," thought he, grinning a little, "I've unteached me own teachings, at that! By being right about Mellissy I have showed the people I was wrong about magic. They thought I knowed the magic, which I didn't at all, I knowed Mellissy. I knowed how frightened she'd be, to be sure.

"I must ask about Mellissy now. Mayhap the man did fright her all too well. Mayhap, instead of being faint, she may be dead or dying now. I must go in and see."

But Mellissa wasn't dead, and she didn't die, although she was a long time ill. Minyanata nursed the baby for her along with her own and McJack soliloquized audibly about the way new creatures knew how to feed. He mentioned birds in the nest, and new-born pigs and described how these last would "tuddle around on their little legs to where the feed be." And he deduced that there was "some guiding power beyond it all too great for men to know." This was while the day was dawning.

Then he grinned ruefully. He had to express his thanks to the red magician, withholding his own private opinion, for when a man has seemed successful one doesn't tell him that he's failed. And, too, when a man, McJack, for instance, has taught one theory and proven the truth of a contrary one, he's in a quandary, to be sure.

"Sure," he confided to himself, "all I can do be to grin and bear it, and prove meself right some other time. For, if things go as they do the now, there will be time a-plenty for to live and to learn and to make me plans. There will, at that."

And so there was on Wahatquenack, the river. There where, outside of the cabins and the improvement in the farmlands, the land looked the same as when they had come. In spite of its changes it was largely the same, along the river and the creeks.

And there the people lived and worked for years. Sometimes there were tidings from the outside world. The white men's world. From Jamestown or Plymouth or from far to the north. More white men coming all the while. Working while the red men waited on Wahatquenack, the river. And some seemed to sense this somber thought, the whim and the will of the white man. The white men who some time would come.

Wawakna and others were growing old. Some died and babies were born. There at the first there were three of particular interest — McJack's second daughter, Mellissa's son and that other, the one who was born to the woman of Menotac's people. This child who had been able to toddle before McJack paid attention, although Nanquemoke had mentioned it.

But one day he stopped and looked sharply. He frowned, then chuckled. Turned the little boy's face around to the light and remembered something, a few words a man had spoken down there by the whale boats, where the sailors had waited for them that would never come: "And some wanted women."

Sir John glanced sharply at the boy's mother; she shrugged her shoulders, sadly. Her husband had done the same. It had not been his will nor hers. The blame lay on a law of nature and a white man's lustful whim. A white man who in a matter of a few short hours had both begat and been gone. He, perhaps, had not carried furs on his back, lacking the time to steal them. That day on the trail. Before the people had come to Wahatquenack at all.

But they had come and they had stayed. All of the people lived in the town in houses made of logs. For summers the wigwams were stretched against them, like a porch. The cabins had fireplaces like Sir John's. With the one white man among them, and with a few of the white man's tools, the men had learned to work more, to chop and hew and build. To do more of the labor in the fields, to plant and tend and harvest. To depend less on the forest and more on the farms. To absorb, slowly, to be sure, some of the culture of one Sir John McJack.

The people were more prosperous than ever before, especially in the winters. The winters when ice crept over their world, over the meadows and the streams. In the nights it crackled with the moving of the tides. Crackled and crumpled and crushed, there in the dark. But the indians could sit by their fireplaces, then, in what they thought was comfort. Their walls did not shake when the high winds blew, shake and shiver and threaten to fall. There in the lee of the cedars. But their world was a-trembling, Sir John could feel it, just once in a while with the coming of news.

There through the years, five or six before a white man came at all. But a wandering few of the inland people came down in the springs, more peaceful than of old. They told the tidings form Virginia shore, the red men cheated in the trade. Some of their own people killed. Many crowded back from their farmlands, deeper into the woods, further up the streams. Did they choose to farm they must clear new soil, and before that soil was fit to farm they must move again.

For the whites were coming, more and more. Growing bolder. More grasping. At first when few and feeble, they had asked; they now began to demand. Sometimes they bought or bribed with rum.

McJack knew what rum would do to a white man; it was bad enough at best. But his indians had never tasted rum and he must learn from others what it would do the reds. The reds, in whom the sullen fires of resentment grew, but controlled when sober by fear. The rum made the heart of the indian glad, briefly. He forgot his troubles and returned to his dreams. Then, with the recoil, came the fear again, and the craving. His thirst was quickly fostered, but his resistance small.

This was the tale that came down to the river. Denied the drink and the dreams, the red man's sullenness grew. And in his brooding mind was born another thought, an impossible one, the overthrow of the invading whites. The regaining of his stolen world, not this world where men built houses and stole farms for locations. Built a church to worship, on hallowed but stolen ground. These were the red man's thoughts.

Thus, on Wahatquenack, in peace and plenty and a degree of progress, the People of the Turtle learned the news of their outer world, as did Sir John. He, at times, looked at his daughters there, with a peculiar light in his eyes. At Yanata, growing up fast. Giving promise of great beauty; she was whiter than her mother, and the small one, too, his half-breed daughters who would grow to be women. In his mind was a plan. A plan to forestall the things he foresaw.

"Sure," he told himself, "it would be the best. There be good injuns and bad injuns, and good whites and bad whites. They, the lot of them, have but the one world to live in, to be sure. I fears it be not great enough. We will see, we will, at that."

He added as an afterthought to his musings: "Could I read, I would teach the lassies, that I would, did I have somewhat of a book to do it. And could I write, I mayhap could tell this tale that be my own of how I came and what I found here. How kind these people be at heart, for none other seems to see it, being blinded by their greed. But I, who have that tale to tell here in the very mind of me, cannot write it down a word, for all me craving."

Thus Sir John mused, there between his red world and his white one. So the years had passed, with his plans and his dreams and his tasks to do, there with his indians. With the one white woman in their midst, Mellissa Mallore. With the little half-breeds who were growing fast: two boys, two girls, Yanata much the elder. And with the red folk of the morrow.

Mellissa seemed more reconciled. After the birthing she had been very ill. Panquenack had been patient; all of the people had been kind to her. She couldn't get away even if she would, so she made the best of her bargain. She and Minyanata were quite friendly again. Quite often they visited. Yanata became quite friendly, too, and Mellissa grew fond of the girl. Not knowing what it would cost her.

So passed the years. Wawakna, he who had been chief and a kindly man, died of his age and was buried, inshore a little, among the pines in his sandhill. He had no son; who then would succeed him? The people, of course, held a council.

There were eulogies and speeches and praise of McJack. Who, better than he, for the chief of the band? More speeches and praises; McJack was amused, and a little bored. Suddenly he realized they were waiting for his acceptance.

"I do be thankful," he told them, "for the honors ye do me. For the kind deeds of the past that ye done. Sure, had ye not been kind at the very first, when I was alone and a hungered, I had not lived so long to learn so much, or so little. And I gives ye thanks a greatly, to be sure.

"But to be your chief, that would not be wise. A red man should be the chief of the red men, though a white man might give him counsel. Do ye choose some other one for chief?"

He could see ambitious gleams in some of the eyes, then. So he spoke quickly: "Now I have a man in me mind, I do. He be not so old he be fearful, and not so young he be a fool. He be Nanquemoke, him that I reckons could well serve the band. Do he agree, I will serve as adviser, to be sure, at that."

Which made it necessary that the speeches begin all over again, in praise of the new chief. The chief be dead; long live the chief! The leader of a band of some thirty men there in the shade, on the shore of the river. With their nearest neighbors some five miles away, on the headwaters of Muskee. On Manumuskin, too, and Menantico.

These were the creeks. The creeks which wandered through the inland miles until they were freshened beyond reach of the tides. There where the pelts of the beaver grew prime. The pelts which the world was a-wanting just then, and wanting badly.

The beaver, harmless and busy there in their wildlands, paddling and puddling and building their dams. Cutting their food trees and storing them safely. Preparing for winter when pelts would be prime.

That's how it was, and how things happened, largely. "What the white man wants he will go far to fetch." And McJack might have added, had he thought, that there would be very few places where he wouldn't go. Few things the white man wouldn't want. He certainly wouldn't bypass the river, Wahatquenack, with Muskee, Manumuskin and Menantico, the creeks, so close together there.

Chapter 13

The first of the white men came in October, around midday. McJack had come in from the woods to find a boat and five strange men on the shore; one of whom was an indian. Many of the red people were down there, too, crowding behind the chief, Nanquemoke, who had sent for McJack, and was holding the men on the little beach. "Sir John will come," he had told them, gravely, "and ye shall stand and wait."

And the men had looked mightily puzzled both by the fact that the chief spoke English of a sort, and that such a person as "Sir John" existed, there in the wilds. The whites were uneasy and curious. Their leader seemed a likely sort of man.

"Who would Sir John be? he inquired, glancing uneasily over at the cabins.

"He come. He tell ye, if he so wish." And that was all that the men could get from Nanquemoke until McJack came hurrying in and stood beside the chief. He eyed the whites sharply, and they him. Perhaps the whites thought that this "Sir John" looked remarkably like an indian. Their leader frowned and was the first to speak: "Are you Jo... Sir John McJack?" He appeared startled by perhaps a sudden memory. McJack grinned his amusement.

"I be one John McJack," he replied easily. "Some claim I've been knighted, and some, I have no doubt, think me benighted. Does that mean anything to ye at all? But ye should come up on the shore; who might ye be?"

"My name is Saunders. Josiah Saunders. I am an agent for the trade company, making arrangements to buy the red men's furs, come spring. We have a sloop down on the bay. I scarce expected to find a white man here, much less..."

Sir John laughed amusedly: "Much less McJack?" Mayhap ye thought me dead, or mayhap ye hoped it?"

But Saunders hastily disclaimed the unkindly thought, and McJack stepped down and took his hand and put him more at ease. He introduced Nanquemoke, and the chief lied bravely for politeness sake, for he wasn't glad to see him at all.

Saunders, trying to be agreeable after they'd come up under the trees, declared he had some good rum in the boat. Would Master McJack and the chief..."

"Hold!" was the unexpected order, and Saunders was startled by the sharpness. "Hold ye there! If ye come to visit or to trade, or for whatever, ye shall give no rum to the red men here! That I will not have at all! Not here, nor on this river, nor on these cricks!"

And Saunders didn't have to ask McJack for his reason; by experience he already knew. He nodded, and shrugged, and perhaps saw the base of his plan crumbling. Perhaps he had made a mistake by coming to Wahatquenack at all. With McJack astride, as it were, of the line of trade, the profits would be lessened, for McJack further explained: "Do ye come here to trade, ye shall trade fair. Give goods and tools of worth for work. Steel hoes. Axes. Steel heads for the arrows. Iron pots for the cooking. Such goods as these, but not one drop of the rum! Ye shall not do as ye do down yonder!"

Saunders nodded again and looked dubious, especially after considering the fact that the indians lived in cabins. "From where came the tools to build this town?" he inquired. "Have others been here to trade?"

McJack laughed, then: "Not here. Ye be the first white man aside from me to see this part of the river. But down yon on the cape, some whalers came. They left some knives and axes and some guns."

"And... some bones?... Me thinks I have heard of bones."

"Aye. Ye mayhap heard the tale. It were not a handsome tale, at that, thought it was their own choosing. They thought to have their murdering will and way, and did not get it." And that was all the warning that Sir John thought necessary.

Then he became a more gracious host. Invited the men to pitch their tent beneath the trees and while Nanquemoke was mostly silent and his people watched and listened, McJack learned more news of the outer world. Of the settlement at New Amsterdam by the Dutch. Of one on the great river by a small party of Swedes. Of the English on Virginia and Maryland shores. English, Dutch and Swedes! And, far to the north and more inland, the French had earlier settled.

McJack frowned and then smiled shrewdly: "Sure, if I know these breeds of whites at all, it will not be long afore each be at the other's throat, and mayhap all will be at the red man's throats. It'll be a gruesome world afore it be a better one, for even in matters like the praise of god each cannot agree with its own, and will fight like mad over their diffrences.

'Now, the red people have a bit more sense: if they don't think alike about the gods, they do not chop a head to change a mind at all. Do one man believe that satan have three horns, and the other think he have but two, each do be free to do his own counting. Do one think a turtle be a better sign than a turkey, they do not make the turkey wear the turtle shell."

Saunders nodded and smiled but had no further inclination for the theological discourse, and none greatly for national politics. He was a man of the moment; his business was trade. And, that being so, perhaps he understood McJack's diatribe the better because of a difference of opinion in even the ways and means of trading merchandise for furs; his own opinion and McJack's.

The trader only stayed that day and night, having asked McJack to spread the news that his sloop would come in the spring. This would save time for Saunders and for the favor he'd be very much obliged to McJack and to the chief and to all concerned. Then the boat went down with the tide, Saunders probably puzzling on the problem of the unexpected trade rules, and leaving McJack to ponder on his own.

One of these was his daughter, Yanata. The girl was thirteen years old and gave promise of beauty as great as her mother's. Perhaps of more, from a white man's standard, for her coloring was lighter. McJack had seen the trader's men watching the girl. Singling her out and ogling lewdly. Rough men, they. Perhaps but lately out of some English jail. Many men of the time were like that. McJack shrugged. Not the sort of man for Yanata at all, and yet of the type she was most likely to meet, among such whites as would come.

And McJack wanted a white man for his daughter, a good one. No scum and scattle. But where, and how, and whom, when the time should come. This was one of his problems, but not yet urgent.

Meanwhile there were other matters: there was that of the coming fur trade and McJack feared it. Feared its ultimate if not immediate effect. If controlled and fair it would be good for the red people. If allowed to run its own riot it would be bad, largely because of the white man's rum. So McJack laid a plan for the coming of spring.

There were two small camps downriver, but when the trade sloop came there were no furs for sale; they had all been taken upriver to a spot on a higher bluff, two miles above Nanquemoke's wooden town. McJack and Panquenack met the sloop in a canoe as the trader came in with the tide. McJack, none too trustful, stayed a gunshot away: "Ye shall follow our canoe; we will lead ye to the spot."

But the trader, too, proved wary. Instead of bringing his craft in close to the bluff he held away, near to the meadows on the opposite side; there was no bank there at all. "Ye should send the indians here to trade," he shouted. "I will not bring the sloop beneath the bank; there are scores of indians there. Were I to come close I could not use my guns at all, in case of need. The red men could..."

"Aye, I know. But ye be not dealing with injuns now; ye be dealing with McJack. Do ye trade fair ye shall have no need of guns at all. But mind ye this: no drop of rum! If ye do as I say, I gives ye the word of John McJack."

"But why will ye not trust me?" shouted Saunders.

"My friend, I be my own captain, but ye be not: ye have yer masters. Ye mayhap have yer orders; I cannot know what they will be. So I say ye this: Ye shall bring yer sloop beneath the bank or sail back down the river; I will not lead these injuns to a trap. The tide be well-nigh flood; on its crest ye can warp yer sloop with ease. Ye have yer choice."

And Saunders decided to trust McJack. When his sloop was under the bank she was half a bow-shot from the trees, there where the red men were crowded. They came down to the deck in small and curious groups to trade, while McJack looked on, watching for their welfare, that they be not greatly cheated. Saunders made no attempt to barter for rum, and a strong friendship was established between him and McJack.

And thus, in that beginning of trade on Wahatquenack, this was the fairest trade post in the land. Trading time, there at the bluff, became an annual affair. A gathering of the clans, their yearly contact with the white man's world, and for half a decade it was peaceful, though each side watched the other. Saunders took this precaution: he refused to sell either guns or powder though he was free with the arrow points of steel. McJack grinned and didn't blame the man at all. His people were prosperous and peaceful; the arrows would serve. Their lives were made easier by the white man's tools. Everybody was pleased, but McJack still had his problems. For one: Yanata. She was rapidly unfolding. McJack exulted in the beauty of the girl, in the tall litheness and the near whiteness of her. Her eyes were brown, not so dark as her mother's, and at times held a twinkle, like McJack's, though his were blue. She was lovely and desirable.

But as yet McJack hadn't met a man to whom he would willingly give her. The red-skinned beaus were becoming urgent; such whites as she met were ineligible. So McJack had himself an imminent marital problem. Protecting his daughter without giving offence. He was compelled to be tactful.

And, at the last, there was still another worry: a probable change in the trade rules. Saunders had played fair; McJack and the indians had little fault to find. But on his fifth trip to the bluff, when Yanata was eighteen, the trader had confided: "This voyage may be my last to this river. Some clerk in the counting room has been adding up the totals. These profits are good, but not near as great as other spots. So, come spring again, we may not come at all, or there may be another master. And different rules, or none at all. Master McJack, I can plainly see your point of view, but it seems the company cannot. So I'm giving you warning now."

That was bad news and after Saunders had sailed away McJack had the thought to ponder on. To plan and prepare for if he could. What would happen another year, come spring? He talked it over with Nanquemoke; neither found an answer while that summer wore away, and autumn came: early part of October. There had been no frost but the leaves were turning. Reds and russets and scarlets, and the reeds of the meadow were greenish gray.

One day, about then, two of the indians came hurrying into town, mystified and frightened. They had been hunting along the main trail, two miles or so to the eastward and near the Muskee ford. There, in the earth, had been many strange tracks of great and unknown beasts. They were stamped deep in the soil, proving the great weight of the things that had made them. And there were footprints of white men, too, for the men had worn shoes. In all probability these men were trailing the great beasts, and there were more man tracks than beast tracks.

McJack himself was startled at the news. In his early days he had heard, and from reputable sources, that satan sometimes trod the earth, leaving footprints there. But then he thought quickly, he had never heard mention of a group of satans cavorting around with people. And he chuckled at the foolishness of the thought, and asked: "Now just how would be the shape of the critters' feet? Ye should draw me the same in the sand."

When that was done he smiled and chuckled again, though greatly mystified. Not as to what the tracks might be but as to how they had come there.

"Mayhap," he surmised, "it be no thing to make light of. Neither the tracks nor the critters could do ye harm. But the folk that's with them might, at that. The tracks were made by horses, I've not seen a horse for many years, yet in my land they be not so rare at all. I have told ye of the same, yet never did show the way the tracks would be.

"But this be plain: white men be in the inland there. We will go to the ford and scout a bit. If the men come by the trail, and they must have done, for the beasts could not pass in the thicketed wood, some of your people may have seen them. I wonder, Nanquemoke, have the whites started trading on the land, with horses instead of ships? I think they have not; it would not make sense. But from where did they come? And why? We will say nothing to the people but go to the ford and see these tracks. See if we can read some sense in them, which I doubt."

At the ford he still had his doubts; there were tracks of four or five horses and of maybe a score of men. There were hand marks at the edges, too, where the men had got down to drink. But the hoof marks got the indians' greater attention and aroused more curiosity: How tall were the beasts? What color? Could they not follow the tracks and see the creatures?

McJack pondered a moment. "Best we had not. There be many men, a score at least. These tracks be five days old, or mayhap more. They lead away, down toward the cape. Yet, they may have turned aside. One thing be sure: if they come to our town they must come back this way, for the Muskee meadow would stop them. So, Nanquemoke, mayhap it would be best to set two men to watch the ford, to see what happens."

But McJack was still very curious. Uneasy, in fact. Back in the town he pondered on the matter, and only grew more perplexed. As far as he knew there was no place from which the horses might have come. He scratched his head: New Amsterdam? The Dutch? They were a long way off. Still: "Nanquemoke, mayhap it would be best if the two of us go down toward the cape. We should know about these men. We can't have them surprising this town and doing the people harm. So do ye think it best we go and see? Scout slow and cautious like, down yonder?"

Nanquemoke nodded. Though more silent, he had been as curious as McJack. So they started at dawn. Some miles down they found the marks jumbled, where the beasts had stopped and stamped about. They had eaten the leaves from the bushes and cropped a spot of wood grass. In the sand were marks where saddle bags might have lain, and in an open space the men had built a fire; but a search of the ground gave no hint as to their identity. So McJack lacked proof but assumed them to be Dutch.

"There be, I reckons now, what with the saddle bags and the beasts, some greater man amongst them. Mayhap he rides one beast while the others walk. Mayhap the bags were to pack the food." He grinned broadly: "Mayhap I be guessing in the dark, for I know nothing at all for sure. But, I think the men be Dutchmen."

For he knew that the Dutch in New Amsterdam claimed New Cigeria too (it was not until Berkley and Carteret took title that the land was called New Jersey). The men with the horses were probably exploring. Looking over the land to see what the gods had so precariously given.

"Sure," surmised McJack, as they followed the trail, "if the Dutch do claim this land there'll be fighting a-plenty afore they gets it. Afore all the tale be told, at that."

The arrived at the side trail that led to Wawakna's old camp — the horses had gone there, too. Their tracks showed plainly; they were all over the campsite. The men had camped there for a night; had gotten their first sight of the bay at the foot of the bluff, reaching as it did over to that other and unseen shore. To the south, beyond the bay, was the ocean. Down there, too, was the headland of the point of the cape; but there was also an autumn mist, when McJack and Nanquemoke looked that way. The land showed dimly.

The Dutchmen had gone down there by way of the beach, for just south of the camp where the bluff was low, the horses had slid and scrambled down. After that there weren't any tracks at all; the flooding tides had erased them. Had erased them even more completely than had the flooding years erased the signs of the red people of the abandoned camp. Nanquemoke was sad as he looked about: the bare soil, tumble weeds growing in the sand. The shells. Bits of broken pottery. Silently the chief picked up an arrow point that the rains had unburied. Put it into his pouch. (Perhaps he or his father had owned it once.) Shrugged his broad shoulders and thought his broad thoughts.

And McJack did some remembering, too, as he stood on the edge of the bluff. As he saw the path by which, so long ago beneath the light of the moon, Minyanata had led him to her people. To her people who now were his people. His voice sounded husky: "Best we had go back to the main trail yonder, and then on down. We must go cautious; there be no cover on the beach at all... Nanquemoke! Down by the point, in the mist! Do my eyes tell true? Do I see a ship down yonder?"

The chief nodded and frowned. McJack reversed his conjectures concerning the Dutchmen. "Mayhap the men put the beasts ashore from the ship? Mayhap they had gone to the north by the eastern trail, and were but coming back?"

They changed their own plans slightly and went down through the woods to the whaling camp; from there they hoped they could see more plainly. Coming into that camp, McJack chuckled: "The whalers have cut the cover from the farmlands here, in case again they be surprised. They've built huts for the workers there, and would ye see the bones yonder on the shore! Mayhap from there we can see more plain the ship."

But the sight told them little. The vessel lay in the cove; she was a tall ship but flew no flag and no men were in sight. So McJack and the chief scouted down that way, skirting the main trail in case a watch had been set. Worked their cautious way around to the rear of the campsite, between it and the ocean, amidst the thickets and trees. The indian had grown very wary: "Mayhap one watches. Mayhap they be not friends."

McJack grinned and remembered the time when he had walked right into the gun barrel of Mundell's sentry. "Best we had take the care, though I doubt these sentries would be out so far; the men be down near the beach. We will come around amongst the laurel, yonder; then we can watch. Mayhap it'll not be wise to go on down, but I would like a look at the men, to be sure."

And he could see plainly, from a distance of perhaps a hundred yards, for the woods down there were more or less open. The two looked over a clump of laurel. Directly behind them was another little thicket. At times they could hear the voices of the men. A laugh or a shout.

But McJack complained: "I cannot see the ship at all, but it would seem that the men be ashore for a lark. Some play at dice. Some seem to sleep in the sun. Mayhap there be two score in all. Two stand on guard between us and the men; the one looks half asleep. Nanquemoke, if we work our way a bit over yonder, mayhap we can see the ship."

So, those sentries being so safe in sight, McJack and the chief moved here and there between the thickets, seeking a better angle. Then: "Nanquemoke, would ye look at the cannon! The many small pieces, and the large ones. And she has a gun deck below; I can see the ports. She carries the guns of a king's ship, and yet I have doubts. One thing: she flies no flag. Another: no watch be pacing the deck at all. And there be nothing in the dress, on shore or ship, to mark an officer from a man. Nanquemoke, I wonder: is this a pirate ship? I never did see one! Mayhap it would not be well that we go down; the crew down yonder looks not so large, and I've small wish to sail the sea again. So, for the now, we will not go down." The two stood watching.

From behind them: *Click!* And a chuckle.

McJack and Nanquemoke whirled. "Sure," said the grinning sentry there, under his green cap with a tassel, "and mayhap ye will! What mean ye, spying on us here like overgrowed pixies from a bog?" This to McJack. Nanquemoke stood haughtily, with stoically folded arms.

The sentry grinned again at McJack's reply: "I be a man as shocked as yerself to meet me here: I be John McJack, the same as looks into yer gun barrel now, and into the Irish eyes of yer own Celt face, and reads the answer to the thing he'd wondered about: What sort of ship be yonder?"

"Sure, ye can tell the master, then, what ship he sails," said the sentry. "Your name means nothing at all to me. Walk to the fore. March! This last he shouted and he poked McJack with his gun barrel. The crew, down there, had come alive; they stood and waited. In the front stood a man with a great red mustache; McJack, marching so ignominiously down, sized this fellow for the captain. He spoke in Lenape to the chief: "Nanquemoke, I know not what lies ahead, but ye should be calm. Watch what I do and say. Though my wits were caught napping there, mayhap I can awake and use them now; mayhap I have a saving thought."

"Halt!" shouted the Irishman behind them. McJack heard the man chuckle. The red mustached man was grinning, too. His eyes were on McJack and the indian. He stood with his feet spread apart and a hand on his hip, while with the other he twirled his mustache. In the crew McJack spotted a very tall Scotsman, and a man who looked Dutch. Said the captain: "What have ye here, McPhale?"

"A man, and an injun," was the ready reply. "I found them watching from the bush. Ye should watch the wit of this one. He swears he be John McJack."

The captain shook his head and McJack was disappointed; seemed that his name meant nothing to master nor men. But they were naturally curious. The captain suddenly scowled. Then be bellowed: "What mean ye? Would ye walk among us and lack the grace to say 'God save the King?'"

McJack, having kept in mind the tales that Mundell had told, gambled on his answer: "That I would not, at all! But I would say this: Ye should hang the bastard from his own bastion!"

These seemed the key words; the men and the captain roared. McJack grinned with relief and amusement. Nanquemoke was both stoic and confused, so he contrived a smile. Watched McJack for his cue. The tall Scot looked over another man's head at the indian. Seemed interested in him, and curious.

The captain stepped forward and took McJack by the hand: "Sure, I know not from where ye came, for we thought there was not a white in the land at all."

So, then, there were natural explanations with a mutual interest. Briefly McJack told his story and learned the germ of theirs. In a way the men were pirate patriots. Seemed that when the Irish shipping had been seized by the English this crew had managed to save their craft, and convert her. There were, so far as they knew, but three others as lucky.

"So, ye see," the captain explained, "we be pirates now, by force of the king's orders, the which we would not heed. We be the Irish Navy, in a smallish way, though lacking the safety of a home port, except in Jamaica, where any pirate ship be safe. If we take goods from a king's ship, or doubloons from a Spanish, these go to serve the folk at home. In dark of night we slip into a hidden creek, in County Cork or Kerry, and leave our goods. But ye should tell me more at length this tale of yer own; I warrant it more strange than ours."

So they sat and talked, and McJack idly picked small pebbles from the sand and doodled with them. One of the crew watched him sharply. Searched McJack's face in a puzzled way. Then: "Master McJack, this world be somewhat upside down, will ye grant me that?"

He nodded, mystified. "Then," suggested the other, "it would seem but fit, such being the case, that a man should walk head down upon his hands; be that not so?"

"How mean ye?" Would it be like this?" McJack chuckled and placed his hands on the ground before where he sat. He bent far forward, found a point of balance, and slowly lifted legs and body into the air, though not so easily as in years gone by. Thus inverted, his face grown ruddy with the gravitating blood flow, he walked a few steps on his hand, then flipped upright again. Breathed a bit heavier, and explained that age was slowing him down. "How did ye know?" he inquired of the curious crewman.

"Aye, did me mind not fail I had seen that face afore, and the acting, but cannot tell the where."

And neither could McJack, but he had to put on a show, of course. Next, the jugs came out, and all drank to the health of this John McJack and his indian friend, and they drank to the health of the crew. To the folk at home. To the degradation of the king. To this or that or the other. A few of the men were already tipsy.

Nanquemoke choked on his first attempt, and McJack watched him sharply, wondered about the chief's reactions, and soon found out: after the third drink a foolish grin took the place of the dignified smile. The green-capped sentry full of Irish devilry, urged the chief to dance a hornpipe. Nanquemoke couldn't, of course, but he obliged with a devil dance, a thing he had half forgotten.

He pranced and advanced and made fierce faces at the devils. Ducked and dodged when those devils struck back. Whooped and yelled and charged and retreated, and made a magnificent comeback and chased one devil into the blazing sunset, out over the bay. Another time he compelled to ignominiously climb a tree. And then, as if satisfied with the good deeds done, Nanquemoke lay down for a nap.

The pirates had roared their appreciation, but McJack's amusement was largely simulated: Would Nanquemoke, once having had his taste of rum, go on from there and become a sot? This, McJack had heard, was too often the rule; he'd never seen a red man drink before. He shrugged his shoulders and smiled; he himself was slightly drunk by then. Some of the crew, having had a head start, were more so.

At dusk, which soon came then, Nanquemoke was one of three who had to be carried to the boat. Slung from boat to deck on a tackle. His red hands and legs hung limply down; his head was a-bobbling; one of the merry deckhands grabbed his plaited hair to swing the chief inboard, and plumped him limply to the deck. The sight didn't please

McJack at all. Nor would it have pleased Nanquemoke, had he been able to see himself, so McJack shrewdly determined to tell him about it.

It had grown quite dark; the ship showed no lights at all. McJack and the captain were sitting on the aft-deck. The shoreline was deep shadow there; the bay showed only a dark-flecked sheen, the ocean not at all.

McJack, with a possible purpose in his mind, had been spinning his yarn in greater and more colorful detail, first about the whalers and then, after the people had moved to the inland, the traders. He explained that, should the next one refuse to abide by McJack's trade rules and barter for rum... he shrugged a despairing shoulder in the dark: "Ye've seen what the rum did so quick to Nanquemoke there! The red people be not bad people, but many be not very wise. They be like children when it comes to trade, even when they be sober. Nanquemoke be a wise man in his way and his world, but a bad trader could cheat him with ease. These things I have fended as best I could, for Saunders played fair when he knew the rules. But he tells that his masters be greedy for greater gain; what he give in trade has greater cost than would rum and beads and baubles. So-o, I have great fear if the next man change the rules by force."

When the captain spoke his voice was bitter: "Aye, it reminds me of the rules at home. The men of King James overrun the land and force the laws. The people have no say at all. The king has made the ruling. Have ye no plan at all, about this trading?"

"What can I do? The land be big to watch. If none be there to guide them the injuns be like fools — they be so easy tricked in trade. If they get the rum they will be greater."

"Aye, your land be big, but so do the seas be wide. And we cannot always go where we choose. Over yonder we must avoid the ships of the king; we be not great enough to fight them. Our men are few; we cannot spare to have them slain in hopeless battle."

McJack smiled in the dark. "Ye be not so few as I, at that, to fight against the men of the king. What right have he in this new red man's world? Did god dispense that the king should own it? Nay, he did not! What right have he to tell the people how to pray and when and to who, and all?"

"But James be afflicted with a heady lust for power and spite," said the captain. "If the people don't abide, his soldiers chase them to the bogs! If a priest stay an hour, he can be hanged! If a catholic man own a horse, and a man of the king should crave it, then that man of the king can set the price and force the sale of the beast! If a man of the faith go five miles from home, he can be clapped in jail! If an Irish ship choose to sail the seas, the men of King James can seize it! What right have he in our country at all? What right with the ships? What right have he in this red man's world? What must ye do yourself when ye seek a port at home? Aye, ye be forced to come home in the dark of the night, and hide amongst yer own trees in a gully there!"

And this was partly how it came that McJack secured his new piece of ordnance to possibly guard his river: a little five-pounder with power and round-shot. He had new friends, too. Friends who, in the uncertain future, might be of help. The next morning the little gun was taken ashore and hidden under a tarpaulin, pending the time when McJack could get it in his boat.

But Nanquemoke was still unhappily drunk, and sick and wretched; his dignity was gone for the time; the chief well knew it and was ashamed. It was late afternoon before he was able to travel, and he was keen to go. To seek his lost dignity in the solitude of the woods. He was wiser and sadder and to McJack's great relief, the first avowed prohibitionist in all of the capelands. McJack smiled and didn't greatly chide. Knowing the chief's sensitiveness he made it a matter of friendly ridicule to further his reformation: "Sure, the men made merry when they slung ye aboard on the tackle. They did that; one grabbed your hair as he would a rope and swung ye inboard like a dangling corpse! He did, at that!" And he knew that the indian would never forget. That he never would repeat, McJack hoped.

That afternoon, having an hour or so to look, they found that the Dutchmen and their horses had been all over the land down there. Finally, some five miles from the Point, when the dusk was coming, they saw where they had headed toward the north, on the eastern trail, the one which skirted the marshes and the sounds. Nanquemoke called his friend's attention to some of the tracks; these seemed to stumble. One fore-track showed a shorter stride.

"That beast be lamed," declared McJack. "It has mayhap trodden in a hole. It'll slow the men. Nanquemoke, how long think ye since the tracks were made?"

The chief held up four fingers. McJack nodded: "Four days? Then best we'd camp here for the night; the air grows chill. We will make a fire." And Nanquemoke, still in rather poor health, was glad to agree. Next morning he was greatly improved.

McJack was surprisingly eager to start: "Nanquemoke, in the night I had me a thought: mayhap the lamed beast will slow the men. Mayhap so much that they'll leave it. Mayhap it be not so greatly lamed it cannot be cured. Mayhap we can get the beast."

They hadn't gone a mile before those stumbling prints grew worse; in one place the beast had forced a halt. The ground about was stamped where the others had waited.

"It'll get weller or worser," opined McJack. "The beast has stumbled again in this pine, the trail so narrow between the trees."

And then, a bit beyond in an open space, they found the horse; but never would he pull a plow. The beast lay sprawled and puffed; its tongue had been eaten and its throat was torn; the gray hair there was rusty with dried blood. The front fore fetlock was badly swollen. Behind its left ear was a bullet hole.

"Nanquemoke," and McJack's voice was somewhat sad, "now ye have seen the sight of a horse. Small good it'll do us, too, at that. Small good he's done the Dutchmen, too; they've mayhap found this backyard too large to play in. Not worth fighting for. Best we'd be heading for home."

And on the way he thought things over to himself, basing his deductions on past observations. Before McJack's time Nanquemoke's people had stayed static for ages. Then, briefly, what with the trade goods and McJack, conditions seemed changing for the better. But Sir John was fearful of the future.

"It's me thought," he silently explained to himself as he walked the trail behind the chief, "that these injuns should come along slow. A change be on the way; they should have time to get readied, have time to let their minds catch up with their matters. On the other hand, sure, we must wait and see." And he shrugged again as he walked, going to his town on the river. The wooden town there, where red folk lived in white folk cabins.

Which is where he waited through the winter, and the spring. Time for the trade sloop, and it hadn't come. McJack hoped it wouldn't, for he feared it greatly. Men came in from the creek-side camps to inquire. Their furs were ready; where was the white man's trade ship? McJack couldn't tell them; he had received no tidings at all.

The sloop was three weeks late and the weather was growing warm. In the moonless nights the doors of the cabins were left open for the air.

That's how McJack came to hear oars in the thole-pins, that night when the tide was in flood. Out on the river — he couldn't be sure. When he went down there was nothing to hear. Just the tide swirls and ripples. The frogs, the laughing loon. Those gray geese talking in their sleep. Some fish splashing as they played near shore. Just the sounds one wouldn't notice.

"Sure," he muttered, "it was me dreaming, at that." And he went back to his cabin. Minyanata and her daughters were all sleeping gently. From far up Muskee came a whip-poor-will call. "It's the first of the season," thought Sir John McJack.

Chapter 14

McJack had concluded, concerning those sounds of a boat on the river, that he had been mistaken. Perhaps a frog had been "cutting a chunk" in the meadows beyond.

However, on the evening of the second day after that he knew better; for in the camps upriver and along the creeks the indians had been having a spree. Rum had somehow gotten into those camps, and into many of the indians. Unaccustomed as the people were, a little of it went a long and diversified way. Some had been hilariously happy; others had been quarrelsome; one or two men had been hurt. Another had beat his woman. Their traditional deference to the authority of their chiefs had been overthrown for the time, and their councils scorned. Disorder was the rule of the rum.

But no rum had been left at Nanquemoke's camp; someone was wary of Sir John McJack. Whoever had dispensed the rum had been familiar with the country, or had had a guide. Perhaps the renegade indian, the one who had first come with Saunders. This last was McJack's suspicion.

"Nanquemoke," he said, "stay and guard the guns, and the people. Let none take up weapons until I say. The trade sloop will be coming soon; I reads his plans. I will go down and meet the sloop. I will tell the man plain. Then, he can do as he please..." McJack didn't finish the threat, but he and Panquenack went down in a canoe. Gliding along with the tide in the still of the evening. The quiet wherein the curlew and the kill-deer called, swift-spotted against the sky.

There was quiet of a sort in the lower camps, too. Their rum was gone. The men were sullen and the women sad. All were bewildered by the thing that had come upon them, and which they craved so quickly to renew. Perhaps no other race on earth was so crudely ripe for destruction nor so poorly equipped to resist. Stoics by nature and the hard lives they led, capable of suffering and privation, and of quick recovery when conditions changed, they seemed helpless against the rum. McJack knew this from hearsay. Nanquemoke had had a brief experience he would never repeat, but he was exceptional.

McJack pondered on these matters as he and Panquenack went on downriver, when the night had come and the ebb was still running. Down to the beginning of the bay; the sun was three hours set by then and the tide had begun to turn to flood.

Inshore were the tree-lines, etched dimly on the dark. Mere shades they seemed, beyond the meadows. On the bay there seemed nothing at all, at first, and Panquenack paddled slowly. Then, downbeach a little, off the mouth of the river, a dim shape showed. Its mast was outlined against a lighter cloud. McJack calculated on time and tide: "Sure, it be the first of the flood now; they cannot move in the dark. Come morn, the ebb will have started again. I will have time, at that. So I will speak to the sloop, but will not go near. It's meself that be lacking the trust, to be sure."

So he held the canoe a long gun-shot away, the night so calm that his voice would carry.

"Ahoy the sloop!" His hail rang clear, yet at first there was no response. Perhaps the watch was drowsing.

"Ahoy!" This from the deck of the vessel.

"What sloop be that?" inquired McJack.

"The *Prince Maurice*. Fur trader. Who are you? Have ye a ship?" Evidently the master was surprised, there in those empty waters.

"Be ye going to Wahatquenack?"

The man laughed. 'Why?" he asked. "Can't the injuns wait?"

"Mayhap. Be ye going to trade with the injuns?"

"We be, when it suits us. And who are ye? And will ye come aboard?"

McJack ignored both questions. "Where will ye trade?"

"Where I damn well please, and where and when it suits me best! Who are ye that makes so bold to ask? Be ye from a ship nearby?"

"I be John McJack, and I be warning ye fair! If ye trade for rum, and do try the tricks, I will sink yer sloop beneath ye!"

"Ho-ho! How bold he talks! I will do as I please, and bedamned to ye! Now get ye gone and stop your gawping. We have men and guns and goods for the trade, and trade we will, me hearty! For rum or for what!"

"Ye have choosed yer course," replied McJack. "All fools be not red fools, at that.

There be a great one on the sloop; he be wearing yer boots the now!"

The master cursed. There came a flare and a musket shot. The ball fell short and wide. McJack fired back a taunting laugh. He could hear the master cursing as he and Panquenack paddled away. Back to the wooden town, to wait and see. To clean the guns and make ready. It was not until the second day that the sloop made for the river, and by then the news had gone inland, passing from one camp to another.

But there had been no prearranged spot for the trading and McJack had advised that the people stay in their own camps and wait. Or better, not go down to trade at all. This last he could hardly hope for; the indians were childishly eager. Besides, there was the lure of the rum. It made men happy.

There was little in McJack's plan that was definite; matters depended on what happened, and where. Location of the sloop, temper of the indians and the terms of trade. The sloop was edging her way up the reaches of the river. At times, with the wind drawing wrong, the boat had to wrap around the bends. It was very slow going.

Apparently the master became disgusted for he anchored in Yak Wak Reach, between the two lower camps and some four miles south of McJack's wooden town. There the east bank was low but firm; from the sloop he could see well inland and, did he choose, could rake the woods with his guns. To the west there was no bank at all. Just tide-flooded meadows waist-high with the reeds.

McJack had concluded to let matters take their course for the time, so he didn't go down. Instead he had Nanquemoke send a dependable man, to scout. In those lower camps McJack's influence had never been as strong as with his own people and those above, on the river and creeks. Both he and Nanquemoke had urged all these people to stay at home and for that first day they did it.

But those below did not; temptation was too close at hand. Twice during the day McJack got reports. Many of the indians were mildly drunk. They were getting almost nothing for their furs, or worse than nothing.

"If that man be crafty as he thinks," declared McJack, "he will not quite stop the rum, even when the injuns' furs be gone. One thing I've learned: a mad injun be a bad injun, drunk or sober."

But during the day none of the people above went down; perhaps they were waiting for the sloop to come to them, but McJack doubted that it would. The trader would hold his vantage point, and do the waiting. There he was not so far from the open bay and the Wahatquenack was treacherous for sail.

So that first day was done. The dark of the night was quiet and calm there on the river above Muskee. Just the tide-swirls, at first. The frogs. A cat-owl. A whip-poor-will.

McJack still sat on the shore at midnight looking and listening in the dark, the dark where one could see dimly. See shadows that slid on the sheen of the water. One at a time, in silence, near yon side of the river. Canoes. The indians going down to trade, too eager to wait.

"So that be that," thought Sir McJack. "The sloop will stay in Yak Wak and that will suit me fine." Then he went to his cabin to get some sleep.

The trading lasted more than a week. Some few of the upriver indians went home, bewildered and discouraged. Their furs were gone, and they had little to show for them. Little that was good, at least; they had headaches and hangovers. When these last were gone and they'd had time to brood, they'd have a temper.

But many of the indians stayed down at the trading, their canoes hauled up on the shore. McJack and Nanquemoke went down to look. They went by land and stood well back among the trees. Most of the indians were still mildly drunk; some were sodden and asleep, there beside the ashes of their fires. A few seemed sober and these were the saddest of them all.

And Sir John thought of Yanata, and he was afraid.

The *Prince Maurice* lay out in the stream, bow to the bay. A larger craft than the other, carrying more men. There must have been a dozen or more; they had taken precautions, too. The helm was boxed around with boards: protection against the arrows. Same with the cannon on the larboard bow: it pointed through a port toward the eastern shore, aimed low to rake the land.

McJack noted these precautions, and then gave attention to the build of the craft; she was shallow of draft and broad of beam. Her stem stood nearly plumb: "That will suit me fine."

Then, still keeping out of sight, he and Nanquemoke went down through the woods to the river. Down beyond the bend, where on the other shore were trees and where the channel was not so wide. The tide ran swiftly there.

"This be a good place," McJack decided. "If we be forced to do it, we will do it here. We will, at that."

And that night they were very busy, going back and forth in the dugout boat, passing the sloop in the dark. Next morning on the shore, McJack had about a dozen men, all from his own camp. He didn't let the other indians know — they were either busy or befuddled, up there near the sloop.

So they cut tall slim poles and made a boom across the river, lashed together with thongs. Fastened at the ends to trees. Its course was diagonal; on the eastern shore it led to just below the little cannon there. They did the work on the top of the tide, when the water was still.

Then McJack became doubtful. Perhaps, unless the trader did worse than he had, it wouldn't be necessary, or mayhap wise. So, pending what the trader would do, he waited. Decided that, in case no further trouble came, he could cut the eastern end of the boom and clear the river. Let it swing down with the tide, and the sloop could go, too.

"The man have his choosing," decided McJack. "May the saints help him to choose right, for I have small greed for murder!"

So he and his dozen men stayed there the night; the next ebb-tide would begin an hour before dawn. By daylight it would be running swiftly; he surmised that the trader would use it. When the ebb began, the boom bent like a tightened bow; the anchor-tree quivered with the strain, there in the first of the morning light. The wind blew downriver, lightly. More of Nanquemoke's men had come down. They were placed along the shore, between the trading and the boom.

"Nanquemoke," declared McJack, "we will not start the fighting, but if it starts, ye and Panquenack shall tend these men. See that they be careful, but keep them shooting at the sloop. I would have the whites so excited that they shall not see the boom. If no fight start at all, then we will cut the boom and let the men go, in case more should come to claim the sloop. We will wait and see."

But they didn't wait long. The shade of the trees showed plain on the river; the tide surged strongly down its crooked course to the bay. The sloop had planned to go with it. With its furs and its profits. With the man who had traded "for rum or for what."

Then came the creaking of gear. McJack could see the gaff and the tip of the sail as they climbed by jerks toward the masthead. Then there was a yell and another. A moment of silence. Then a whole medley of whoops and yells. Splashes in the river. Some musket shots and then the boom of the cannon. The yells were mingled then with screams.

McJack's face grew white and his jaws set grim. The battle light came into his eyes. "The man has choosed his course," he shouted. "There be no choice for me!"

While the yells and screams continued, the sail flapped loose in the breeze. Then it began to jerk again. And, just as the gaff rose tilted to its top, Nanquemoke's scout came running.

The first stirring on the sloop had roused the indians on the shore. It seemed for the first time to have brought full realization: the sloop was leaving with their furs! And with the remainder of the rum, too, for the trader had been unwisely frugal at the end. Why waste it to no purpose when the trading was done?

As a result many who had been pleasantly drunk were at least part sober. Sober enough to realize their wrongs, and as McJack had foretold, they were mad to the bones of them.

An old indian had gone out in his canoe and demanded the return of his furs, gesturing with his empty hands. Then he had tried to climb over the rail, and had been kicked into the river. That had started the yelling and the arrows had begun to fly. Some of these reached the deck, or the planking, some even fell short. From where the indians were crowded together it was a long bow shot to the sloop.

And there where they crowded was where the shrapnel caught them. Men dropped their bows and writhed on the ground. Some lay still. The tail-line was cut and the sloop sailed away down river.

Then the indians with the muskets began to fire; bedlam broke loose on the deck; the traders hadn't known about the guns. Two men were struck and the others tried to hide, lying flat, or crouching behind the housing. From there they fired their muskets back. The indians fired from the shore.

The sloop went on downriver. The sail drew full and in that sail small holes began to show. There were holes, too, in the boards of the fencing that was designed to withstand the arrows. The helmsman crouched low; he couldn't see so well downstream. Steered more or less blindly in that racket of guns and yelling, with the two wounded men on the deck.

The wind held fair and the sloop would soon near the bend. Once there and with the changing course, the sail would swing to larboard and hide that eastern shore. The west bank would be out in the open then but the helmsman daren't stand to see it. He only dared raise his head a little, steering in part by the tops of the trees. But someone on deck saw the western end of the floating boom and signaled. The helmsman swung to the larboard then and the middle of the river.

On the eastern bank near the end of the boom McJack was waiting. The sloop struck at a long, soft slant; her course slowly changed, heading for the eastern shore. The master raved and shouted, he was excited indeed. And frightened; one could hear the fear in his voice.

The change in course had set the sail abaft and it swung to starboard; the sloop slid slowly along the circle of the boom.

And the indians with McJack let loose their yells and their musket balls and never was panic born quicker. Panic and helplessness; the press of the sail swung the bow upstream. The craft lay broadside to the cannon set up by McJack, the cannon gifted by those genial Irish sailors. McJack fired it. The piece bucked with the recoil and turned half over. The cannonball struck the planking just above the water and went clear through to the river.

The range was then so short that the indians used their arrows. More men came running down the shore. Panic and death were there on the disabled sloop and the devils were loose on the shore line.

A man leaped from the sloop and tried to swim the river. But the current caught him; it swirled him with it. Panquenack, there on the shore, saw the man swimming. Being carried swiftly away. So the indian followed downriver and out toward the middle. The two heads showing and the flailing arms, the white and the red. Panquenack was gaining; the white man was already winded. The indian rolled as he stroked, swimming strongly; the man saw him coming. He seemed to be choking.

And when the red fingers closed about his throat he choked indeed. The two of them went down. Panquenack loosened his grip a little and the man breathed water. Black water down there from where the surface showed green. But only Panquenack saw the green and when he surfaced he came alone. Swam to the shore slantwise to the current. He must hasten back; there was more to do. Panquenack, whose woman was Mellissa.

The sloop had foundered, there against the shore. The indians had swarmed aboard and McJack had gone with them. He found two men hiding in the hold; one was the trader, white-faced and shaking. The indians wanted to kill them, but McJack and Nan-quemoke, with the help of Penoke, an upriver lad, got them both ashore, the indians because McJack had asked it and from no kindness of heart at all. Neither was McJack inclined to be kind, but those men must serve a purpose.

The indians recovered their furs and what other loot they found. McJack was busy with the whites on the shore.

"I be John McJack," he told the trader. "The same as was speaking to ye down on the bay. Mayhap now ye have learnt a lesson, and I be only sparinh the worthless life of ye that ye may pass that lesson to them as sent ye. If ye should reach the place from whence ye came, and I hopes that ye do else I've spared ye in vain, ye will tell the lesson that ye learned. Tell them that it do pay to be fair with all men, red or white.

"Ye have done great harm to the people here, and not in pounds nor in pence could ye pay at all. Not ye, nor them as sent ye. There be no need for more speaking the now. Nanquemoke be bringing ye a boat, and mayhap some stores if can find them. And now before the injuns change their minds, ye had best begone! It's Sir John McJack that sends ye; see that ye not forget."

And on the ebbing tide the boat sneaked down the river. When the trader looked back he saw smoke arising; the *Prince Maurice* was burning where she lay, left grounded by the ebbing tide. She and her master had been sent to mend matters. Small matters of profits pertaining to trade.

The white man's world might be angered; but the red man's world was shaking more and more in spite of their temporary triumph. McJack could foresee it and feel it. It was the thing he hoped to forestall, at least in his family affairs. He knew the general trend would only be briefly stopped; there was always that motive of profit. In furs or in farms. In one thing or another. For cat-paw or for king.

"Sure, there be Yanata, and the small one. Yanata be tall as her mother now, and as comely. She be half-injun, but I be proud of her! The bucks be casting eyes her way even now. I have noted them often. But I cannot let harm come upon the lass, if I can stave it away!

"So keep yer eye on the lass, me Sir McJack, for the red-wing will call and the urge will be strong, be it red urge or white, and ye cannot change it with yer craft at all. There be two worlds in which for the lasses to live; I have placed them half between the two. The white world will build; the red will fall, I do read the signs of the times the now. Saints grant the lassies have a chance!"

And so he pondered, forming his plans. Feeding his hopes. Trying with the craft of him to direct the course of destiny. To build a boom across a muddled bloodstream, as it were, and change the course of the lives that were on it.

"They cannot," he determined, "go back to the injun for they be of the line of John McJack."

And that was the year that the surveyors came, and changed the name of the river.

Chapter 15

That early summer was sober and more or less sad. Foreboding the future, some of the indians cherished dreams of vengeance. A bad time for white men to come into the land.

It was along in July that a runner came from down the river with startling news. A ship had come into the bay and put out two boats at the mouth of the river. The ship had gone on but the boats came in. Stopped here and there at the bends. It was all very suspicious. The lower camps were preparing to fight. Would Sir John bring his muskets and cannon?

McJack was perplexed; the tale didn't make sense. Evidently the men hadn't heard about the *Prince Maurice* or they would scarcely have dared in open boats.

"Nanquemoke and me will go down and scout," he told the runner. "Make haste and bid yer people hold their hands and force no fight at all. Afore, ye did not heed me; ye should so now. We will go down and see."

McJack and the chief went to the lower camp in a canoe. The boats were still some two miles down, beyond the bends. A scout reported they were on a point of the western shore where the beach was gravel. The men had set up a strange little gun; it stood on three sticks and a man aimed it here and there. As yet he hadn't fired it. Besides, there seemed nothing to shoot at or did the white man have some magic gun that would kill silently and from afar?

McJack smiled. "Nay, there be no such magic in all the white man's world at all. Bide here; Nanquemoke and I will go and see."

But as he and the chief paddled across the river and hugged that shore, while going down, McJack had a vague suspicion. A thing on three sticks and a man aimed it! McJack chuckled. Hoped he was right. Then, on second thought, he wasn't so sure, for it meant that the whites had plans for this red man's river. And those red men weren't ready.

There was a narrow beach of fastland on that western shore, skirted by trees and reeds and bushes, and Nanquemoke suggested that they take to the land and scout from the covert. Thus hidden, they worked their way down and soon saw the men. A bit closer they could hear them. The older one was taking down his magic gun and a younger one had a board across the bow of a boat. There were eight men in all but only the two seemed busy; the others idled about. One was fishing. McJack couldn't quite understand what they were saying.

He grinned at the chief: "I think these men be friendly, and they be not on guard at all. I will give them a bit of a fright; ye should watch them come alive!" And then, still in the covert, he shouted:

"Ahoy! Ye on the beach! What do ye here?"

McJack laughed silently and Nanquemoke smiled at the sudden and startled commotion. The scrambling and grabbing of guns and the attempt to stand at the ready. With rather wild eyes they scanned the cover. But the bushes and reeds told nothing.

The surveyor, the more elderly man, seemed calmer: "Ahoy the bush! And who are ye?" They young man left the boat and came to the surveyor's side. Alert but undecided. McJack rather liked his looks.

"Ye should speak first," McJack replied. "Who be ye? What do ye here?"

The man had gotten the directions of the voice. "We are surveyors to the British Crown and we come in peace. Are ye him that is known as Sir John McJack?"

"I be that same. Ye should place yer guns in the boat again, before my men come out in the open. Ye shall have no harm if ye do it."

McJack chuckled again and felt the prestige of his "title" when the surveyor made a gesture and the men, some of them reluctantly, placed their guns in the boast, glancing meanwhile at the bush. How many red men were hiding there?

"Now, ye shall stand a bit away and I will come out and speak ye fair." McJack was grinning his amusement as he and the chief went out to the men.

"I be McJack. This be Nanquemoke, the chief of one of my towns. Nanquemoke, this man be...?"

"My name is Richards. Simeon Richards. We are surveying. This young man is Adrian Bogard, my assistant."

There was hand-shaking then and the young fellow smiled at McJack and the chief and seemed very pleased to meet them. He had a sort of daredevil look in his eyes. A handsome young chap with wavy hair. McJack's quick liking increased. Perhaps, for a fleeting moment, he thought of Yanata. Of his plan for her.

"I am very glad to meet ye both," Adrian was declaring. "These are our men." The men seemed glad and relieved.

"Ye should bring your force to the open now," suggested Richards. "Or," smiling with sudden suspicion, "have ye already done so?"

"I've done just that," confessed McJack. "It would seem at times that many men who be not there serve just as well as if they were, if things are rightly planned and all."

Adrian laughed then with the others. "Sir John, ye must have survived quite largely by your wits. I have heard some tales of your shrewdness."

"Aye," and 'Sir John' chuckled, "were all things told ye might have heard tales of my dumbness, too. But there be one ye have not heard at all. Did ye meet two frightened men in a boat?" This to Richards.

"No-o. We have seen nothing but a single canoe, downriver."

And then McJack explained about the trouble with the *Prince Maurice*. "I tell ye now that ye may sense the temper of the injuns here and the cause for it, and be gentle when ye meets them, to be sure. Be gentle, but be wary. For a time it'll be best I keep ye in my charge, in case some may think ye harm. Ye will come to my town, and all." And then he thought, indeed, about Yanata. Yanata and the lad with the daredevil eyes and the smile. And the waving hair and the youth and the strength and the hope of him. And the ageless eternal urge.

And Adrian thought about Yanata, too, as soon as he saw her and through the days and nights that the Englishman spent in the indian's wooden town. For Yanata was distinct among her kindred there. And different. Because of her poise and facial and physical beauty. Bashful at first, she maintained her dignity.

And Yanata? It was natural that she should be drawn to the lad, even from the first. And McJack and Minyanata were greatly, though secretly, pleased, and as secretly afraid. Sir John was puzzled about marital matters, in more ways than one.

For there had been Penoke, an upriver indian, the youth who had seemed so willing to help McJack get the trader ashore from the *Prince Maurice*. So anxious to help McJack that the latter had wondered why at the time. Later, he knew. Penoke, smitten by Yanata's charms even before the fight on the river, was seeking her father's favor. A fine-looking Lenape, he had protracted his stay in the wooden town. As best he could, which wasn't so well, he had spoken of marriage. Had offered three bearskins and two strings of shell money along with himself. The matter had required tact on the parent's part.

"Sure, Penoke," he had explained, "ye wants the girl and so do many others. Ye see, Penoke, I be a bit uncertain about it. Our young men do reckon that she should belong to one of them. That makes for muddle in me mind. Ye should hark to this. Ye should go back to your own town and people, when ye gets readied, of course no haste be needful, and give thought to the thing. Yanata still be very young. Ye must wait, Penoke, and even if ye wait I cannot tell nor say."

And McJack had smiled, and thought he'd handled the matter well, and had waited to see Penoke go, he hadn't succeeded. Penoke prolonged his visit; he was still in the town when the surveyors came. He was not at all pleased with Adrian. The other men didn't matter to Penoke, but they did to McJack. For they created a social and sexual problem as well as a racial one. There were not many unwed women in the town; McJack hoped that the whites would leave them alone. It was a muddled sort of little world. Sir John found himself in a rather ambiguous position: he himself had taken an indian girl for a wife and he encouraged Adrian to court his daughter, yet did all that he courteously could to prevent those other white men from any attempt to do likewise. Hoping greatly for his daughter while as greatly fearing those very hopes, because, if successful, Adrian would take Yanata away.

So Penoke was only a minor problem, or so McJack thought; he wished the youth would go home. But Penoke, silent and persistent, stayed on.

The surveyors planned to camp in the town for two weeks, living in their tents. They aimed to make a chart of the river and to search along the creeks for mill sites. For minerals and soils and timber, so that the whites might know if this red man's world was worth the toil of taking. Another ambiguity for Sir John McJack, and all he could do about it was shrug his shoulders; it wouldn't concern the immediate future. Perhaps he wouldn't live to see the ultimate results of those surveys, important though they were.

And the evenings at the town were very important, too. Sunsets and afterglows. A canoe on purpling waters. A young man and a girl. Perhaps walking among the pines in the dusk of day. Just being together. For Yanata the red-wing was calling aloud: "Come over-he-re!"

McJack and Minyanata were both glad and afraid as they watched. "Me lady, the ways of this world be changing now; our lass must go to the red or the white. We can but wait, and pray, and see what happens to the lass."

And something did seem to happen, though not what McJack had planned for. It would prove both serious and somewhat ridiculous. It had been a long while getting to the wooden town, because in its genetics and geography it had started afar.

Down on the cape McJack had come ashore on his mast. He had stayed and been busy. But before his time other men had been busy, too. There had been Captain Mey and Captain Hudson. They had skirted the shores and mayhap landed. Mey left his name on the cape, Hudson on his river and bay. And later than that the pilgrims had gone further north and settled in New England.

There had been the Jamestown people, too; and down on Maryland shore the calverts had come. The new world was being settled here and there by English, Dutch and Swedes. They stayed on the coasts, or near them.

But long before them had come the French, ancient enemies of the English. Further north and inland. Founded Quebec. And, too, even before the pilgrims had come, they'd worked their way along the Father of Waters*. Building a town or a fort. Making ready to take over the land. The mid-country for certain, the coastlands could they get them.

Very early in the century Champlain had, unwisely, helped the Huron tribes against the Iroquois, and thus made enemies of the latter. But, sensing the unwisdom of the act, and realizing too late the power of the Five Nations (the Tuscaroras as yet hadn't joined) the French made many overtures for peace. With some isolated bands they succeeded for a time, and briefly, they used them. Later the united forces of the Six Nations would be against the French, but in McJack's time this hadn't happened. The French were vaguely laying their plans.

They were hundreds of miles from McJack and his people and his river. Up there in the inland north of west, putting French notions into indian minds. Sowing the first seeds of the French and Indian Wars which they knew would come unless they could get rid of the English and the Dutch. There were not many Swedes anywhere, just then, though they would soon be coming. So, in the minds of the indians the French planted sundry notions, thinking they were planting the nucleus of a nation.

One theory was, the whites being so few in the Long Land** and the Lenape still masters of the soil, that the Iroquois should go down and spy out the land. Convert the Lenape to that French idea. Kill off the English when and if they landed. They hadn't heard of McJack at all, didn't know he was there. Though they surmised that the traders would come in the springs.

The older red men, more wise and not yet filled with thirst for the white man's blood, preferred not to go. It was a long way to the Long Land, and if the Lenape were unfriendly the red men might have a war of their own. A needless and profitless war, at that.

But a score and a half of young hoodlums had listened to the new idea. It appealed to their youth and their yearning for adventure. So, come springtime, they'd go exploring. They'd visit the Lenape and propound the thought. They, at least, could go down to the sea.

They wore their hair in the defiant scalp lock, roached fore and aft. They were nearly naked, for they were traveling light. They had a long way to go; warm weather was coming. They came to the river above where later would be Trenton. Crossed on the shelf-rock there. Wading. They were in the southern half of the Long Land then. They'd seen the Great River*** (and it hadn't seemed so great at all) but they hadn't seen the sea.

They did not go along the shores of the Great River, for down that way were the larger towns. The Lenape towns. Inland, the camps would be very small and mostly transient. So they went their way, around the headwaters of Rancocas and then down. There were the little camps on the little streams. The Lenape were compelled to be civil. They listened and pretended to agree. Conceded that the English and the Dutch were rascals.

* Mississippi River
** New Jersey
*** Delaware River

Stealers of land and cheaters in trade. Perhaps the French white brothers would be very much better.

So the youthful invaders, having the arguments their own way and finding the Lenape compliant, became puffed with premature pride. Grew a bit more arrogant. When, down-country a little, the dialects changed and they weren't understood, they'd be impatient. At the little camps they demanded food and generally got it. They molested the women. Feeling the power of their relative numbers, flushed with the feeling of their own superiority to these weaker brothers, they had begun to be bullies. So they bullied their way toward the capelands, toward the Wahatquenack and McJack's wooden town. They were having great fun. The small camps of the natives weren't.

But after the Iroquois had gone the Lenape shrugged their shoulders. The intruders had done small actual harm. Such things had happened before. This raid was not worth the trouble of gathering the small clans together to resist, for by then the Iroquois would be far to the south. Let the people down there take care of the matter.

Chapter 16

It was evening at the town on Wahatquenack, and calm. Upon the river the afterglow lay, with its trees in the water, and its clouds. Pinks and purples and ambers and greens: distinct, yet mixed and muddled. Not muddled to mar, as a man might mix them; not that at all. The Artist Instinct in the Hand of the God, dawdling with its pigments as the day died there, dawdling for a moment before the dark should come, had made perfection, briefly. It wouldn't last; it couldn't.

All things move; when the world stays static it is but resting for the change. Sometimes briefly, sometimes long. That afterglow would live its lovely moment there, then it would move when the night should come. Come silent on its unseen feet to slowly dull the colors there, as if it wiped the canvas clean, to try again tomorrow.

"I wonder," said Sir McJack. "I wonder many a time on all of this. This night there be beauty here, in all the quiet and the peace. Mayhap tomorrow will come a storm. With lightning and thunder, and all.

"And that will be a beauty thing, as well as this, though mayhap men will be frightened. There be some might of power beyond it all, and that same power can guide the searching lips of new-born babes to suckle! I wonder."

Richards just nodded; he, too, wondered. But more at the man than at the sunset scene. And at Yanata, too.

But Yanata wasn't as talkative as her dad; she said very little and thought a great deal. On this, or that and on Adrian mostly. On sunsets and sand cranes, on moonlight and moccasins, when her moccasined feet wandered out beneath the moon. With Adrian. Walking in the shade of the overarching trees, the oaks or the pines. Or just walking in moonlight beside the still river with the dark of the cedars beside them. Living and learning, for good or for ill.

It was late when she crept beneath the tepee, then. Very happy, a little bit afraid. Her mother, lying there where the girl must pass, reached out a hand. She drew her close: "My lassie, ye be happy now?"

"My mother, I be very happy, to be sure. But I be somewhat afeared."

"Lassie," the mother whispered, "ye make pray. Make pray the spirit gods. Make pray the saints. Make sure, at that!"

A mosquito was pesting about McJack's right ear. It buzzed and it bothered, and then it bit. And he daren't slap the thing at all, since he pretended to be so soundly sleeping.

The dawn came in from the red-rose east, and it was day. The breakfast fires were burning. Women brought water from down at the brook, where it ran in the midst of its cedars. At the surveyor's tent the men made ready to go. That day they planned to work along the Manumuskin. McJack came out to join them.

"Sure, it'll be warm the day. If we... Wait! What comes? A man a-running!"

Swinging down the trail came a tall Lenape. He came on across the camp and down to the shore. "Iroquois!" he panted. "They come. As many men as here!"

"Do they come in peace?" McJack's face was sober. He had never seen the Iroquois but had heard bad tales about them. Richards and his men were listening; the men and women crowded around.

"They come into camp with the war dance. They eat the food of the camp. They laugh at our people!"

"Have they the guns?" All of the twinkle was gone from the eyes of McJack.

"No guns. Bows and little axes. Sharp." The man was from the Manumuskin camp. He was regaining his breath after the five-mile run.

"Have they hurt your people?"

"Not my people. My people be few; they must do as the Iroquois say. By signs. My people cannot speak with them; the tongues do differ." The man pointed back toward the inland. "Not far," he warned McJack. "They come here."

"Then," said McJack, "we will make us a plan. We will, at that. Call in the people that have gone to the farms. But, and listen well, the whole of ye, let none fireball or shaft untill I say.

"Nanquemoke, what think ye? Will the red men come into so big a camp, what with the cabins and all? Will they not be suspecting there be white men here, and mayhap guns?"

"First they will scout the camp, and see," said Nanquemoke. "If they see many men

they will loiter in the woods. They will steal the game from our hunters. They will steal our women as they go for the berries or the fuel. This is the way my fathers say they did afore. But they were Lenape; I do not know what the Iroquois will do."

"Most likely they will do as the Lenape did," said McJack. "They be not out to kill, but to frolic. Nanquemoke, they would make fools of us and our people, as they have made fools of the smaller camps. But I have me a plan..."

"As the Iroquois come near, ye shall go out from some thicket and walk right blindly in their way. They shall capture ye." McJack grinned at Nanquemoke's sober face. Then the chief smiled, and nodded; he had play-acted before, though this would be more risky.

"I shall tell that most of our men have gone away? I shall lead them to the camp?"

"Aye, Nanquemoke, ye be a shrewd injun; ye shall do just that for the sake of the people. This be not a battle of blood, but of brains. We will set them a trap. We will, at that."

So they, the white men and the red, made ready for the reception, and Nanquemoke went out to watch the trail. There was a bustle and a hustle, and then there was quiet.

An hour or so had passed. It seemed very peaceful among the trees and cabins there. The women and children kept close to their homes, but mostly where they could be seen. The only men in sight were in that group in the open near the center of the camp. Away from the cabins, and men picked for the purpose.

There were but five of these. They seemed to be holding a council, but the eyes of those who faced the trail would stray that way, watchful. There was a tiny fire in the center; one of the men held a pipe in his hand.

Behind a corner of a cabin stood Sir John McJack, where he could see down the trail. Just out in front Minyanata sat sewing; Yanata was pounding corn. Mellissa kept out of sight, McJack's suggestion, lest the Iroquois should suspect the presence of white men. The scene looked very domestic and natural, but there was tension in the air. And a crooked smile on the shaven face of McJack.

Then, down along the trail, he saw some men. Perhaps half a dozen. He grinned, then set his jaw. Standing haughtily with the Iroquois was Nanquemoke, arms folded across his breast. Pretending. Then a scout came forward to spy into the camp, slipping from tree to tree. He could see the women there and some children and those five men in the centre around the little fire. He went back to the others on the trail. They seemed to be consulting. One of the men spoke again to Nanquemoke; the chief stared haughtily back at him. Shrewdly, the chief had first told his tale; then, seeming to have repented, to have taken on that stately silence. Seeming to regret what he'd told.

McJack chuckled because he'd seen the men come on. Stealthily at first because Nanquemoke seemed reluctant. Appeared to have sensed that he had betrayed his people. McJack beckoned Yanata to come to him. Told her to walk down toward the trail. Then, seeing the Iroquois, she was to scream and run back into the camp. This, McJack figured, might hasten matters.

And it did decidedly. For the Iroquois came after Yanata with whoops and yells. The thirty young red men. Out into the camp they came, swinging their little hatchets. Out to where those five men were sitting, apparently in council, seeming to be the only men in camp and so frightened that they couldn't move. The women had run to the cabins by then and McJack hadn't had to urge them.

The racket was terrific and terrifying. Out they had come, on a prance and a run, those Iroquois lads from the northland. Casting their panic into an unprepared camp, just for the fun of the matter. Just to make something to boast about back home: a tale of their prowess. Or so they thought as they danced and yelled and threatened with their hatchets those innocent men in the middle there. These men seemed too frightened to move — perhaps some weren't acting, at that. But McJack had told them to stay on the ground to be out of the line of possible fire.

So at first they sat and gaped. The women watched from the cabins; some of them screamed; that wasn't play-acting either. A little aside was something in a tarpaulin; McJack crouched behind it. The indians didn't see him as first, too intent with the men on the ground. Whooping and yelling at them; having the fun of a lifetime there. All according to plan — but the plan was McJack's.

Sir John gave the signal by yanking the tarp from the cannon. The piece was empty, but the lads didn't know it. It seemed to have sprung from the very ground, and suddenly they realized it was pointing straight at them. Ready to belch out its bullets and bolts.

And out of the woods had come white men and red men, with guns. Out of the cabins had come more of the same. The Iroquois were suddenly surrounded. There by the cannon stood McJack with a flare!

Those yells were now sticking in their throats. Each way they looked there stood men with muskets: as many or more than they were themselves. Mayhap more, and there was that cannon aimed directly at them. McJack waved the flare as if ready to fire it. The Lenape in council lay flat on the ground. The silence was so sudden it hurt.

It was the north lads' turn to fear and gape. There was no way they could run at all. Every direction, except in the line of the cannon's blast, were those muskets; and the shrapnel from the cannon would tear the Iroquois to bits! They couldn't fight; they couldn't run. Seemed the young bullies couldn't even think, at first.

All except one; he saw that mock council, lying flat on the ground, beneath the line of fire. Quickly this lad saw the scheme of things: the men with the guns wouldn't shoot their own people. With a yell he dived into the middle and hugged down close to the soil. Quick as a flash went more of them, so fast one couldn't count them. But not all. A dozen or so were of sterner, if not wiser, stuff. They had their tribal and personal pride to sustain. So they simply folded their arms and stood, silently glaring defiance. Bewildered but haughty. McJack admired their pluck; they were fine-looking bucks at that. Though helpless they still were proud; the others were wriggling in the heap. Trying to mix and muddle with the Lenape there so that the other men wouldn't fire.

It had only taken a moment. Many of the Lenape and whites were laughing, it had been so ridiculous. The men quickly formed a circle about that heap in a huddle and the dozen lads standing. One of the council had gotten out of the heap; the other four were trying. But they couldn't; the lads grabbed their legs and held them down for protection while those who were standing continued to glare.

McJack had the defiant Iroquois disarmed first and ringed with guards, then laughingly turned to the others. Some had ventured to raise their heads to see what was doing. Their scalp locks looked funny instead of ferocious; the fright in their eyes showed plainly.

But instead of looking into the barrels of the muskets, instead of seeing death thrust into their very faces, instead of murder they saw mirth. Not a gun was pointed at the heap. Some of the whites bent over and guffawed and slapped their knees and pointed. More than that, the women had rushed to the outer circle and they, too, laughed. Laughed and squealed and derided. Only the little ones stayed frightened. They were pop-eyed, perplexed. The bucks who'd stayed standing ground their teeth in impotent rage — women were laughing at them!

For just a moment McJack didn't know what to do, especially with the lads on the ground. Some whites of the times would have murdered them; would have taught the reds a lesson. But not Sir John McJack. His methods could be murder when they had to be, but not in a ridiculous case like this.

His merriment died to a kindly grin and stepping closer, he beckoned to one of the lads. He got to his feet and McJack took away his hatchet and knife; his bow was still lost in the huddle there. McJack had Nanquemoke and Richards do the same with the others and in a few moments there was order of a sort. But the dozen who had dared to stand, McJack kept by themselves, under stronger guard. Seemed there were two kinds of Iroquois as well as of Lenape.

They had made their merry way for two hundred miles and more, to get into a mess like this. And not a bow had twanged, not a gun had banged. But there they were, humiliated so that women made ridicule! Just what had happened? What whim of the spirit gods, perhaps, was this? And who was this white man who had charge of it all? The clean-shaven one who grinned like an imp? Whose eyes still twinkled with the fun he had had, the fun he had stolen from them?

Up among their own rocks and rivers and trees they'd never heard of John McJack. But, as they had come down into the Long Land, from camp to little camp or smaller, and as they'd rollicked closer to Wahatquenack and its people there, they had heard the name mentioned. Just Sir John McJack. But what it meant they hadn't known, the dialects so differed.

And he himself was so different; acted so queerly and did such strange things. His speech was so queer when he spoke to his men. They'd seen him speak to the women, too, who were still laughing and pointing, but warming the food by the fires while their men stood guard. Their men who held their guns in the crooks of their arms, all ready for mirth or for murder. As ready for one as the other.

When the food was brought their wonder grew; these were strange people indeed. And more than one Iroquois eye was directed at Yanata. Their eyes would follow the girl about and McJack was quick to note it.

"Lassie," he told her, "mayhapit would be best if ye'd keep more out of sight."

But he hadn't time to explain just then and Yanata stayed more by the cook-fires. Watching. Watching the Iroquois and the Lenape and the white men. But more often she watched young Adrian — he too had been having his fun. So had Penoke, the upriver youth who hadn't gone home. In spite of the excitement he found time to watch her. Penoke who hadn't forgotten.

The proffer of food was one of Nanquemoke's ideas, a bit of political planning. It was a sign of good wishes, and as the youths got the idea, they reluctantly ate. Under the circumstances, they would be polite if it killed them, or saved their lives, they scarcely knew which.

McJack had them placed so that he could talk with them: "It be like this," he began, "mayhap ye cannot know a word I say, and I will ask Nanquemoke, he be the chief, to help ye understand. I get a small sense from your tongue, to be sure, but mayhap between us all we can work out a plan. Always I likes me a plan." And he grinned over the luck of the last one.

As he, aided by Nanquemoke, talked with the lads, one would nod his head. He'd gotten the sense of what the chief had translated. He would pass it along. And gradually the idea soaked in, with the aid of gestures and of drawings on the ground. Some more of the Iroquois nodded. A few frowned and were sullen. But the gist of the talk was this: The Lenape of the Long Land were men of peace, yet they would not be put upon. If visitors came, and if they minded their manners, they would be welcomed. They would be fed, were they not too many.

But they, the Iroquois, had not minded their manners. They were but young men, not overly wise, and the Lenape would be lenient. Why had the young men's fathers allowed them so far away from their homes, in a strange land? If they met with men of evil minds, they might come to great harm! But they had been very lucky at that for the Lenape were not of evil minds and had no desire in their hearts to kill, though the Lenape had been offended.

Might not also the spirit gods have been offended? The Manitou of the Iroquois could not approve of such bad manners! Though the Lenape would forgive, perhaps the Manitou couldn't. Perhaps the Manitou must mete out punishment, send bad weather, or frighten away the game, or make sickness come, either or all of these, while the very young men were strangers in a strange land! But that was for the Manitou to decide.

McJack had predicted that the day would be warm and he'd been partly right in the earlier morning. And the evening before, when the afterglow was showing, he had said that the next sunset might bring a storm; in that he'd been wrong. Wrong by a matter of nine or ten hours, for it came in late morning.

While they'd been busy with the Iroquois and more or less excited by the doings at hand, no one had though to look upriver. There was nothing there but a cloud at first. A lead-colored cloud with white on its edges. There had been a million such.

But time in its passing proved this cloud different. Not a great time either; perhaps only an hour. It failed to darken the sun because this cloud was high and downriver a little. Perhaps that was why at first no one noticed the cloud at all in the north-west. The tide on the river was strong on its ebb, going down to the bay in a hurry. The leaden cloud grew almost black; the white of its edges had turned black too. There came a rolling of thunder.

McJack and the others, just about ready to give the Iroquois back their weapons and send them down to the cape, started in surprise. A few of the Lenape went out to the beach to look, but most stayed where they were. They didn't want the young bucks to run away, get scattered and hang around the river; nor did they want them starting back too soon. They were afraid that out of spite, and in order to regain a sort of perverted self-esteem, they might wreak some vengeance on the smaller camps above.

And the Lenape, considering that the Iroquois were so very young, would stay their hand; were the red men not all brothers? Yet the men from the north were too many for the town to feed and shelter, so the Lenape would show the young men where to go to find that food and shelter.

McJack drew in the sand a chart of the main trail on down to the cape. To the whaling beach where the shanties were. He knew that the whalers had gone for the season and so far as he suspected, there were no indians there at the time. Some more of the young men nodded; they'd gotten the idea. But if it hadn't been for Nanquemoke, McJack's words would have been useless.

The Iroquois, too, had looked toward the north. They couldn't see much because of the trees of the camp and the cedars above, but they could tell that the north was dark, even though the sun still sparkled its dimpled shade upon them there. They were perplexed and bewildered; even the weather was behaving strangely. Perhaps there'd been something in what Nanquemoke had said about the Manitou being mad. Mad at the young men of "bad manners."

Upriver the world had gone gray and dense black. The clouds were rumbling there. Below the blacks and grays were tinges of green, streaked up and down. These seemed to twist and turn.

One of the Lenape came running in. "Wind comin'," he announced. McJack shrugged and nodded and was compelled to quickly change his immediate plan.

From far upriver they could hear the roar but the lightning came before the wind, scarcely ahead of its thunder. It crackled and ripped across the sky, there where it had darkened. There where the clouds had already rolled almost to the sun. A minute more and the sun was gone. More lightning came and thunder.

Many of the women had squealed and run to their cabins. A few, not so nervous and perhaps less thoughtful, stayed out to watch the clouds roll down. But most fastened down their summer tepees and otherwise made ready. Some of the men pulled the boats up on the shore. Richards was trying to tie down his tent. Even before the wind, the earth seemed trembling. Pulsing with the power of the thunder.

Next came a moment of quiet, while McJack rubbed his eyes. "We must get the people into the two cabins in the center," he told Nanquemoke quickly. If the wind comes these lads may break and scatter. We must hold them in the cabins."

And they had none too much of time what with a few of the Iroquois balking a bit, having to be urged inside; for the storm came quickly. The town was protected by the dense cedars, but the wind proved a twister. It howled and reached long fingers down and tore at things. Twigs flew at first, then branches. Out by the river a tree went crashing down.

The river rolled where before it had rippled; waist-high waves and whitecaps there. They roared and pounded the shores. Lost their whitecaps in the gale; formed others and these blew away in spray.

Then came the rain in torrents: slanting and driving torrents. Richards and his men, working in the rain, had to restake their tent to hold it. Lightning struck a tree behind where the captives were and splintered it to its base. Some of the lads were stunned.

The cabins were sturdy but the tepee halves were frail; the wind tore some away. Wrapped them on the oaken limbs and fluttered and tore them. The treetops bent and writhed; more branches fell. Baskets raced and rolled across the ground.

McJack was on guard at the Iroquois' cabins. His face held a grin which the rain couldn't erase. It seemed that Nanquemoke's prophecy had come quickly true. McJack beckoned the chief to him, close: "What be these lads doing?" And Nanquemoke, ear to the doorway, listened.

McJack read the indian's lips: "They by praying to the Manitou. They be frighted." McJack grinned again and nodded. "Sure, they be bad injuns in good times, and good injuns in bad time, same like some of the whites; there be small difference. But these lads have the fear, and a thought in their minds, mayhap it'll serve a while to keep them good. I hopes it will."

The storm raged strongly for an hour. It was noon when the wind died down. Then, amongst the minor wreckage, they brought the Iroquois out into the open, preparing to send them down to the cape. McJack had small faith in their permanent repentance, once they were free and the sun would shine. So he gave some good advice which he knew they couldn't understand. But McJack didn't mind talking; he seldom did. And his imp was active again.

"We bids ye glad farewell," he announced very gravely. "We do, at that. We wishes ye well, and did we have a well we did not want, we most wishes ye was in it! It would ease our way of thinking for a while. But if ye go back to yer homes and yer people, ye should have tales to tell. Tales of the people of the Long Land; and do not forget to tell the tale of how ye did prank us! And ye must have tales of the Great Sea ye have seen, to be sure.

"And do not forget, ye scum and scattle, to mind yer manners the while ye're here. Go on down to the sea but take great care that the clams do not bite ye!

"And down there ye will find the bones of the beasts of the sea laid on the shore. These be the bones of the beasts our people have slain, our men be that great and strong! And nights when it be dark the ghosts of the beasts will walk the land; if ye don't mind yer manners they will do that same!

"So we gives ye yer weapons and sets ye free. Four days ye may stay on the cape, then be ye gone to your people. Give the same our good wishes. And tell your fathers how sad we be that they begat such silly children as yerselfs."

Then Nanquemoke, wisely omitting most of the insults, but emphasizing the ghosts and the limit of time to stay, interpreted as best he could. He thought some of them got the idea. And when they had gone he placed scouts on the trail to be sure that they didn't loiter. The lads would make new footprints on the new washed trails, and the Lenape could tell.

Then after the Iroquois had gone McJack wondered if he'd been wise. Perhaps he should have insisted that they go directly home, but Nanquemoke shook his head. They must see the Great Water, and tell the tale to their people." And he further explained, in his own way, that any added humiliation might be more than they could peacefully stand. That they might come back and, not rollicking then, have sought their vengeance. Perhaps even lurk about Wahatquenack and cut off some of the people.

"Sure," conceded McJack, "mayhap we did do right. I hopes we did. Most injuns, if ye treat them fair and prove ye're smart and crafty, will give goodwill and friendship. But some be surly. We will watch and wait and see."

The surveyors did not go out at all that day. It was too far spent and until they knew for certain where the Iroquois went and what they would do, the men stayed close to the townsite.

At dark when the afterglow was again on the river there, the scouts came back. The Iroquois were well on their way to the cape. McJack looked his relief. He looked, too, out on the river, upriver a little toward the meadow shore. A canoe showed there on the water. Shadowy, among the ripples that it made. Drifting with the tide mostly. Symbolic perhaps. Adrian and Yanata.

While he was watchingm, Mellissa came down. 'I wishes them well," she told McJack. "I most sure do!"

And so did he. How deeply none knew but himself. Not even Minyanata, who in her prayers took no chances of being partial; she prayed alike to the saints and to the Manitou. For Adrian and Yanata.

But there was one who frowned and was ill pleased. Penoke didn't like the state of affairs. But he said very little; just waited.

Chapter 17

Some two hours later... The afterglow had faded and the night come down, but not the dark. The moon which had climbed from beyond Muskee had seen to that. Silent, riding amongst its little clouds on high, it played its part in the plan. Worked its way and will with the tides of the river; and on that flood was the lunar sheen. On the forest floors were those dense or dappled shades. And, too, the moon worked its way with a man and a maid.

Their canoe had come in from the river. Adrian and Yanata had strolled upstream a way, across the logs which made the bridge for the brook. There at the end of the cedars there was shade and gloom, the cedars towered so high and dark. Beyond, on the narrow beach, the sand lay silvered, between the trees and the little tide-bay.

Out in the light, beyond that shadow of the trees, they were alone. Adrian and Yanata with their youth and their night.

"Yanata," he whispered, "I want that ye should wed with me! Will ye do it?"

She was half-frightened again. Something of that blood-bar was thrust upon her mind. Suddenly, but not for the first time. Before, she had pushed the thought away, that half-felt fear. She feared, even more than could her mother, on that night of hers upon the capeland. Yanata was born of that night, of McJack and Minyanata. Straight-bloods each, they'd been.

But she, Yanata, was fruit from mixed races. Not one, not the other. Half-red, half-white.

But she was just as human as either, or both. Had all the urges of the same. Felt all the longings; mayhap she felt more. But she felt fear, too. Fear of the mystery of her own romance. For she was of the line of Sir McJack; she had a calculating brain. Even against her will her thoughts would come.

Once, down on the capelands, when the first of the whalers had come, McJack had said to Wawakna, to him who had been the chief, and her own grandfather: "Wawakna, d'ye see how it be? If ye lose yer fear and yer wisdom, and yer cunning and craft, and puts yer trust where ye fails to put yer thoughts and fears, ye cannot live. Not now! Ye and yer people be like little Saint Pat: ye cannot be overbold nor overfriendly with those who come here! So I would say to ye now: Hold fast to courage and fears alike, for ye have need of the both this day. Ye have, at that!"

Yanata hadn't heard him say it, to be sure; but she had heard him speak many times since then. With her mother or Nanquemoke or with the whites. They all built up to a sense of that blood-bar between her own people and Adrian's. Between his personality and her own; his education and hers. Despite all of his learning, Yanata knew Adrian was headlong and impulsive. Sometimes heedless. But...

"Yanata, I asked would ye wed with me?" He was asking again, not taking her for granted. The moon showed the eagerness in his eyes. The wave of his hair. "Did I have priest or parson I would wed ye now, Yanata," and he put his arms about her. Held her tight. Looked into her eyes. "Yanata, do ye know how beautiful ye are, here in the light of the moon?"

Then something happened to Yanata. The same that had happened to her mother and to millions more. Though the moon was bright, and she could see, she would kiss blindly, love blindly, give blindly and live!

"My mother," she whispered, while he held her there, "was wedded by the moon; there was no priest at all. She told me the tale of it, so she did!"

"Then so shall we two be wed, by the moon of the Manitou there in the sky!"

And so it happened. Just the two of them and the Manitou Moon. But Penoke was watching from the dark of the cedars, a crafty Penoke who was not at all pleased. Adrian and Yanata of course didn't know. Perhaps they wouldn't even have cared.

Chapter 18

That evening, from far to the south, McJack and Nanquemoke heard rumblings of thunder, often repeated.

McJack chuckled: "If they have a bad storm down yonder so soon as this, them lads will think their Manitou be mad with them, for sure. They will, at that. Mayhap," and he grinned his amusement, "if they think the storm-devils be on their very tails they will use them tails for tillers and steer for home. I hopes they will. I cannot live with ease while the lads be in the land."

And perhaps he was right to be so ill at ease; no man loves to be outwitted. Neither would the Iroquois want their story told when they should go back home. They might mention the name of Sir John McJack, a very remarkable white man whom they'd met. A man who had cannon and muskets and men at command, in his wooden town in the Long Land. Something to confound the minds of the Frenchmen.

And they could tell of the country: how it contrasted with their own. Of the sea, after they'd seen it. But in order to see it they must go down to the Cape. Through the deserted camps and forests. What farms they saw were overgrown. There were no man tracks on the trails. The land was empty. Perhaps some of the sense of it bore down on their spirits. They didn't rollick as they went along.

Instead, they went slowly, fearing that the land had been accursed. Perhaps there was truth in what Nanquemoke had told them; there may have been devils there. Storm-devils for certain, for that night the rains beat upon them again with thunder and lightning. It was, in fact, a period of little, local cloudbursts, first here, then there, seeming to follow them wherever they went. Especially after that idea of the wrath of the gods had been implanted in their minds.

Next morning was fair and they found the side trail to the whaling beach. There were the shanties on the land. The stumps of trees and the litter of last spring's camp. In the ends of the waves were the skulls and bones of the whales. And there was the bay, so wide they couldn't see across it. They failed to differentiate between the bay and the sea, for they never went down to the Point at all.

That, in addition to the storms and their superstitious fears, was because of a sudden suspicion in the mind of one. McJack had told them to stay four days on the Cape — why the four days? What sinister things would happen at the end of that allotted time? Was this another trick of Sir John McJack's for which he needed the time to prepare?

So, homesick had they admitted it, the lads decided to outwit McJack. Come morning they would shake those accursed sands from their feet and start homeward. Leave the empty land to its empty self.

That was how it came that, near dusk of the third day, they came again to Muskee ford. Stopped briefly to drink and then went on toward the north. Nanquemoke had set a watch; the Iroquois seemed headed homeward. The scouts reported them in something of a hurry. The people in the wooden town were greatly relieved. They could relax and resume their leisurely ways.

So, next morning, Panquenack and three others took a boat and went downriver to tend their turtle traps. Adrian, in the tent, was busy on the chart. McJack, with Nanquemoke and Richards, went up and across the river to look at the fastlands there. The others, both white and red, were busy or at leisure as they pleased. Or so McJack, with his friends on the fastlands, supposed.

In the afternoon there was another of those freakish storms; the rain fell again in torrents. It came from the northwest and went across river and over toward Muskee. McJack's party waited a while for the river to calm and then paddled leisurely down and across; they couldn't see the town because of the bends in the stream. From the surveyor's viewpoint their errand hadn't accomplished much, but they all felt complacent because the Iroquois had gone. McJack's canoe went slowly, the tide being wrong; they kept to the eddies along the shore.

But when they came in sight of the town, Nanquemoke pointed. McJack frowned: "Something is wrong. The women are waving in haste, and there be no men in sight at all. I do not like the looks of that."

Minyanata and another woman had been ready to launch a canoe, but waited on the shore. There was a babble of excited and wailing voices. McJack, as the canoe came in, could see that his wife had been weeping. He heard "Iroquois!" and "Yanata!" and

"Mellissa!" And somebody was dead and somebody had run away.

"Hush, the lot of ye! If ye all talk, none can hear." Then he got the story and his face went pale and grim: Yanata, Mellissa and three others had gone out to Muskee to gather swamp berries. The Iroquois had come back. They had killed Mellissa and carried Yanata away. McJack's voice wasn't steady: "Where be all the men?" Young Adrian had taken charge. He and the other whites and all of the indians who were at home had gone in pursuit of the Iroquois. Upcountry, along the main trail, though there had been no tracks to follow because of the rain. The Iroquois would have had some two hours start, after the murder and abduction, and McJack had been waiting for the river to calm!

He muttered a curse; then in the silent soul of him he called on the saints for help. It couldn't end like this, for his Yanata! From downriver the boat came drifting with the tides; Panquenack was in that boat. Panquenack whose woman had been Mellissa, and whose face went nearly as white as his woman's had been. At first he obeyed McJack in something of a daze.

"Minyanata, ye should go to the house and give each man a gun, with powder and ball. There be little more than an hour of the sun, but a moon will show. Let the women make a litter for Mellissy; she cannot lie in the woods the night."

Nanquemoke led. Then McJack and Panquenack and the three other indians. Richards went last and was well-nigh spent when they reached the Muskee.

There were the muddled tracks of the other women and of Adrian's party, made after the rain. On both shores of the ford the imprints showed, and then led off on the northern trail. Toward the east and beyond the ford was the cross-trail, the one that wove its winding way toward its junction with a straighter one to Tuckahoe.

Over there a little way, Mellissa lay in the wet where her friends had dragged her from where she'd been hid. She lay on her side and sprawled. She was almost rigid; the fingers of her right hand entirely so, for they gripped the handle of a short sharp knife. McJack noted the blood on the blade of it.

His voice choked: "Lissy, ye did fight for the lassie, and die for the fighting! I gives ye thanks for what ye tried to do!"

Panquenack knelt beside his woman. Felt her face with his fingers, but drew back quickly; the face was cold. It did not have that warm, smooth feel that it had had before. There was nothing there to thrill his blood; instead, it chilled it. But just for the moment, for Panquenack had a task to do, in memory of Mellissa. He placed his hand on the top of her head as if to swear by it.

But he looked up quickly at John McJack. Signed that he too should feel. A bit reluctant, he complied. Then he sat back on his heels... "Our men have gone off on a wrongsome trail," he announced. "The Iroquois did not do this thing! See where the blood be clotted here, afore it dripped to make the pool. There be the shape of a musket stock in the very bone. And the injuns did not have the guns! Nanquemoke, there be white men in the land; they must have come by Tuckahoe Head, for ye had scouts on the trail to the Cape."

Nanquemoke searched in the dusk and found the rain-washed print of a boot heel; the man had been going away, toward the east. The chief indicated this by pointing and again they dog-trotted, McJack counting the distance and the probable time. To rescue Yanata seemed hopeless, but McJack had a sudden thought. He stopped the men; by that time it was almost dark, there under the trees.

"Nanquemoke, these men must have had a boat. To have a boat they must have had some sort of ship and even a small ship would not come so far in the river, yonder. There be a point where a ship must hold and wait. Be there a trail that would go more straight to such a spot?"

Nanquemoke said there was; about a mile further east it branched off into the upland. "But it be not good," he explained. Richards, who had been breathing hard, began to cough.

Then one of the indians held up a hand, listening intently.

'Help!" The voice was very faint. It came again and from down the way they'd been going. It quavered: "Help!"

"We must use the craft," advised McJack in a whisper. "If it be a trap we shall not spring it."

But there was no trap; the man lay in an open space beside the trail. They could see him dimly and McJack placed a hand on Panquenack's shoulder. "Ye shall not now," he told him. Mayhap the man will talk."

McJack went close and nudged the man with his foot. "Who be ye? How come ye hurted?"

"I be Sam Grinnet. I be hurted bad with a shaft."

"Ye lie, in part; for we know how ye was hurted. Where are them who was with ye? Quick, now!"

The man seemed too weak or too frightened to speak and made a feeble motion down the trail.

"Was the lass with them? And how many men?"

"She was not hurted. I did not do it! It was them others."

"How many men? Where be your boat?"

"There was six. The boat be in the little river."

Then McJack wanted to know: "Why did ye do this?"

"For the twenty pounds." The man's weak voice was eager, then. Perhaps he could buy his life with what he knew.

"Which twenty pounds?" McJack, in spite of his haste, was curious. He hadn't heard of any twenty pounds.

"The coin that the company posted for them that would bring ye to terms. If they fail, they will send a force, and burn yer town. Will ye help me now?"

"We have not the time," and McJack walked quickly away. Panquenack was the last to leave. The others heard a squeal of terror and a thud. Panquenack didn't speak when he joined them. He'd been helping Mellissa in that last task of hers.

And then, although it had grown so dark, the low hung moon only beginning with its little light among the trees, Nanquemoke found the branch trail. This, to the navigable point for ships on the river, would run almost straight and save half the mileage which those other men must make.

It was at this branch trail that Richards was forced to stay behind; the others went on at a speedy trot. McJack's only plan was the gaining of time on the straighter trail; by this it would be ten miles to where Nanquemoke thought a ship could be. Perhaps, if prayers to the saints availed, they might intercept the boat on the narrow and winding stream.

They had made half of the way and were breathing deep and sweating. At a little stream they stopped and drank. Dashed water over their heads and shoulders. Nanquemoke suddenly straightened, and sniffed: "Smoke! From yonder, by the river." Then the chief was thoughtful, seeking his bearings: "Here, the river be not far; a great bend comes close, then goes away again."

"Aye, but the men would not stop to build a fire," said McJack.

"My people live yonder, beyond river. Very small camp. Mayhap they come to river. Mayhap they have seen boat."

And when Nanquemoke led them close, the red people not only had seen the boat, but they *had* it. By the moonlight in the open, McJack could see it moored to shore, near the little fire where four men sat. Apparently they were in council, deliberating what to do. Not very cautious, nor exceedingly wise, they were less than a gunshot from the southern shore.

"They've found the boat! whispered McJack, quite unnecessarily. "Nanquemoke, whence come these men?"

"Up yonder," pointing to the north. "Mayhap a mile. Small camp on little stream."

"They will not have caught the whites — and Yanata?"

The chief shook his head: "There be but four men in the camp."

"Then the whites will be on foot, in the land?"

Nanquemoke nodded: "Shall I call my people?"

"Best ye had not; they would take the time in the talking. We should go back to the trail and haste near the ship. Mayhap the men be lost in the woods."

And when they had gone so far that the straight trail merged with the crooked one, and when they found no footprints there, they waited. And McJack sweated while he wondered: What was happening to Yanata, somewhere there in the woods? What had already happened? Why didn't they come? They had had the time. Yanata, alone with those scum and scattle! McJack fretted and fumed and wondered some more, standing in the shadows of the trailside pines.

As to the answers: Yanata and Mellissa had crossed the Muskee ford and were on the southern side of the stream while their companions were on the other. Mellissa had found a laden bush and stopped. Yanata went on, perhaps some fifty yards beyond. There, down a little lane from the trail at the edge of the swamp, the berries hung in clusters.

Yanata was busy, facing toward the swamp. It wouldn't take long to fill her basket there. She heard a small sound behind her; Mellissa must be coming. Yanata, smiling a little, didn't even look to see.

That was how they caught and gagged her before she could even scream. Bound her hands and dragged her out to the trail.

Then Mellissa came; she came too late but in all of her fury. Once, she herself had been caught and bound by just such men as these must be. Been taken by surprise, as had Yanata.

"Ye scurvy twelps!" she screamed. "Let loose the lass! If ye do not..."

"Devils of hell!" yelped one of the men. "Another of the bitches and a white one at that! We cannot let her loose to tell! Catch the she bastard!"

But they didn't catch Mellissa, for she didn't run. She, that short sharp knife gripped in her hand, went into the battle. A hell-cat for certain. Fighting for freedom and for a friend. Knowing that there was no pity in the men. She who had fled that other time from a sailmaker's needle and from another woman of righteous wrath.

The men had laid down their muskets to catch and bind Yanata; they were surprised and panicked by Mellissa's fury. She slashed at a man, and he dodged. At another; she missed, but the man tumbled into the bushes. One tripped and fell backward; Mellissa came on toward Yanata. Had almost reached her. Her knife had found one man's shoulder. Another it had slashed across the forehead, just above the eyes.

And then it had come: the musket snatched from the ground and swung down hard. Mellissa never knew it; she died fighting. Yanata was dragged down the trail.

The men cursed and looked backward. Two had dragged Mellissa into the bushes and tried to hide her. Sam Grinnet groaned; he was bleeding badly but his companions wouldn't stop to staunch the flow. The one with the gash in his forehead had at first to be led. Cursing. Trying to tie a rag about his head. The wound, being where it was, was hard to staunch.

And then the storm had come suddenly on. Behind them the trail was washed almost clear of their tracks. But behind them they'd left Mellissa. And further on, between them and their boat, they soon left Grinnet. The others with Yanata, went along on the crooked trail. Hastening away from the vengeful McJack and his red men. This hadn't been their original plan at all; it had been plotted at Muskee, on the spur of the moment. As they fled they doubted the wisdom of it. But their greater doubts came just at dusk, when they reached the river and found their boat gone.

The first man exclaimed: "Damn! This be the place. There be the split oak tree. I thought we hid the boat in the grass."

"Aye, we did that," another conceded, "but we was dumb. The tide was ebbed; with the flood the boat raised and someone saw it. The master will not be pleased with the loss of it."

His tone was uneasy; he had other thoughts than his fear of the master's wrath. Could McJack have been even here? Some uncanny fear crept into their bones. And when, a bit further, along where the trail came close to the stream and they could see a fire down there in the almost dark, they stopped. That fire might be on their side or the other. How many, and what men were there? They knew it was none of their shipmates.

"Best take to the woods and go around," suggested the man with the bandaged head. "We can come back to this trail again from there." As he spoke he wiped more blood from his eyes, so blinded he must depend on the others.

His idea seemed good, but the men were not woodsmen. Perhaps they'd been born and bred in the heart of London, and they failed to take into account that long bend of the stream toward the south. The one who might have sensed direction from the rising moon was hardly able to see. And when they entered the woods again, they drove Yanata before them. Followed blindly for a little while. Followed Yanata who had been born in the forest, of the crafty McJack and her indian mother.

So, sooner than they knew, they were hopelessly lost. In greater panic, too. They sought a trail and couldn't find it. And time was passing, as Yanata had hoped.

Finally, however, they found a trail. The moon had risen then and the man with the bandage motioned toward the east. Seemed to at last get his bearings.

But as they walked, weary and frightened and looking behind often, they failed to see those footprints so faintly in the path. But Yanata saw them, and her heart throbbed with hope. Moccasin tracks, in moon-lighted spots on the sand. She looked for a shoe mark, but failed to see it. Adrian hadn't been there and that made her heart sink a little. Perhaps these tracks were made by some strange red men. Yanata couldn't know. But as she walked, then in the middle of the line, she was alert. They were coming to a dense pineland. Walking blindly into the gloom. Those moccasin tracks had led there, too, but the men hadn't noticed.

The man with the bandaged head never got up from the ground at all; Panquenack bent the barrel of his musket when he crushed his skull. The others were stunned for the moment, and their hands were soon bound behind them. Yanata had thrown herself sideways to be out of the struggle. McJack helped her to her feet.

"Lassie! Lassie!" was all that Sir John could say. Yanata clung to him when her hands were untied; and released also from her fear, she looked at the others. Nanquemoke, Panquenack, and the three indians. "Where be Adrian?" she whispered.

McJack could have laughed, but he didn't. It seemed so ridiculous, then: Adrian away off there to the north on his wild goose chase. But he didn't blame the boy. His mistake had been natural. None of the others had held any doubt. Not even Penoke, who helped lead the line, along with Adrian. Yanata's two lovers; McJack chuckled a little.

"Where be he?" Yanata insisted.

"He be seeking ye, Lassie. He be, at that. We divided our men to scout a wider ground. He be all a-duddered with his fears for ye, and be still a searching."

And that was good news for Yanata.

They brought the captives out into the moonlight; one was a man who had been with Saunders. He stood shaking with fear; he had immediately recognized Yanata as the daughter of McJack, who scowled at him, and then said to his own men: "Let me see the one who is down; drag him here to the light. Seems I have seen this ugly face afore: It's the master of the sloop that we sunk. He would have his vengeance, and try for his twenty pounds. Which gives me a thought: I must go down to the ship; I think she and her master be not far away. I have a word to say to the man."

The sloop proved a mere half-mile away; she lay near the northern side of the stream, by the meadows, where she couldn't be approached because of the mud. On McJack's side the fastland went clear to the river. The dense shade of the forest reached out on the water, dappled on its outshore edge. The sloop lay at fore and aft anchors; she tugged more strongly at the stern, for the tide was ebbing. It had some two more hours to run.

The moon glinted down on the craft; everything aboard was quiet. In the forest, too, except that a whip-poor-will called. So did McJack: "Ahoy the sloop!"

His voice rang clearly; there was exultation in it. A tone of triumph, but the sleepy watch failed to note it at first.

"Ahoy the shore," the watch finally responded. Then: "Master, here be the men come back." And next he seemed to sense there was something wrong: "Where be the boat?" A doubt had flicked into his mind. Into the mind of the master, too; he had come to the rail; McJack and Nanquemoke could see him.

"Who be ye?" he shouted.

It was then that McJack let loose his exultation, with a laugh. A wild and exultant laugh. It rang over the river and along the wooded shore. It would echo, too, in the minds of those men on the sloop, so long that they'd never forget.

"I be Sir John McJack!" came the voice from the dark. "Him ye would trap and fool, had ye the guts and the wits, which ye have not at all! But I will give ye good advice: If ye have any sense at all ye will be up and begone!"

McJack waited for a reply, but there wasn't any. Perhaps the master was racking his wits out there. Wondering what had happened.

So McJack explained: "We have your men, tied tight and good. Sam Grinnet be dead, along with him who was once the sloop's master, the sloop that we burned on the other river. And in the morn the four shall hang for the deed they done! Did ye think ye could beat Sir John McJack when ye sent such fools on yer errand? And if ye be polite, I'd ask ye this: What would that errand have been? It lacked the sense, it did."

Perhaps the master, in such close contact with the mysterious Sir John, the man who piled men's bones along the trails and sank invading sloops with his cannon, thought it wise to be "polite."

"We was told to find a back way to your town," he explained.

"Ah-h! And what do ye know of the twenty pounds, and the threat to burn that town, and all?"

The man hesitated. Mumbled something that McJack couldn't understand. And then he lied; McJack felt sure he was lying: "I know nothing of them at all."

"Hah! Such being the case I will give ye this tide to begone to the sea. If ye do not move the now, I will sink yer craft where she be! If ye do go now I will warrant ye safe. But haste; the time and tide will serve but brief!"

McJack and the chief listened. Then they heard the captain working; saw the men on deck. They hove in the anchors and manned a boat to help with the steerway, in that ebb of the tide. This eddied here and there near shore; out in the open it swirled toward the bay.

Assured that she was leaving, McJack chuckled again: "I did forget to mind me own manners: never did I ask the name of the sloop, nor of her master, at that! It were an oversight. I did not mean to be rude at all." And Nanquemoke smiled in the dark.

And McJack pushed back his worries then, for the time. He chuckled again as they went from the river. Went from one river toward the other: from Tuckahoe to Wahatquenack. Going home. He and Yanata and five of their friends. And with the men who would hang the next day.

McJack sobered, when he thought about that, for he knew he'd have to do it. Besides, to hang the men would be a kindly deed: he'd overheard the indians mention a fire and a stake. They mustn't do that at all. These men hadn't killed Yanata; hadn't greatly harmed her. So on that score, McJack was glad.

Then his face grew sad when he remembered Mellissa. He'd say a prayer for the woman. And while they wearily walked in the night, with the moon going down over where they knew their town to be, he did it. That was before they'd come to the Muskee trail, before they had rejoined Richards.

Chapter 19

The dawn had been come an hour before McJack and his party got back to the town. When they were within perhaps a mile or less, Nanquemoke had sent out his piercing code-call... "We are coming home and all is well." This winged its way along the trail and woodsy airways, clear to the town itself.

So the women had met them on the way. Minyanata came among the first, panting from her running. She and Yanata clung together for a moment; they laughed and cried. There was a babble of questions too great to be answered. The men were almost to weary to smile or even boast.

When Minyanata saw the grim face of Panquenack she guessed what had happened to poor Mellissa. "Ye be bad men!" she exploded and cuffed one's ear before he could dodge. The other women began to jibe. One took a poke at a nose, but missed.

"Hold! Hold!" McJack ordered. "It'll serve ye nothing to cuff an ear which cannot wag or fend for itself at all. Stop the nonsense and tell me this: Has anything been heard of those who went out first?"

That sobered the women, for they'd had no news of their men. All night they'd sat in their little groups and waited. They had heard the frogs, the owls, the loons, the whip-poor-wills; the ducks across the meadow once in a while. The squawks as the birds had flown over. But there had been no news at all.

Adrian and his men must still be somewhere in the north. They would likely be scattered, the stronger men leading, chasing after the Iroquois lads, who hadn't further offended. Perhaps should they over take them there'd be a battle, and a useless one.

But McJack needn't really have worried, for they hadn't caught up with the Iroquois. Almost they had; they had gotten close. But instead of the strangers they had met with a Lenape, one of their own red people. He had seen the men from the north. The men, or lads, with the scalp locks.

No, they had no captive. No girl at all. They were walking wearily along, traveling at night because this was cooler. This last was the Lenape's thought.

So, discouraged, they all turned back, going slowly because they were so tired. It was well toward sunset when they reached their town on the river.

As for McJack, wise in his forethought and impish in his humor, he had planned for a welcome, in case all was well. Always he liked to have him a plan. So, after his own party had rested a while, he had Nanquemoke send scouts to the trail, but not to use the code-call. McJack arranged for a little surprise.

Adrian, leading the straggling line of men, footsore and weary and very forlorn, came up the trail toward the camp. There was only one person in sight; she stood at the edge of the town. Out in the open and she smiled.

"Yanata!" Adrian fairly yelled the name. "Yanata!" And he ran to the girl and took her in his arms. Held her close and kissed her there, for all of their watching world to see. For Penoke, too. Penoke, who scowled.

McJack grinned. He wiped a hand across his eyes. This by the code of the world that they lived in was a wedding and as binding as bonds. Always McJack had liked to have him a plan! He'd planned for one thing or another along through the years. For a long time, then, he'd had a plan for Yanata. For her and her children, of the line of McJack.

Forgetting for the moment that they were tired, the people were briefly merry. They laughed and shouted. They wished Adrian and Yanata well. Forgetting in that same moment that they had a hanging to do. And, just for that moment, forgetting Mellissa. But not for long.

For Mellissa lay on her carrying bier, there in the open, before the tepee half of what had been her home. All in the camp had grown very still. Mellissa's white face was turning a little blue; Panquenack sat beside her. He had that right, for she had been his woman. The fact that she had been other men's woman didn't matter; not then. Not to Panquenack nor to little Johnny Pank, nor to Nanquemoke nor McJack. Nor to the saints, nor to the Manitou, mayhap.

She was dressed in a robe of white doe skin. On her feet were white moccasins. Her light hair was combed and braided, and the blood didn't show at all.

McJack knew he would have to hang the men, for there would be no point in letting them go, even if the people permitted. Down at the *Prince Maurice* he had allowed two to go. Men fully as guilty as these. One had been more so, in fact, for he had been the master.

The one who had ordered the killing of the reds, and planned their plunder at the trading, "for rum or for what." And now he was the one who lay on the Tuckahoe trail beyond the pines and swamps of Muskee. As still as Mellissa, or was he? There were buzzards out there at times. And beasts.

But there had been a point to releasing those other men: someone had to take the news to the masters. To the trade company. Otherwise they'd have sent a ship to search for the ones who were missing. Perhaps they'd have come in force enough to win; McJack hadn't dared that other time to take the risk.

This time it was different. The master of the sloop already knew. The masters of the master would learn in due time. So these four men had to be hung, either hung or burned at the stake. McJack might have shot them, but the hanging would be more dramatic, and almost as quick.

Four ropes from the wreck were over the limb of an oak, all in a line, each with its noose. They sickened McJack when he saw them there, not far from where Mellissa lay. This nearness had been the indians' notion: they wanted the spirit of Mellissa to be satisfied with their vengeance, that she might sleep the sounder. Her spirit, according to their thought, still hovered around her, watching. Richards' men had gone upriver.

"Bring out the men that will hang." McJack's voice was hoarse when he said it. His hands shook a little and his face was white. As white as the men who came from the cabin. One walked erect, his head held high; the others had to be dragged along. Nanquemoke and Panquenack helped to bring them. Panquenack was not gentle at all. He had no qualms, for there lay Mellissa. She'd been his woman and these men had killed her. The men who stood with the nooses on their necks.

The ropes above them were all a-quiver, clear to the oaken limb. McJack's voice squeaked a little when he began to talk. He coughed and then: "I would say a word with ye, I would. I would tell ye how sad I be that this must be done. But ye have made us do it, ye have at that. Ye have but to look upon this woman here, ye have but to look to see why we do it. For what ye did, and ye did it for no good means at all, ye four must die. That be the law of the land where ye did live afore; it be the law of this land, too.

"This hour ye die! If we had a priest I would let him do the talking. I would, and be glad of it! But we have no priest. So I will ask ye this: Have ye anything to say?"

None of the men answered. Perhaps they realized how useless words would be. McJack swallowed hard, then went on: "I gives ye good graces for where ye be going the now. I know not where that be at all. I would ask that ye say just this: 'God save the soul of me when it shall please! If it be thy will, may I find peace, when at last I have paid the price for the same!' Would ye say just that?"

The voice of McJack was pleading. Three of the men tried to mumble the prayer; the other remained defiant.

McJack raised his hand and the deed was done. The ropes quivered again and jerked; they almost thrashed about. But not for long: just the time it took for the men to strangle, then go limp. Yet many of the people did not see them; they had turned their faces away. Some looked out on the river. Some saw the woods. But Panquenack gloated as he saw the men die.

By and large the people had gotten small pleasure from the punishment for the crime. It was a time for duty and not for a dance. McJack had made that thought sink in. It had cost him a lot, but he was glad that he'd done it — Sir John McJack, Lord of the Land Where He Lived the While.

And then, in the deeper dusk, they buried Mellissa. They carried her out to the pine-land and the sand. The women eased their nerves by wailing for her then; Mellissa had, of late years at least, been a friend to them all. And she, in her white doe skin shroud, was covered with the sands, lying prone. Not covered so deeply, perhaps, as were some in the hold of the *Phoenix*, the ship that had cast her on to the sands of the Cape, but for as long.

There was no sea to sing its song to her, but she had the songs of the winds in the pines and of the birds. And Panquenack, and little Johnny Pank, could stand beside her. They could know: Here lies Mellissa. Mellissa Mallore. Wife and mother.

And more than once, in the dusks of such days as they lingered there, they did it. The two of them. The tall red man and the little boy. And Yanata, too, and Minyanata, and the others. In the little time that the people were allowed to stay there on their river.

As for the men who had been hanged, Nanquemoke explained to McJack: His people did not want them buried there. They thought their soil would be polluted. They did not want them even near; they had a plan. Sir John didn't like it; he frowned, and then he nodded. It really wouldn't matter at all. The men wouldn't know. The red men had a right to some of their opinions. McJack might not entirely agree, but he wouldn't force a turkey to wear a turtle shell. He wouldn't, to be sure.

So that night when the tide was started strongly down, the bodies were lashed to a dry cedar log. Towed out into the current and sent down to the sea. Downriver. McJack prayed that they'd reach the bay before the turn of the tide; perhaps they did for they never came back.

But Richards and his party did; they returned in the morning. The men had been hanged and the bodies were gone. There was nothing to show, and the sun was shining. But Richards looked troubled. McJack appraised him shrewdly. They were there beside the surveyor's tent at the time. McJack sat on the trunk of the tree that had fallen in the storm. He was doodling with a couple of pebbles: "Do ye be thinking the thoughts I think ye be — that mayhap we've just begun with trouble?"

"I'm afraid so, McJack. The mere fact that the company took the time and the risk to get a line on your location from the rear shows that they plan something. The attempt to kidnap Yanata was probably conceived on the spur of the moment."

"Sure I did think the same," said McJack, "yet I liked not the thought at all. I be some-what wearied with the strife. I would have peace, could I get it fair, but I will not sell; I will not, at that!"

The surveyor nodded again; he still seemed very thoughtful. McJack made another guess at this thought, as he smiled shrewdly: "And what about yourselfs? What if the traders try to make a case at court, and learn ye was near us at the time of the hanging?"

"That, too, might cause us trouble. The traders pay a tribute to the Treasury of the Crown and we take money from it. Not much, but a little, by way of pay and expense. Place the case of profit against that of cost, and profit would probably win."

"That be true, and it be bad; but the thing be like this: They on the sloop did not know ye was here at all. They had no way to learn. Them who did know were the ones who were hanged; they will not tell. And never will we.

"Ye should go upstream, the now. If your chart show that ye've been up there, no one can tell the when ye went, nor prove that ye was near the hanging at all, or that ye knew. Always I would tell the truth, could I do it honest; but, if to be honest I must tell a lie..." McJack shrugged and smiled.

Richards did the same and agreed to the other's plan. It might, with a bit of "honest lying," prove a valuable alibi. The surveyor, like too many men of too many times, was compelled to play both ends against the middle.

Adrian came out of the tent just then. He smiled and nodded to McJack. To the surveyor: "Master Richards, I've finished the chart, so far as we've gone."

The three of them went into the tent to look. McJack studied the drawing carefully: "Did ye ever hear what did cause it to be so filled with crooks and quirls?"

"Natural erosion, I suppose," said Richards. "In the beginning it sought the easiest way to the sea, though not the shortest."

McJack gravely shook his head. "Sure, but the injuns tell the tale like this: One time, even afore the red men came, the land was empty and very quiet. And a great serpent did come out of the sea to rest from his wriggling. He, the serpent, was very tired, and the sea was cold, and he looked on the land and he said to himself, there being none other to speak with at all, 'I will go on the shore and sleep in the sun.'

"'Best, though,' thinks the serpent, 'I had go with the tail of me first, so I can keep me an eye on the sea, in case something should happen, a ship sail by, mayhap or a whale for me supper, always I must keep the watch upon the sea.'

"So this serpent did back himself upon the land, miles and miles and miles of him, and he took a smallish nap. The sun felt good, after the cold of the sea, and it dried the skin of him warm. But the warm made an itching on the serpent, and he twitched a bit whilst sleeping. Just stirred the skin of him a bit, but the great heft of him pushed the soil aside, where he lay. But the itching would not be cured and he stirred himself some more, and the earth were pushed aside the deeper with the weight and his stirring about. And when he, the serpent, went back to the sea, he left his very shape upon the soil, and there was a river. And even until now it be the same: the shape of the serpent, with crooks and quirls, the tail end in the inland there; a brook so small a man can stride it."

"That," declared Richards amusedly, "is very nice to know, although I still stick to my own idea of erosion, present-day serpents being what they are. But what is the awkward name of this stream? I have trouble to remember it."

"Wahatquenack that be the injun name. I have heard it so oft it be easy for me."

"Suppose, this is just a suggestion, we change the name to something a bit easier?"

"Like what?"

"Suppose," said Richards thoughtfully, "we give the trade company something to remember it by? They have a craft down there on the shore. Shall we call the stream the Maurice — Maurice River?"

"That be good, to be sure," declared McJack. "Good for white folk. But, be it Maurice or be it Mud, it'll still be Wahatquenack to the injuns and me."

He watched young Adrian trace the name on the course: Maurice River.

"Would ye" — there was a plaintive tone in Sir John's voice — "just do a bit for me on a piece of the stuff? Would ye just write down the name of me: just 'John McJack?' I would like for to see it, the once."

"I should write the title, too: Sir John McJack." Adrian's eyes were smiling.

"But," grinned McJack, "if a man be a 'Sir' it should come from the king, and the king, so I have heard, be mad with me, in a roundabout way. He would not knight me at all." He chuckled at the fancy.

Just then they were diverted by Johnny Pank, who stood in the flapway. Curious. Serious. There were tear marks for Mellissa still there on his face. But Johnny Pank smiled shyly.

"Hello, Johnny Pank," greeted Adrian. "Ye're just in time to be witness, and I appoint ye gentleman-in-waiting to Sir McJack. Ye will do his bidding and serve his will while we're gone upriver."

Adrian laughed and patted the boy's head and Johnny Pank would have something to remember while and where he should live. Something for the moment to please his thoughts, though he didn't understand it. Only the kindness. The touch of the hand upon his head. It eased his grief for Mellissa and diverted his thoughts, Johnny Pank, the half-breed, while the men went out to adventure.

Like when, after another day or two, the surveyors went up the river. They would be back by the time of the frosts, Adrian told Yanata. They would go up the crooked and brackish stream to the headwaters of the "Maurice." Up above the tide-lines where the water was fresh and clean and sweet. Through the great swamp which would some day be a lake, but which, just then, as for ages, was briar and bramble and cedar and gum and sumac and maple. And bracken at the borders, too, and vines which coiled and climbed the trees.

That was where they thought they'd go, when they left the town. At the last minute Penoke appeared. He asked if he could he go with them, and so he went along. No one thought much about it at the time, though McJack was a bit relieved. It would get the indian out of the way; he wouldn't bother Yanata. Yanata, who waved to Adrian as the boats went around the bend. Her man going away for a time, his work to do. A task to finish before time of the frosts. Yanata would do the waiting. The watching and the hoping. Yanata and her mother.

And McJack? He had plenty then for thought. More time to think it. And it wasn't good thinking at all, because any doubts he might have held about the tale Sam Grinnet had told him, about the planned invasion of his town, were soon dispelled.

It was three days after the surveyors had gone that a strange Lenape appeared in town. He inquired for John McJack; he bore tidings from far way. Saunders, from down Jamestown way, had proven his friendship for McJack; he sent the warning by the red man. A sloop was being fitted out with many men and some cannon. The Lenape had been two weeks on the way. He did not know how soon the white men would come. But Saunders, in some way that the messenger didn't explain, had done the red man a favor; in return the red messenger had trudged the trails and begged the crossing of the many streams in borrowed canoes, fording the smaller ones along the way, and had brought the message to McJack and his people. There was no longer a doubt about it; sooner or later the invaders would come. To burn the town. Get clear of McJack. Clear the track, as it were, for their trading. For rum or for what.

McJack always liked to have him a plan, but what could he plan against the things he definitely knew? Against those things that he didn't know? What could he plan for Yanata, then? And doubts would creep into his mind. Doubts about Adrian.

He liked the lad immensely. But he knew he was headlong, impulsive. He might, mused McJack, be more or less fickle. He, McJack, had been fickle, too, back when he was young. But after taking Minyanata he'd been true to her.

But then Minyanata had had small competition; for many years there'd been no white woman at all. Not until Mellissa had come, and Mellissa had held a certain lure for him. He remembered Minyanata and her needle and the race for the thicket, and he smiled. And sighed a bit for Mellissa's sake, remembering how she'd died. Her death and her doings, taken by and large, merited a prayer for her soul and Sir John gave it.

But he, in the past, couldn't have gotten away to any white women had he tried. And now, he couldn't go even if he wanted, which he didn't at all. But Adrian could go, almost when he chose, when his task for the season was done. Would he, up there in the woods with the time to think life over, choose to go alone? Without Yanata?

And if he did take Yanata, and left McJack and her mother, they wouldn't like that either — with his own future so threatened that he would have small chance to see her again. Ever.

McJack knew this: Adrian had been carried away by the beauty of Yanata. By her manner and her poise. But, there hadn't been any other girls — no white girls there in the woods along the river. There where Yanata had fitted so well. But, when jewels were as plenty as the "diamonds" on the beach down yonder, could Adrian take Yanata home and be as proud of her as he had been in the woods?

So wandered the thoughts of John McJack, in spite of himself. And there were other things to think on. About the plans of the traders. McJack, for once, hadn't a plan of his own. He was puzzled and worried. He must make a plan!

So he would walk in the woods and ponder. He couldn't leave the indians there, the people with whom he had spent a score of years. The people whose cause so long had been his own. They depended on him for guidance and council; they had depended on him for battle, too. And up until now, Sir John had won, because he always had a plan.

But now, though he walked in the woods he could find no answer. Not a right answer. If twenty pounds had been posted before, what would they post now as the price for his head? When the sloop would go back and report: two of their men killed in the woods, four of their men hanged by McJack. The next time they sent a force it would be something he couldn't cope with. Neither he nor his people; and his people, as a camp, had been doomed to extinction. The whites would "clear them out." For espousing the cause and culture of John McJack over all of those years. Because he had cherished theirs.

They, the red people, had taken that culture of Sir John McJack because they'd had faith in the man himself. They had taken many of his thoughts, his ambitions and plans. Taken them kindly and for their own, even before the traders came.

And then, with a few of the white man's tools and "goods of worth," they had bettered their conditions, increased their comforts and slowly were learning a new way of life. Pacing the path that would lead to their progress were they not too hurried on their way. Coming slowly, not being forced, and allowing "their minds to catch up with their matters."

But their "matters" were moving too fast for them now; or other mens' "matters" were. For while on that pathway of their own progress they were in the pathway of profit, too. Of the white man's profit, and that white world didn't like the obstruction at all. It wanted more profit, and it wanted it now. Wanted it badly enough to pay twenty pounds, good money. It would be more. More money. More men. Too much and too many for McJack and his people. He couldn't think of a plan at all.

Perhaps he had better consult with the chief. Perhaps they should hold a council.

"John McJack," he complained to himself, "I thinks ye're confounded for good! For long ye have been Sir John McJack, the Lord of the Land Where Ye Lived the While, but yer day be done. Ye have come against that which ye cannot quell. Ye be an outcast in the land of yer own people; and ye be helpless here with the red ones.

"Ye have brought great doom on the red folk, too. Ye who was smart and bold with craft! Ye who would say: 'Do this! Do that!' Me John McJack, ye was merely dumb. Ye would boast and brag and threat. And ye was but a fool of a sort, for now ye know not what to do.

"I will talk with Nanquemoke, that I will; he may have a thought where I have none."

So he went to sit at the feet of the chief and tell his troubles. And Nanquemoke smiled kindly and wisely. He had a plan where McJack hadn't any. Not any at all.

Chapter 20

There be no way we can hope to win, if the men send a force to fight. For the force will be large; they will have the guns and the men, and have nothing but the fighting to think about, at that. No trading, nor whaling, just fighting to kill! And I have helped to bring this on the people here!"

McJack's voice was tired and slow. Discouraged. He sat with the chief, who was smoking his pipe. He had been meditating deeply, there before his cabin, under the tepee half of it. A gentle rain was falling; it pattered on the skins of the tepee top. Dripped off its edges. The chief placed a hand on the knee of McJack; that was when his grave face smiled: "My brother, he be sad this day; he be, at that. He takes great blame upon himself; he should not do it, to be sure.

"He thinks he has brought trouble to my people. But it be like this: that trouble would have come much worse had he not helped. There at the first, and through the years, in the days just done.

"I will tell ye a tale: It be like this: It rains. We come to shelter in case we be wetted. We sit where it be dry, and watch the falling of the rain. It gives for the thinking. This be an old land, and a good land. A Long Land, but it be not wide at all. Almost, in some two days, a red man can run the width of the same. Even from the Great River to the sea he could do it, did he choose.

"If a red man can do it, so can a white one. This land be easy to come at; it be hard for the red man to hide, and he would. It would be worse if many white men did join the seeking, to be sure.

"For long our fathers did own all of the land; no white man sought them at all. It was a red world, for the red people. Our fathers did have the woods, the trails, the meadows, and the streams and their shores. It was their own; they had it all.

"Our own people, we lived in the land as our fathers had done. We knew no better way to live at all. But the troubles that we had were all our own; they were red troubles; we knew how to take care of them. And we lived.

"But with white troubles, in a land so easy to come at, with the trading for the rum, with the white man's greed for the skins and the furs, with the white man's scorn of the red man's life, this land be too narrow.

"So I have talked with our men; so we made us a plan. We did, at that."

Nanquemoke smiled at McJack, who might have been listening to himself. The chief had stolen so much of his friend's crude culture that he even thought like him, at times. Used his idiom always. McJack had noted this fact before, but never so clearly. He smiled at the chief and waited. Nanquemoke went on: "So we will do as our fathers did when living was bad. When it was very bad, at that. As we ourselfs have done before, as when we left the Capeland and come to the river.

"We cannot change the land that we live in, now. It has been a good land, but now it be bad. And it will soon grow worse, when the many white men come.

"We cannot change the land, so we will leave it! We will seek a wider land, and in that land we can mayhap live in peace. For it will be hard to come at, it be so wide. So," and Nanquemoke smiled again, "just as we do come in from the rain, in case we be wetted, so we do leave the land, lest we should die!" But his smile, it wasn't a glad one at all.

Sir John McJack had listened. The fighting spirit within him didn't like the plan at all. It rebelled at the idea of defeat and indefinite flight. But he listened in silence while the chief went on...

"Our plan be this: Our corn be ripened on the farms; we will sell it to our people who stay. We cannot carry the corn and beans, the way be so long and hard. We will take our axes and knives and hoes and spades, but we will leave the guns. They be too hefty, and our powder be gone. Where we go, the arrows must serve. They served our fathers who made them first, before we knew of a white man.

"So, when all be readied, then we shall go." Nanquemoke's tone was final.

"Where will ye go?" McJack inquired weakly. It sickened him that thought of flight. The thought of leaving the land. And the town that he built. The river, and all.

"First to the north, to where we can cross the Great River. Then toward the setting sun, to the land that be wide*."

McJack nodded. There seemed no use to protest. The chief and his men had made up their minds. Without consulting McJack at all. "Sir John McJack!" It sounded laughable; his reign seemed ended indeed. His authority set at naught. Would Nanquemoke and his people leave him to his fate, and he with a price upon his head? Saving themselves when they knew his life was forfeit?

McJack felt low indeed. He wouldn't have thought it ever could happen. "How soon ye be going?" he inquired. He wouldn't let Nanquemoke see how he felt. Or at least he thought he wouldn't. But he himself was looking at the ground and didn't see the face of the chief.

"Before the frost, if we can sell the corn."

"Sure," said McJack, trying to smile. "I wish ye good going, and all. I do, at that."

Nanquemoke smiled again. He was amused. This was a new Sir John McJack: one who was licked and who knew it. Not the cocky McJack so ready with his banter. With his new ideas and plans to fit almost any occasion.

McJack stirred himself, getting ready to go. "I gives ye good going," he repeated lamely. For the first time in all of those years he didn't know how to talk with the chief. And he'd been that chief's advisor.

Then Nanquemoke told him quietly: "Ye will go with us."

McJack shook his head. "Sure, I could scarce do that at all. I must bide here. I must keep Yanata for Adrian; for if I went she could not stand to wait alone. Ye could not spare the time to wait for them, if ye go afore the weather. So I will stay; I will, at that."

Nanquemoke looked him levelly in the eyes: "Then our people will stay. We have talked in council. We have made the plans. We must go afore our people get the rum, afore the wrath of the things that come. But, if our white brother will not go, then we shall stay. And if we stay, we die. And that be that, for nothing can change us!"

McJack tried to look hard at the chief, but he couldn't see him so well. Nanquemoke sat as still as before, but he seemed to be swimming in a haze. Something was wrong with the eyes of McJack; when he brushed his hand across the same, the back of the hand was wet.

Then the two of them arose, the white man and the red. McJack held the other's hand for a moment; he could see the chief quite clearly then. Could see the fine lines in the face of him, the strength in the quiet smile. And the stoic purpose in the mind of the man. If McJack choose to go, Nanquemoke and his people would go with him and live. If the white man stayed, then they would stay, and very probably many would die.

McJack's voice was husky. "I will think on the plan," he told his friend. "I will, at that."

And there were angles and phases and themes in that thinking, but the way he decided would depend on them all. On himself. On Yanata and her mother. But, more than on anyone else, it would depend on Adrian. On what he did, or didn't do. On that he had some doubts, some doubts that he couldn't strangle.

But Yanata hadn't; she had no doubts at all. Her faith was firm in the man she had chosen. She, of course, had her fears for her people, for the plan had by then been made more or less public, following the council while McJack walked in the woods. Even the children knew, more or less vaguely, its cause and its purpose. It was to save them from the wrath of the white men. The wrath which was sure to come. McJack couldn't stop it, nor could they.

Nor could the surveyors, for by then they would be gone. Or would they? The people thought they would. Didn't doubt it. Still, they might be mistaken. So thought McJack while he walked the trails, head bent, eyes on the ground but scarcely seeing it at all.

But with the eyes of his mind he could see disaster. See it too plainly, in one phase or another. For him and his people, and for the line of McJack. For Yanata and such children as she might bear. For the hopes he had held, and the dreams. Disaster to those hopes if he went with the people before Adrian came. Disaster to all of his hopes if Adrian failed to come, if he failed to keep faith with Yanata. In spite of himself he couldn't entirely still those doubts. He feared that, having all this time to think and plan, Adrian would change his mind. He had fallen heels over head in love; would he fall as quickly out of it? Would Adrian, like McJack when he'd been young, be fickle, too?

But Yanata, back in the camp town, waiting, dreaming, her eyes oft looking up the stream though she knew he couldn't come so soon, she had no doubts at all. Her worries were for her people and not for herself.

And the others gathered their corn and beans and for the first time that any could remember, made ready to sell. But no bargain had yet been concluded, for McJack hadn't made up his mind. He was biding in hopes that Adrian would come and that he would take Yanata away. Then McJack would feel more free to go; he knew he couldn't stay. For the people wouldn't go without him, unless he could escape to safety. In that they were determined.

The September days were wearing away; October would probably be the month of frost. McJack, walking with his hands behind him, eyes on the ground, suddenly straightened. Held up his head. "I shall quit with the fretting," he told himself. "It be the time to do instead of to doubt. To help instead of hinder. I will talk with Nanquemoke again."

He found the chief on the shore of the town; he was looking upriver at nothing at all. McJack could read the thoughts of him there: Leaving the homeland! That was the theme.

"Nanquemoke," said he, "I have been thinking some thoughts: There be just one way we can fend off them that will come. We have some friends, but I know not where they be. D'ye recall the pirates on the Point?"

Nanquemoke nodded and smiled. That mess of merry marauders who sailed the seas and "took their tolls." The chief recalled them clearly, and with both amusement and a sense of shame. For they had swung him, the chief of his people, up to their deck on a tackle "like any dangling corpse."

McJack explained: "I will go down and see if they be there now. At times they have come in the fall, but not this early. They mayhap will not come for a month or more; I cannot tell.

"Now the men that we fear, the ones who will come to burn the town and clear the camp, and hang McJack if theycatch him at all, will try to come afore the freeze, so that in the spring they can trade as they choose with none to hamper.

"This be my thought, and it be not so good a one at all. If I can get the pirates to head off the sloop, and with their guns they'd do that same for the love of the prank of it, we can mayhap be safe for the time. We can mayhap make the cost so great that the masters will give up their trading and all. It be a wild plan, but our friends be wild people. Prankful, even though there be no profit."

McJack grinned. He hadn't done that for days. Nanquemoke smiled and he nodded. He placed his hand on the shoulder of McJack.

"Go ye down and see, do ye think it best. But," he hesitated, "why not go up the river, to Adrian? Ask him what he will do? I have watched the mind of my white brother of late; there be doubts in his mind of what Adrian will do. Why not go up the river?"

But McJack shook his head: "Sure, the lad must tend his thinking by himself. If he come free, and not change his mind at all, then that be good. Mayhap then when I gets back from the Cape, he will have come, and we will know. So I will go to the Cape the while."

He went down to the Capelands alone. Along the trail, at the hurry. He had his adze and his arrows; a gun was too hefty for haste. His weapons were light to carry. Lighter than the burden of his added years. A score of years since first he had come. And now, traipsing the trail again.

Between the thickets. Through the oaklands. Under the pines. Up the little hills and down them. On the Indian Trail to the Point of the Cape. He didn't go out to the bluff at all, nor to the camp of the whalers. From the Point he looked out on the sea and the bay and each was empty of what he sought. Far as he could see there was no ship on the waters. None near the shore.

But there were people further up the beach of the bay. Some indians were gathering clams; he went up to meet them. They were people from the river camps, come down for a picnic and to make shell money. "The river people had learned that the corn would be for sale?" asked McJack.

The man whom he asked shook his head. "Boats," he told McJack. "We buy boats, ye sell?"

"Mayhap. If we must go, and ye should stay, ye would have use for the craft. We would not where we go; a boat will not climb a hill, unless that hill be water. Have ye seen anything of a ship at all, down near the Point and the pond?"

"No ship. No boats."

McJack called himself a fool for the hoping. If the pirates did come it might not be for weeks. Perhaps not until early November. He himself couldn't wait. He had a great deal on his mind. Adrian might be coming back; indeed, as McJack trudged homeward that hope took hold. Made him hasten. He had been a fool to come to the Cape at all, and waste the time!

But if Adrian should come when the surveying was done, and take Yanata away, to help the line of McJack come back to its own that it might survive, then McJack could go with the people. Lacking any other refuge he could lose himself in the "wide land" beyond the Great River. Far inland among the hills. So far that the streams would only flow one way; there'd be no tides at all. No ships. No comings and goings perhaps for years. And no tales to come out to the white man's world of the doings or tauntings of Sir McJack. The "Small One?" She was a problem for the future. Yanata's was *now*.

So McJack tramped the trail, going back to his town. He went under the oaks and the pines and the maples again; this would be the last time! He went around the thickets and climbed the little sandhills... and it seemed that the dead men there just sat and watched him go. A shade of a man would reach for his pipe and he'd light it, and smoke it and watch McJack. Watch him go northward and the shade would smile a sad and wise smile: All of this traipsing of trails was so futile and foolish.

So McJack wasn't merry, trudging toward home. He hoped, though, that no more had gone wrong; that something had been right. Like Adrian returning, eager for his bride. That would right the world for Yanata; that was what she expected.

She had been sad, of course, that her people must go; but Yanata was young. The young are hopeful when in love. The going of her people wouldn't be forever; somehow the saints or the Manitou would attend to that; she implored them earnestly enough. So Yanata had been expectant and watchful, when her father left for the Cape.

When he came back, things had happened. He found the girl stretched on her bed in the cabin, broken of heart. Refusing to eat or to talk. Not weeping, but lying in silence. Not heeding her mother who tried to console. Who worried and wept, and yet in her heart was a little bit glad, being selfish with love, like a mother. For Yanata wouldn't go away at all, out to the white world and be lost.

It seemed there would be no parting, unless Yanata died of her grief. Indian girls had been known to do just that; the tales that were told had said so. Minyanata was fearful; she prayed to the saints and the Manitou again. But they had seemed to do nothing about it.

"How come all of this?" McJack had inquired. Nanquemoke had come over and he and Minyanata told him: It happened the day after McJack had gone. It had been sunset and the river was still. Only the shades and the tides and the eddies there, and far upriver, at the bulge of the bend, a coming canoe. There where the last of the sun shone clear. There were two men in the canoe; they paddled slowly with the tide. From the bulge of the bend they came straight toward the town. Or almost straight: the bow would sometimes slack with the tide; the stroking paddles would mend the course. Coming to the town.

When the canoe came in a man stepped ashore. Tall and straight and middle-aged, he was a stranger to them all. An upriver man, from where the tides had ceased to flow.

From the sweetwater country above. He used the Lenape tongue: "I am sent to seek Yanata."

The girl's heart had jumped at that. Adrian had sent her a message. But the voice of the messenger was grave; his face was sober. Yanata suddenly felt afraid.

"This is Yanata," Nanquemoke had said. "You have tidings for her?"

The indian nodded. Turning to his canoe he took out a parcel; something wrapped in a bit of tarpaulin. Yanata's hands trembled as she took it. Her mother helped her unwrap it.

First, a sprig of woodbine.

"That means marry," Minyanata told her daughter. Yanata's eyes began to shine again; she smiled. Of course there would be a marriage. Indeed, Adrian had already taken Yanata to wife, there before the eyes of them all. Of course there'd be a wedding, when they could find a priest. They'd expected that.

But the torn tarpaulin held something more; beneath another fold lay some beech leaves. Just three beech leaves.

Minyanata gasped. Yanata looked at her mother quickly. "That," explained the mother "means 'Forget me forever!'"

Yanata didn't seem to comprehend. She unwrapped another fold; her hands were shaking as she did it — a broken wildflower and some wild pansy leaves. That was all. But too much, at that.

"They mean 'Farewell!'" Minyanata explained; she only whispered it, but Yanata heard. So did Nanquemoke, the chief.

"What does this mean?" he asked of the upriver indian. "Our brother had brought bad news in the tongue of the flowers. What does our brother know?"

"Only this: these things were brought to the chief of my people. He was asked to send the token here. He was to tell that the white men with the boats had gone far up the river. They had gone so far that the white men knew they would be only a day's walk from the Great River. So they had left their boats and walked on the land, toward the setting sun. They would not come back this way at all, for there was a ship in the Great River there.

"So the young man who was with the others had sent these tokens and tidings to my chief. He had given my chief a knife and a hatchet as pay for the errand. I have done the bidding of my chief; that is all I know. I am sad at the heart if the news be bad; but for all I can tell it is true."

So that was the story which McJack heard told. It was, too, the story he had more or less feared. He'd had some doubts. Come to think of it, Adrian had been very reticent about his past life. Had told almost nothing at all. Had been so busied with his work, and in courting Yanata. Beneath the moon, on the sand, out in the pinelands, in a canoe on the river.

But not in the gloom of the cabin where McJack had found his daughter. "Lassie, it be like this," he was trying to console her "ye be young. Yes, lassie, I know not what to tell ye now! But ye must be brave. Ye cannot lie here in the gloom and wear yer heart away, at all. Ye cannot do it; I be telling ye so!"

But apparently Yanata thought that she could or must. She just looked at her father dully. Reached out and patted his hand. But she wouldn't get up at all.

"I will talk with the chief," concluded John McJack, and he went out to find him. "Nanquemoke," he said, "we will go with ye; we will at that. If we go we should be starting. Best ye'd make haste with the plans."

Nanquemoke smiled; he was greatly relieved. He had been almost as worried as had been McJack about Yanata; and time had been passing while the father made up his mind. And time was of such importance. They had a long way to go; the winter would be coming to meet them. They must reach their new land in time to prepare.

So the corn and beans and the boats were quickly sold. If they were lucky the shell money would buy more for the winter. They would have to take their furs and skins along. And their tools. But not the grindstone to sharpen them. "Mayhap we can make one, where we be going — it would break a man's back to heft it so far," said McJack. "It be a sorry task, this leaving the land; but we must go. We must make ready for to do it. We must get Yanata on the move; we must, at that."

"And, thought Nanquemoke gravely "we must get ye going, too, my friend. Ye have been too broodful here of late."

So McJack, having been forced to make up his mind, became more like his younger self: busy with his plans and the doing of them. It was about the first of October; they would start the next morning.

Chapter 21

Their packs were made up and ready: tools and furs and skins. And a few of the pots and cumbrous things. The guns, they had done a strange thing with the guns: they'd taken them in the dead of night and sunk them in the river.

"Sure," said McJack, "I be afraid to leave them. There will be none to lead or give council, and, if the injuns get the guns, and somehow some powder, and more likely some rum, they would make trouble. So we will sink the same." And they'd done it, except for the cannon. These they left mounted on the shore, trained on the river. One last and humorous gesture of Sir John McJack's.

When morning came they were not merry at all. The men nor the women; some of the children ran lightly around, eager for the going. Too young to regret the leaving of the old land, not old enough to fear the new.

Some of the folk from the other camps were there to see them off. To wish them well. To regret the going of Sir John McJack. They themselves had little to fear or so they thought. According to what they had learned, all of the spleen of the traders would be vented on McJack and his people. As long as they could control them the traders needed the indians to trap the furs, else there'd be no trading. It was simple enough: the traders needed a source of supply for furs and a market for their trade-goods and their rum. They needed a market, but no McJack.

It came time to go soon after the dawn was done. Along the eastern shore the river was shadowed by the trees: the oaks, the maple and the gums. And by the giant cedars, too, where the brook ran down.

To the west: the waters and the land, and the meadows lay still in the sunshine that slanted down. White cranes were standing over there and gulls. And the tall blue heron. The tide was nearing the top of its flood, the water smooth. It shone but did not shimmer. Curlews called as they flew.

They looked their last and went their way, the people. Fleeing from the wrath with which they could no longer cope. Going with their burdens along the trail. First to Muskee, and then toward the northland. On the trails which their fathers had made for them there. Packed hard by the millions of moccasined feet through a thousand years of time. By feet which were dead because the years had flown away. Perhaps, there at first, the men who had made that trail had been fleeing in fear. Perhaps, behind them then, they'd left a power with which they could not contend. Or they may have been adventure bent. No one could tell, not even the dead men who sat beside it. The first of the story had been lost. Muddled in mystery; no one knew.

The people left the ford at Muskee. On to the Manumuskin. Cutting a bit toward the east, to reach the shallows.

From Manumuskin to Menantico; it wasn't so many miles. Just four or five, there in the woodland. They were still in their own country; most of the men had been there before. So had McJack. And Richards and his men. And Adrian; when McJack looked at Yanata his thought of the boy was bitter.

But it was well for Yanata that she was on the move. At first the shock had thrown her mind into a sort of stupor. There was just that one and bitter thought: Adrian had failed her! In spite of their troth, in spite of the hours in the afterglows there, in spite of the gilded Manitou moon. Adrian had failed her and gone away!

He hadn't been man enough to come back and tell her but had sent a message; had gone out that other way. He had crossed the land to the Great River; there had been news of a ship that was there. Perhaps that was the way the men would go home, on a ship. Adrian had been going to take her away, on a ship. And some day he would bring her back to visit, on a ship.

Such dreams and plans, and he had proved that he was only a coward! Afraid of two things: afraid to take her out to his own white world and afraid to come back and tell her so. Afraid to tell McJack and his people, Adrian was a coward! The thought was bitter but in its way it helped. It and the fact that her people were going away, helped to break her stupor. But it didn't make her happy at all.

Menantico, winding first between its meadows and then its woods; they crossed it in the woodland. Wet their feet and slaked their thirst, and then went on. More than a hundred people they were in all: men, women and children. Luckily there were none so old that they couldn't walk, but on the whole they went slowly. In a long and straggling line, each with his burden. All of their wealth they carried with them.

It was one of those times when they stopped to rest that Penoke came striding down the trail, and he was alone. The last McJack had seen of him was when he'd gone with Richards. Going upriver; he had said he was going home. Penoke. McJack frowned when he saw the youth; would he bother Yanata again? But at first he seemed surprised to meet the people and didn't pay attention to Yanata at all.

"Where have ye been the while?" inquired John McJack.

Penoke pointed to the northwest; it was there that his village lay. "With my people." He spoke in the Lenape; he hadn't yet learned the idiom well. "My father has died. I walk in the woods with my sadness."

McJack just nodded. Nanquemoke asked: "Have ye seen the white men who went north in the boats?

"I went a little way with them, then left and came back to my people. But my people heard that the men had gone across the land, to the Great River. I do not know; I did not see them go."

Nanquemoke seemed satisfied with the answer, but McJack frowned. He didn't know what was wrong, but he felt something. Nothing definite at all; just a doubt. He shrugged; it wouldn't matter. But when the line had started again and he saw Penoke along toward the rear, with a pack he had taken from one of the older women, he frowned again. What was the injun up to? There was only one answer: Yanata. The thought was the cause of the frown.

They made a score of miles that day and camped at night on a branch of their own river. A branch of Wahatquenack: Indian Run. Only ten feet wide and sweet water.

But the indians didn't run when they came there; they walked wearily in the late of the day. They couldn't see the afterglow at all, the trees so dense. The stream so narrow that it lay in the shade. Only at high noon would it sparkle and shine.

It was a branch of their own river that they knew. Mayhap Adrian had been there at that very spot, but there was no sign. McJack doubted it; the stream was too narrow for the oars; the water wasn't deep at all; the stream bed was of pebbles. Cousins to the "diamonds" along the bay. But they didn't slide and grind in the wave-ends, there were no waves. Just a gentle current, going down. A one-way current, feeding the river. Taking nothing from it but always giving. Sweet water; that was why Wahatquenack wasn't so salty as the sea: sweet water coming down.

It, that sweet water, wouldn't be quite so sweet when it touched the shores of their little town, the town with the cabins and all. Up here in the woods the water passed any given point but once down there it would pass that point many times. First down, then up, then down, then out to the bay and the sea. Salt water then. Deep water. Up here it murmured; one had to listen to hear it. Down there it could roll and thunder in a storm and do its part to wreck a ship!

McJack and Nanquemoke talked about the wonder of the thing; Yanata listened. Her father was pleased that she did so. She hadn't shown interest in anything before; had just walked along with her burden. Too sad, in fact, to be afraid.

McJack's thoughts were seldom away from her and in thinking of the girl he wondered again about Penoke. He suspected that something more than chance had induced the youth to join them. He asked of Nanquemoke: "Did ye hear that Penoke's father had died?"

Nanquemoke nodded; there was a little quirk at the corners of his mouth.

"When did ye hear it?"

It was then that the chief smiled broadly: "Five winters agone. He was killed by a bear."

McJack grunted. Penoke's grief was lasting long. McJack wondered some more as to what the youth was up to, but the etiquette of the woods forbade him to inquire. But what had the indian been doing since leaving the camp of the white men? He didn't ask Penoke; McJack just watched him.

The trail went on; so did the people. Another day; another score of miles. Here the land was rolling. The hills were longer and higher than they'd been down-country. Not so high nor so steep that the trail must wind around them, but high enough and steep enough that they were wearisome to walk. And they could only see a little way because of the hills and the trees. There were no rivers, nor meadows there at all: just now and then a little stream. A river, perhaps.

On the top of a hill they came to a fork in the trails. One went to the left, the other bore slightly to the right. The left fork would soon reach the Great River, they had been told.

But Nanquemoke shook his head; so did McJack, although that was the way that the Lenape messenger had come when he came to bring Saunders' warning. But that man had been alone; a hundred people could not so easily beg a crossing. Opined McJack: "Do I get the lay of the land aright, it would make no sense to reach the river now; we cannot cross it. Yon other fork, the injuns say, do come more near where we want to go."

So that was the trail that they trudged along, the five score and more of the people. The easterly trail would lead to the head of Rancocas and then around it. When they started from the fork McJack was near the end of the line; he helped a woman to adjust her pack. Yanata had gone on, but her father saw her bend her knees, mark something on the ground. She did it quickly, then went on.

When McJack came there he saw the sign: an arrow. It pointed the way of the inland trail. "That be for Adrian to see," he muttered. "He who has gone the other way!"

Then suddenly McJack stopped short. But no, Penoke had had nothing to do with the bringing of the news about Adrian. Another indian had done that, by order of his chief.

"But it be queer," he muttered again. "None saw the men go over the land at all. I wonder."

But he had to go on with the others. On and on and on. It was the seventh day when they reached the Great River. Deep water there, and wide; there was no sign of a ford.

The trail went on beside the stream, on the slopes of the hills, beneath the trees. In the afternoon sun the water would shine; on the trail there were shadows until they came down to the ford. Then, shelf-rock in the stream, all of a sudden and clear across. A little way down one could sail a ship; there on the rock they could wade the river.

There were rocks on the shore, between the trees: pebbles that giants might have dropped in their play. The people wondered; down where they'd lived there had been the pebbles on the beach, and sandstone in the inland, all small enough for a man to lift. The pebbles, a child might fling them. But not rocks like these. The people looked rather fearfully at the ford. It was so wide! Three times as wide as the river they had known so well. They'd have to feel for footing here. The current was running down. Down toward deep water. If, laden as they were, a weaker one should stumble...

"I not like that!" declared Minyanata.

"I be not overmuch pleased meself," replied McJack. "It be a risk, all laden down like we are."

But they must cross, so they made a plan: One man, lightly laden, would go at first, to feel the way. The other men would follow with the heavier packs. Then they'd return and help the women and children, many of whom would have to be carried.

They could do that, or they could make a raft to freight the goods across, could they find some dead cedars. But they couldn't; there were no cedars; just the hardwoods, and those were too heavy. The green logs would hardly float their weight.

The people were weary; some wanted to wait until morning. But Nanquemoke pointed to the marks on the rocks: "The water be low the now, and not so strong. If a storm should come up yonder" he pointed up river to where they could see the hills all crowned with trees, hills so much greater than they'd ever seen before, so great that they awed the people, "it would be much worse. Best we go the now."

The other men agreed, as did McJack: "Sure, did the water flow more swift, and deep at that, we could not do the task at all."

So the thirty men, laden with the heavier packs, made the crossing. The women waited and watched. Nanquemoke led; he carried a pole to feel the way. To search out holes and hidden stumbles.

Up to his knees; he could see the rock and didn't need to feel. They waded slowly; most of the packs were heavy. From each man's legs the eddies swirled, down-river; and bubbles. Those little bubbles caught the sun, at first; near the western shore they would be shaded by long shadows of the trees. Evening shadows on the water. But they hadn't reached them yet; once in a while a man would falter, off-balance. The young fellows laughed. Nanquemoke, in the lead and taking great care, was sober. The water was up to his waistline.

He had to feel for the footing then. Carefully and slow. Poling with his pole; if he found a hole he went around it. Each man made but one eddy then, from the waistline; the bubbles floated down.

The men made the crossing, but they were tired so they rested a while. Rested briefly in the new land, the "wide land" beyond the Great River. The land so wide that they could walk for many days and seek that place where the white men might never find them. In that land so wide between rivers. Between the rivers and the sea. For the white men came by way of the waters. In ships. Where a ship couldn't go they made shallops and sloops, but they had to have rivers to float them.

In this wide land the red men could mayhap hide among the rocks and trees. Hide from the white man and his rum; Nanquemoke feared the rum more than he feared the guns. No ships with rum could come among the rocks of the inland there, where he and his people would go.

There was a rock right close to where they'd come ashore, the greatest they'd ever seen. Ten times as high as a cabin, it was; ten times the girth. A hard-stone rock which stood alone among the trees. How came it there? The men wondered. They walked to it and around it and looked up at the top of it; they felt its base with their fingers. They looked, too, at the trees. The age-old trees around the older rock; the young men marveled greatly. The moods of the Manitou, when the world was made, must greatly have varied.

They wondered and went back for their women.

They, the women, had taken off their clothes and stood in breechcloths like the men. They must keep their clothes dry, for the night would bring chill. Penoke looked at Yanata; there was a shine in the eyes of him. A covetous light; McJack could tell the reason Penoke had chosen to come. He knew for sure; Penoke was seeking Yanata. Though Adrian seemed to have changed his choice, Penoke hadn't. He was patiently seeking, biding his time; knowing more than he seemed to, Penoke.

McJack frowned; and then he smiled and shook his head. He didn't blame the injun. Why shouldn't he want her? Then Sir John looked sad for a moment, the line of McJack! That bloodline of himself which he had hoped to send back to its own. But the sire for that line wouldn't be found in the hills, those hills where only the reds would be. The red men hiding from the whites. Or so they hoped.

McJack turned then to Minyanata. She stood at the edge of the river, almost as naked as that night when he'd wed her, on the shores of the bay. He grinned, remembering. In a matronly way she was still good for the eyes.

When the line of the people made ready to cross, the shadows were long on the western shore. First, Nanquemoke, then his woman. Then his son; if the lad couldn't wade he could swim. Only the men bore the heavier burdens; they wanted to neither lose their women nor their goods. McJack and his wife and daughters were near the middle of the line. He carried a search pole. In that wavering line it would be easy to lose the way; there were no footprints on the water there. Just bubbles and swirls.

The people, crossing the stream on the shelf-rock. The small children borne on the shoulders of the men; the larger ones swimming and having fun. Yanata, being young and strong and for the moment forgetting her grief, bore a pack on her shoulders. Across her bare shoulders; it hid them from Penoke. Penoke was a little way behind. He helped an older woman along, but he kept his eyes on Yanata.

They had come to the place where the water was deeper at the beginning of the shadows on the western shore. It was up to Yanata's thighs. She was looking ahead, careful for her mother. Minyanata was doing very well, she thought. She was proud...

"YANATA!" Someone was yelling the name. The voice came from the shore they had left. The people turned slowly to listen; Yanata moved quicker. "YANATA!"

A man came running along the slope of the shore, back there. Rushed into the water. Wading across: "YANATA!"

The face of the girl grew radiant. "It be Adrian!" she screamed. "It be Adrian!" "He be coming to get me!"

She thrust her pack into another's hands and started back to meet him. He was her man; he had come to get her! When she went past Penoke she never saw him. Didn't see the others, either. Only Adrian, splashing through the water. Following the others.

And all of them stood still to watch, up to their waists in the water. All, that is, except Penoke. He went quickly on to the other shore. Passing the others, but they paid no attention. They were watching Yanata and Adrian, coming closer. Yanata laid herself down and swam; she made more speed. And then she swam straight into Adrian's arms. Both of them panting, he held her there. And Yanata was very happy indeed! The saints, and the god, and the Manitou had all been very good to her. All of a sudden.

Chapter 22

That night they camped in the lee of the rock. The October air was somewhat chill; the fires at the base of the rock felt good. Many of the people went quickly to sleep.

Adrian, too, was tired; he had dog-trotted much of the way following the signs of the arrows. Though Yanata had grieved and gone away with her people, there had been a little hope in her heart. Enough to cling to and to make those signs.

"Son," said McJack while they sat by the fire, "do tell me this: When ye was charting the river did ye lose any of your tools?"

"Why, yes; I believe we did. A couple of hatchets and some knives."

"Was that when Penoke left ye?"

Adrian thought a moment: "It may have been, although we didn't miss them until later. He went with us as far as the swamp, then left and went back."

"Aye; he had him a plan, from the very first. So, with the message in the tarp, and the tools for the paying, he goes to his chief with his tale. The chief had no cause to doubt it, though why he did not send Penoke with the news I do not know.

"But Penoke, he keeps quiet. He goes out to the trail, for he must have heard of the plan to flee. He mayhap kept an eye on the town the while, a-biding his time. He were bound to get Yanata, but he could not do sit whilst ye was there at all, nor whilst she hoped ye'd come.

"So he makes him this plan to make ye look bad, and he nearly done it! I be sad to the heart to think that he fooled me; I were not so crafty in that at all. So, lad, will ye give me your pardon, now? I craves it purely."

Adrian laughed and gave his hand. "I will that. Most hearty, and glad! Most likely I would have done the same. What became of Penoke?"

Most likely the indian was hiding in the woods and McJack yawned. Adrian stayed awake long enough to briefly state his plans

Richards would be looking for the sloop in the bay. He was to meet it and hold it for Adrian, if he could. But his men were eager to be gone; none had cared to join in Adrian's "fool errand." So there was great need for haste to get back to the bay.

"And then?" inquired McJack. "What shall I do? Shall I grow a beard and hide beyond it?" He chuckled, but Adrian looked troubled, in the light of the fire. He shrugged his shoulders. He hadn't planned that far ahead; McJack being proscribed among the whites, could not go openly. But he seemed less troubled than Adrian by the thought. So he yawned again and chuckled and told the others they'd better get their rest. "It'll be a hard day on the morrow," he predicted.

Most of the people were already sleeping. Being in a strange land, two sentries had been posted. Adrian and Yanata slept side by side; in sleep she held fast to his hand. So passed the night.

But in that night a sentry saw a man; he came out of the woods above. Went down to the shore and along to the place of the ford. He seemed a shadow as he waded the stream, going back to his home and his people, and perhaps to some indian sweetheart. Penoke.

McJack dreaded that morning, but it came; mornings had come for more than a score of years since first he had known these people. The younger ones had been born in his regime and learned many of his ways. There was Johnny Pank and that other half-breed boy and some older ones who were almost grown. There were Nanquemoke and Panquenack and all the others. His own people, for all of that score of years.

Minyanata had made her choice the night before. She hadn't hesitated. "I go with ye," she had told her man.

But where would they go? McJack had that price on his head. "I will grow me some whiskers," he explained. "I will be some other one the now, in case I must." But in the back of his mind he had the germ of a plan. A very wild plan at that.

The people had come out to the shore and the sun. The sun felt good. It sparkled on the waters there; the east shore was in shadow. McJack and his must go across, and back, to the east and south. The people would go on to the south and west. Seeking a home in the solitudes there, amongst the woods and rocks of the "wide land."

The parting was hard. "I be sad to leave," he told them, there in the sun. "Sad to see ye go, at that. Words will not tell the tale at all. When first I came to ye down yonder, ye did not know my speech at all, and yet ye took me as a friend. That night I took the hand of one and all, and of them that be gone now: Wawakna and the many. That hand clasp served when speech could not.

"And now, because I cannot speak the more, it must serve again." So he took the hand of each and all, and of Nanquemoke the last. The two men simply stood and looked. Neither of them spoke a word.

McJack stepped into the river, onto the shelf-rock. The women wept as they followed. Minyanata, Yanata and the "Small One." Adrian went last; his face was sober. The line of McJack, going back to its own. Crossing the river again. To their knees. To their waists. To their knees again. To the shadows of that other shore there in the morning. The eddies and bubbles had disappeared; the water ran smooth and clear.

From there they watched the Red People go. The long line of them, their backs a-burdened, wound around to the shoreline in the sun. One hand held high in a last farewell. They went then into the shadows. Nanquemoke, he who was chief and had the care of his people, led the line. Panquenack went last; Johnny Pank rode on his shoulder pack. The line of the Red Men, seeking to hold their own. There in that land which they hoped would be wide. "Harder to come at" for the whites. But taking a strain of that white blood with them: Johnny Pank, Mellissa's son, and that other, the son of a whaler.

But McJack and his family had their own things to do: first they must go back to the land of the Cape. On down to the bay to meet the sloop; this was Adrian's plan, so they backtracked themselves over the weary miles. Through the rolling lands to the level ones. In four days, the Manumuskin; the next would be Muskee, at the ford. From there the main trail would lead on down to the Cape; the side-trail would lead to the wooden town.

"No need to go that way again," declared McJack. "It would pay us nothing and would take the time. Best we keep on to the bay."

For he didn't want to see the town again, with the cabins he had built. With its graveyard in the pineland there: Wawakna and his woman and the others they had known. And Mellissa. Where would Panquenack be now? How far would he and Mellissa's son have gone? That white line of Mellissa's would go back to the red and be lost; McJack's was bound back to its own again, thanks largely to Mellissa. But for her, Yanata had been carried away, that other time at Muskee.

They were nearing Muskee on the trail. The wind had lately changed; it blew lightly from the river. Minyanata sniffed the air. "Smoke!" she declared. Soon the others could smell it, too. Coming nearer, they could see it in the air, just faint little wisps above the trees. It rode to the inland on that new wind from the river. On the wind that blew over their town.

McJack frowned. "That be cedar smoke!" he declared grimly. "Dry cedar, a-burning there. I wonder."

But he didn't have long to wonder; they met an indian, a man from the upper Muskee. He had been scouting near the camp when the white men came. Some had come in a shallop, and they had cannon. More had come on the land, from the mouth of Muskee.

They had found the town deserted and had burned it. The men were still on the river shore, to the windward of the smoking ruins and the fire-blasted trees. They were making merry and passing the rum.

"Sure," declared McJack, "we did flee none too soon. Mayhap, do the men stay there, and the saints be with us, we come back not too late."

But he didn't explain; he was thinking his thoughts. Minyanata made dire threats of vengeance. Yanata was looking beyond the ford to where Mellissa had died. Adrian remembered his pursuit of the Iroquois, just for a moment.

"Best," advised McJack, "we go down to the bay, lest these men be searching. If the men be on the land, and it seems that they be, it'll mayhap prove a race between them and us. Mayhap it will, at that."

So they went on down to the lower land, past those trails which led to the river. They used great care, but it wasn't needed; they met no one at all. They were far to the south of the path of the smoke clouds.

"We should search for the bay," suggested Adrian. "We must be near it now and Master Richards said they would wait on the shore, near the mouth of the river."

But getting there was another matter and not so easy. When they came out of the woodland they found the meadows. Great spaces of grass as high as their knees. Acres and acres of man-high reeds. Islands of little trees and vines. They couldn't see the bay at all. Neither could they see the mud-holes that were hidden by the reeds.

Minyanata, although she had never been there before, pointed their direction. McJack nodded: "Keep as much as we can to the shorter grass, and watch the mires! Should ye step in a splotch-hole ye'd be mudded to the middle. We have no time for that at all, for the night will soon be coming. If we have luck we may find a trail; if not, we must thrash it through."

And they found no trail, so they "thrashed" it. At times they waded almost to their knees; they forced their way through the reeds when they couldn't go around them. Adrian went first and broke the way. The "Small One" was so weary that she cried; her father carried her on his back. Mosquitoes buzzed and green-flies. Dragon-flies darted here and there.

Then they came to a little knoll; stunt trees grew there and brambles. Far as they could see, above or below, the land was the same. Reeds and grass and stunted trees. And salt ponds; ducks arose from these and quacked as they flew. There were plover and cur-lew on the wing. Mud-hens and bittern and a few great herons, which stood and watched; they seldom flew away.

"They think we be fools," remarked McJack. "Mayhap they be right at that. This be no land for people at all, lest they have wings for the flying." He panted a little.

They were muddied to their knees and nearly exhausted, but they struggled on. They mustn't be caught by the night out there. They came to reeds that were tall and dense.

"We must push through." McJack was getting desperate. "There be nothing else to do the now. We..."

But Minyanata had stopped him. She held up her hand. "Water!" she said. "Little wind on water!"

They all could hear it then, the bay. It must be near; the waves would not be loud at all. Above, they saw some trees; they pushed that way through the reeds and mud. They came out on a bit of fastland. A sandy knoll beside the bay; that was where the trees were.

In there they found where had been a fire and a tent; the holes of the stakes were still in the ground. Adrian's face grew long. Richards had been there and gone. There was no boat in sight. Just the empty beach, the tide being low; the waves and the water and the bend of the land toward the Cape. The mouth of Wahatquenack just above. Ducks on the water. Curlews called from the air as they flew. Gulls were feeding on the beach and sandsnipes. No men. No boats. No ship on the bay. And the night was almost down.

They had little time for looking. Minyanata made a fire while McJack and Adrian found some clams and oysters. These they ate in the almost dark. They weren't very merry. The "Small One" brought a few more sticks for the fire. McJack had been looking out on the bay, perhaps looking for a light out there. A light might show where a ship would not, but there was nothing but dark. Off over the land, though, was a light spot in the sky; the moon would soon be showing. He heard Adrian speak sharply and turned back to the fire.

Adrian held a small board in his hand; he had snatched it from the fire. It was already scorched and smoking. "It's a message from Master Richards!" Adrian exclaimed. He held it close to the light of the fire.

"What reads it?" McJack inquired.

"I... I can't be sure. It's smoked and dim. I make out 'Pirates' and — yes — the word 'night' and that's all I can read."

So between them they interpreted the message to mean that there were pirates near and that the sloop must escape in the night and hadn't been able to wait.

Adrian was discouraged but McJack almost chuckled. "Mayhap it'll be best, at that. Now, we should sleep. In the morn we shall see what we see."

In spite of the disappointment they needed little urging. The five soon slept beside the fire. McJack snored and Minyanata groaned with her weariness and the "Small One" huddled to her for warmth. The moon came up and went down; the sun was two hours high before they awakened. First, McJack looked out on the bay and shrugged. There was nothing there. And up toward the river, from where the traders' men would come, the water was empty.

Asked Adrian: "Master McJack, why should ye be grinning now?"

"Because mayhap we be not too late. I have me a plan, or mayhap so. Come; we must haste to the Cape. Best way now would be the beach; it be good going with the tide at ebb."

"But that's a score of miles and more."

McJack nodded and smiled. Adrian could see no cause to smile: "But those men are pirates!"

"Aye, that they be, of a sort. But it's likely they'll be the friends of mine," said McJack.

Adrian smiled, then. "You have a strange assortment of friends, but if you can chance it so can I. But I'm afraid for the women; the pirates are bad men at best."

"Mayhap they be, in some of their ways; I will not gainsay that at all. But mayhap in ways they be good. I have small fear of these pirates, me lad, but I hold great fear of the trading men. They do but serve and do the will of them that hire them; it matters small what harm they do. Mostly they be scum and scattle; they lack the brains to make their ways and feed their bellies on their own. Best we had go to the Cape, to meet me friends the pirates."

Then they walked down the beach, the five of them, over the first three miles of the empty sands. They saw some signs that indians had been gathering clams. They hoped to clear the meadows before the flooding tide narrowed the beach to the dunes. Come to the fastland they'd likely find a trail.

But they hadn't known the lay of the land nor reckoned on the creeks. The first one was small; they waded to their middles to cross. But the next one, a mile or more down, was deep and rather wide, and there was no trail on the meadows.

So they swam it and came out wet and bedraggled. They had few goods to carry; the sun was warm and their clothes would soon be dried.

McJack had shivered and then he chuckled; next he appraised his worldly wealth: "Sure, I have less goods than when I came at first to the people yonder, Nanquemoke having the adze now. But I have had the years, to be sure: more years and better than many a man, at that, for these troubled times. And I be not alone at all, nor half as frighted." And Sir John grinned.

And he had his plan; he was compelled to see if the thing would work. He frowned a little, then hastened on. The beach curved to the south of them. They came to another creek; it was wide and the flooding tide ran swift. They stopped and pondered, and searched for a trail. The creek came into the bay from the south of east and Minyanata found a faint little path toward the inland. She looked at the sun and at the line of the bay; this little path should lead to the main trail, the one that led to the Cape.

Off there to the southeast would be where Menotac's camp had been, beyond the trail. Minyanata was pleased that she could show her man a thing or two. She pointed to the little path.

"Sure, me lady, I thinks ye be right. There be too many of these small creeks to swim, if we keep to the beach. Best we had to the inland there, and down."

But before they went he scanned the upper bay. The air was clear; he could dimly see its distant curve to the north. Could almost find where the river joined. He was looking for a sail; he didn't see it. This appeared to please him.

"They could not have come on the flooding tide, the scum and scattle that burned the town. And the ebb will be mostly in the dark; they will not come until the dawn, if they come then. One thing be sure; they still be in the river now."

An hour later and two miles in the inland they found the main trail. The time was past mid-morning. Minyanata was of the opinion that they hadn't made even a mile in a direct line, and that they were still some twenty miles from the Point of the Cape.

"Aye," conceded her husband, "I think ye be right. But from here we should have good going."

On down the trail, mostly in the shade; here and there the sun broke through in dappled figures on the ground. They went past a path which led to Menotac's old camp; Lagunaka was there, with his sorcerer friend. Perhaps their broken brew pot lay there still.

Then they were nearing the camp on the bluff, but McJack thought it best not to visit there. It would not be a pleasing sight and they couldn't spare the time. "Best," he advised, "we should go to the camp of the whalers; from there we can see to the end of the land."

When they came to the trail where she had first met her man, that magic man from the other world, Minyanata smiled and her husband grinned. Since that time much had happened. The people had migrated to the river; had built a town. Had migrated again, and McJack and his woman were without even a home. Then they went out to the bay.

The beach was littered with wreckage of the whales but on the sea was nothing at all. Down by the Point the harbor was empty. So, it seemed, was Sir John McJack. "I thought mayhap they would be here," he muttered. "We have come a long way to be stranded here, to be sure. What with the winter close at hand, and all, and the land all empty, and the sea!" And in his mind he saw a man with white whiskers, watching the sea. Hoping for a ship to come. Growing old and daft when the hope had failed. Walking the woods and the beach at night. Becoming the Gray Devil against whom Lagunaka had made his magic. Frightening the people away from the Camp of the Curse. And he so alone that he died of his loneliness!

The others were watching him, so McJack said "Damn!" just by way of oral relief. "Best, seeing we have come so far, we had go on down to the Point. Then should the ship ever come at all, we will be readied. If it not come, we must make the hut to bide the winter through. But I like not the thought at all. And there be another thought that do not please me: the traders' men still in our river. I had hoped to see them again. I had, at that!"

Then he watched for a moment the sinking sun; he squinted his eyes to see. Off there white clouds had built themselves a castle, and a golden stream ran before it. A short way to the north was a mountain, green and gray and purple, and slowly fading. As slowly, the castle tumbled down.

McJack shrugged his shoulders: "Would that be a sign?" he wondered to his silent self. Aloud he repeated: "Best we'd go down to the Cape. One thing be good about the coming of the night: the traders' men cannot do the same; they must wait for the day."

Chapter 23

Because they all were so weary and there would be no shelter at the Point, and because McJack had the luck to shoot a careless racoon that had come to the beach to feed, they ate, and spent the night in one of the whalers' shacks. During that night the breeze went half around the compass; it blew gently from the east. Over the woods from the ocean, but not very strong. There was only a little suggestion of a coming storm and in the morning they went down to the Point.

McJack inquired rather despondently of himself: "For why should we go at all? There be no ship. Mayhap none will come; few ever do. Mayhap we must spend the winter in the whalers' hut. But we will not pay a penny in rent, to be sure!"

And Adrian wondered why he so suddenly chuckled.

Neither at the beach nor at the old camp by the pond could they find a sign that a ship had been there and they scanned the sea again for a sail. They were standing on the shore, down on the Point at the end of the headland. "It be as empty as the wind!" declared McJack disgustedly, referring to the sea.

But Minyanata suddenly held up her hand. Stood taut with her listening. "Wind be not empty," she affirmed. "Little sounds, like slow woodpecker! From yonder!" She pointed up the coastline, a little toward the inland. With one finger on the palm of her other hand she timed the tapping. At first none of the others could hear it, then Yanata joined her mother in her gestures.

"It be like a man that pounds," Minyanata explained, but the ears of the white men were too dull. McJack, interested and intent, spoke quickly: "Ye all stay here and rest, but one must always watch the sea, and up yonder on the bay. I will go more close to these sounds that ye hear, and whet me ears to listen. A sound of pounding? I have me a thought. I will go by way of the ocean beach. I will soon be back." And he appeared in a hurry as he walked away.

Up the beach to where the man with the beard was buried, though there was no sign of a grave at all. Past where the *Melrose* had been shoaled; but when he came to the place where the *Phoenix* had been wrecked, out into the dune-lands and the open, he heard the sounds quite distinctly: *Ping-ping, ping-ping, ping-ping*. He thought he recognized them, too. They came from up beyond a grove of stunted trees on a marshland island. And then, above those trees, he saw the masts; the ship seemed out on the meadow there.

"The men have found the inlet"*, he told himself. "She be the first to do it. But why? Me pirate friends? They creep in hidden creeks at home!"

And when he had waded to his knees in the meadow and come to the island he saw the ship; it was the one he had hoped to meet in the harbor. She sat upright on a mud-flat in the water; men on a raft were working. Calking the craft between wind and water, where more often this was needed. There was an eighth of a mile of mud and water between the ship and the island.

"Aye," concluded McJack, and the thought pleased him, "she be too filled with freight to careen on the beach, so they have set her down in the mud on the flood of the tide, to mend her seams on the ebb."

Ping-ping, ping-ping, ping-ping: the sound of the mallets on the irons.

"Ahoy the ship!" shouted John McJack. But the mallets kept on pinging. "Ahoy," he yelled. "Ahoy-oy!" That time the sound of the mallets stopped.

A strong voice bellowed, McJack knew it was the master: "Ahoy the shore! Who be ye there?"

"I be John McJack. Will ye send a boat?"

But the boat could only make half the way, the tide was so low. But speech was comparatively easy. McJack received welcome news: the mending was almost finished, then the ship would come out on the beginning of the next out-tide. She would come to the beach by the Point for water. The men would be pleased to meet again with Master McJack, but why was he there on the shore at all?

McJack shouted a brief explanation and heard some sympathetic profanity. Also the eager inquiry: "Will this sloop have goods worth the taking?"

*Cold Spring Inlet

"I cannot tell. If ye get free in time ye shall be judge of that. So I will meet ye at the harbor?"

And it was a more jaunty McJack who strode back toward the Point and his people, even though mudded again to the knees and none too filled with food and wearied to the bones.

* * * * *

The crew popped their eyes and made audible and perhaps inelegant comments when Minyanata and Yanata went aboard; but, because they were still in such need of rest, the captain gave them his cabin and they disappeared. Adrian went with them but McJack stayed on deck to explain his latest plan, for the traders' sloop hadn't shown on the bay.

"First," he requested, "set me right on this: How far do it be to the land over yonder?" Pointing south and west.

"Three leagues or more. Over yonder lies a cape."*

"And up yonder in my river be the traders' sloop," said McJack. "What goods she freights I do not know. Mayhap none at all, for she did not come for the trading. Now, even though there be no profit, and because the sloop in a sense serves the English king, would ye lend me yer ship for a prank, and all?"

The captain pulled his great mustache: "I must ask the men. I be master here, to be sure, but my men serve free. They have a voice."

And indeed they had; called aft and consulted they assented with a roar. Anything for a prank that would spite the king. Anything that would serve Sir John McJack. And Sir John grinned and thanked them; he made an elegant bow. Then, while some still listened, he explained that Adrian and Yanata would be wedded as soon as they could find a priest.

That time the captain roared: "A priest? Why wait for a priest? I be the master of this ship; I be entitled by law to wed or to whip! This deck has seen a-many sights, but never a wedding. When the lass gets rested, and we have the time, to be sure we'll have a wedding!"

And McJack knew better than to protest. As he explained to Adrian, just as they were setting sail, "Ye and Yanata must do it. These men have set their hearts upon it; we must nurse this flare for the fun, and all, for they can help us or hang us, the which they choose. We must keep these men well humored."

The ship sailed the edge of the ocean, where that ocean joined with the bay. She leaned a little with the press of the wind; her canvas curved on the yards. She sailed a-quartering with the wind; they could hear the thrumming of the shrouds. Her forestays, too. And the play of the waves on her planking; she rolled, for she quartered the troughs of the seas.

Cape Mey grew dim; Cape Henlopen plain. And the ship dropped her anchor out-

---

*Cape Henlopen, Delaware

side of the point, four fathoms deep in the water there. Her sails were furled while she waited; no sloop showed out on the bay.

The sun seemed sinking into the land, but beyond that land was the bulge of the bay; one couldn't see there at all. Yet across the bay on the line that the sloop would come, the view was plain; the sun as it set didn't dazzle the eyes; that part of the bay showed clear. A lookout was at the masthead, too. He could see the bay and the sea and a part of the shore which was a mile away. But the wind died down with the sun.

The moon instead of rising from behind the trees came from out of the ocean; first it showed a silver glow, there at the rim of the watery world. And then the glow grew to be an edge of the moon, and half a moon; and next that moon was almost full with small white clouds beneath it.

The vessel swung at her anchor a mile from the shore. The night was calm but the swells of the seas kept rolling. A smaller boat would have pitched with those seas as they rolled, but the pirate ship rode steady. There was a path of silver on the sea, out to the moon. On shore the land showed as shadow.

And McJack stood by the rail and thought of this and of that. Of the sea: how friendly it could be at times, how fierce at others. Unpredictable. Pranking or plundering. The sea was like the pirates who sailed it: friendly or fierce.

As of that moment they were friendly; in small groups they seemed to be planning something. A surprise, perhaps. Something that pleased them at least, for they laughed and swore and clapped a hand on a shoulder. But McJack knew that they weren't drunk and he wondered. He hadn't seen the captain for a quarter of an hour.

McJack frowned. He hoped he hadn't made a mistake by bringing the women aboard. The pirates hadn't seen a woman, and they were a tough lot, this piratical "Irish Navy," being in the Irish sense no pirates at all. They were, to use a softer sounding word, "privateers."

Suddenly McJack was frightened. A wailing sound had come from aft, from where he knew his women to be. He took one quick step, then stopped. The wail came again; it made him think of Mellissa at her birthing, there in the town on the river. Of the sounds she had made; but suddenly he grinned. It wasn't a woman at all. For on the stillness of the moonlit night the bagpipes skirled.

'The Campbells Were Coming' was the music ringing out from out of the poop-deck. And they came in fitting splendor: the tall Scot, with his tunic and his vest and his kilt. With his stockings gartered below the knees; with his fur-covered sporran dangling down; with the long plaid scarf and the bonnet there. The bonnet with its feather. With his strut and his stride and his skirling pipes: He and the Campbells were coming!

And the moon rode high among its little clouds; it gleamed on the decking there. The masts cast shadows athwart that deck, and the Scot he strode among them. His shoulders swung as he strutted up deck and down, a-piping.

The captain came down to the main deck, too. Red coat, plumed hat and his sword and all. He bowed and strutted. He beckoned McJack and then he bawled: "Bring out the bride! Bring out the groom! By the hills of the Highlands we'll have a weddin' here! Sir McJack, bring out the ladies!"

Then the captain, with his great red coat and his hat with the plume, fell in stride with the piper. Aft-deck to fore-deck, down port and starboard, down deck and aft and around. With a whoop and a holler the men joined the march, and the bagpipes skirled above it all — 'The Ketchlins of Kerry' he was piping then, and the men kept a-marching to it.

And the ladies were half scared to death at first by the racket. But Adrian brought Yanata out; McJack he brought the mother. Adrian, as bridegroom, felt fittingly foolish.

And then the captain, the pirate, he made a grand bow, and swung his hat low, and made Yanata take his arm and Adrian's arm and McJack took Minyanata's arm, and away they went in the wedding march, for 'The Ketchlins of Kerry' were playing. With the Scot still a-strutting with his shoulder swing and the captain stepping high and Sir John McJack doing the same, and all of the others. For this was the night of the wedding!

And Sir McJack was proud as he walked, for Yanata had played up bravely. So had her mother. And after a moment they didn't have to pretend; when their fright was gone, and when they'd caught the spirit of the fun and 'The Ketchlins of Kerry' had got into their blood, though they didn't strut — they walked erect, heads high, eyes lighted. Swinging themselves a little then, pacing with the piper. While the Ketchins kept coming and the men kept a-shouting; and the moon kept a-climbing the sky.

And the captain read the service then, from out of a book. He did it well. Gravely and with reverence, too.

Thought Sir McJack: "This moon be not so light the man could read; methinks he knows the word and all. Mayhap, this being a sudden changeful world, the man were one time a priest. I wonder."

And McJack, surmising, may have come close to the truth, in those changing times, when men changed masters and masters changed men.

So Yanata and Adrian were wedded again, while the Manitou moon looked down on them. Looked down on the ship and on the sea and on the land beyond. The land which showed as a shadow.

And on that land red people stood. They listened. They wondered: What manner of men were they on the ship? What made those weird and wailing sounds? Why were they shouting so long and loud? Were they frightening great devils away?

And, long after the shouting and laughter were done, out there on the sea, the red people watched and listened and waited. They could see the ship in the light of the moon; her masts and her spars, silent there in the westerly light, when the revelry was done. It was almost as silent in the dawn. Once in a while a voice on the breeze, for the breeze blew in from the sea.

But nothing happened. Not in the dawn nor in the morning nor in the midday hours. The ship lay waiting at anchor there, the watch at the masthead, scanning the bay and the sea. But mostly the man watched the bay.

Down on the deck McJack was counting: "It be nigh four leagues in the river, what with the bends and crooks and all. It be nigh eight leagues down the bay; this wind be light but it would blow on the beam. Mayhap they could not make the bay so soon.

"The sun be westering now; the most of the day be done. On the morrow, or mayhap the sloop will pass in the night. That would be bad! That..."

This from the masthead: "Sail ho, on the bay. A sloop, I makes her. Wind a-beam and sailing south!'

McJack and some others ran up on the ratlines. They could see the sloop dimly. And, in case some on the sloop should look, they might see the ship; she lay so close to the line of the land.

McJack looked inquiringly at the captain. The latter grinned and nodded: "The ship be yours for the time, and all."

The blood of Sir John was tingling. He, supposedly far in the inland there, was in charge of the ship. He looked over the side at the current; its trend seemed down the shore.

"Up-anchor a bit," he told the men. "Not far. See would she drift beyond the land, so them on the sloop cannot see us at all, while we make ready." And the drift of the ship hid the sloop from their sight, so the sloop held her course, bearing down. In the middle of the bay, in deep water. They didn't seem keen on the watch out there. Why should they be? Their dangers, they thought, were behind them.

Her deck was crowded with a small army of men, those who had gone into the river to chase McJack away. To burn his town and teach him and his red men a lesson. Thinking that task done they were relaxed and lazy; some of them slept on the deck. Mostly the others sat; there wasn't much room to wander around. Her little cannon was covered well; they had done their task, at least in part.

They hadn't gotten McJack, to be sure; but they had burned his town and driven him far to the inland. Their trader masters soon would know that the days of McJack were done. They could trade as they pleased, "for rum or for what."

And the sloop sailed on, side-slipping a little, her keel so shallow. The helm held hard; her prow didn't point quite true on course. She would hold that course until well past the Cape, fearing the land on her lee; her master was a careful man. And satisfied and complacent now; he hummed a little ribald tune. They would clear the Point before the dark; there would be a moon, and all was well indeed.

He stood looking south, toward Henlopen. Then his chin dropped down; his eyes popped wide.

For from behind the land a tall ship showed; she was headed for the bay and the sloop. She flew no flag but her sails were filled and drawing well. Wind was on her starboard beam; it was larboard on the sloop.

"Hell's fire!" exclaimed the master, then. "And what be that?"

On the ship Sir John was a sight to see. His eyes were alight and he had dressed with care, for this was a great occasion. He must appear at his very best. He wore the great red coat of the captain's and the broad hat with the plume. Around his waist was a bright blue sash and he wore a cutlass in it. He strode the deck in his glory, but was not too exalted to confer with the captain: "What think ye — should we board the sloop to seek for cargo?"

"It would not be wise. Small chance they carry goods at all, and there be too many men to board. Rats, caught in traps, might fight the hardest; we have no men to lose in fruitless fight. Ye should play your prank, and we will forego profit."

McJack nodded and grinned: "A point more to starboard, mister!"

The sloop was half a mile a-bow. "Send up the bones!" said Sir McJack. And up went the black flag with its whitened skull, a thing that was fit for fear indeed.

And it fitted for fear the men on the sloop and the master. "Hard helm a-lee and head for shoal!" He shouted so loud that the ship could hear. Could hear and grin as they watched the "prank."

The sloop came about with the wind astern; the ship did the same and the race was on. Headed for shoaling water. The sloop could sail in there and live; the deep ship couldn't. But she was taller and caught more of the breeze; she gained, though slowly.

The men on the sloop knew panic, then. Panic and fear, with no room for flight. The deck so crowded they could scarcely move. A blast of shrapnel; they could see the ports of the guns agape. The grim black muzzles there. Closing in at quarter then, they would rake the decks and slay...

"Helm a-starboard!" the sloop master yelled, but when it was done it did no good. For the pirate ship sailed faster and leaned the more. This would depress the line of the cannon; the close aim would be lower; the men on the sloop could see and fear. One man started to yank a tarpaulin from a little gun.

On the pirate ship a man was standing on the rail, his left hand clutching a shroud. In his right was a trumpet; the last of the sun made the metal gleam. It gleamed, too, on his cutlass. And on the broad hat with the feather, on the red coat and the bright blue sash. They could see his face clearly. Some of the men stared harder than before. One of them yelled a name. This couldn't happen! That man, he was putting the trumpet to his lips.

"Hi-yi! Hi-yo! Ahoy the sloop! Hi-yi!-Hi-yi! If ye fire that gun I will murder ye all! I be John McJack, and I do as I say! Hi-yi! Ye scum and scattle!"

And the ship was bearing down the while; she had stolen the wind from the sails of the sloop. On the sloop was bewilderment and panic.

They had thought this man afar in the inland, and they had burned his town! For that he would pay murder and arson. They had thought he had fled because he feared to fight. And there he was before their eyes, the master of a ship! A pirate ship, with many guns and those guns were being brought to bear. They would rake the deck and kill every man; they knew he would do it! He was Sir McJack, there wasn't a doubt. "Hi-yo-hi-yo! Hi-yi! Ye scum and scattle!"

That pirate ship was closing in; the sloop could never reach the shoals. Any moment now those guns...

"Hard a-starboard!" yelled the master, and the sloop lost her way as she came about. "Hi-yi!" yelled Sir McJack and he gestured to the gunners. The cannon bellowed and boomed and smoked and stank. The pirate ship shook with the shock. Through the smoke yelled McJack, there on the rail: "Hi-yi! Ye scum and scattle!"

And from the sloop the mast and the gaff and the tip of the sail fell into the bay. The boom, caught a-center when the sloop came about, fell fore and aft on the housing. A score of men were under that sail and it heaved and hove as they scrambled out. But what good that? They were out in the open. The sloop was adrift; the ship had gone on.

"Hi-yi!" had yelled McJack as he passed. "I will be back! Ye will burn me town! Ye will harm my injuns! Hi-yi! Ye cannot flaunt Sir John McJack I tells ye now! Next round I will load with shrapnel! I will murder the mess of ye there."

The pirate ship bore away, and about, and back. The panic on the sloop was madness. Men sought to hide from the slugs. Some lay flat behind the rail. Behind the low housing, the mast, the waterbutts. Many dived down through the hatchway. The pirate ship was closing in to loose her hail of shrapnel.

"Hi-yo!" yelled Sir John McJack, the master of the ship, for now. "Hi-yi! Hi-yi! Ye scum and scattle! Get forward there, for in a trice ye shall have no stern at all. I will blast it away, I will, at that!"

And the rush of the men to the bow of the sloop nearly swamped her. The ship went past without firing a shot. And Sir John hollered: "Hi-yi! If ye come to my river ye had best stay away! Ye scum and scattle and rats on a raft! Ye sneaks and snakes and murdering mice!" And Sir John brandished his cutlass.

His crew lined the rail and jibed and jeered and swore at the "rats on the raft" as long as their voices would carry in the last of the light of the day. There where the moon took over. And Minyanata, forgetting that in a way she was by right a queen, cast dignity aside and yelled with the others. "Rats on a raft!" she hollered.

And of her own great man she was mightily proud, with his great red coat and his hat with a feather. The most beautiful sight she had ever seen.

"Mister," inquired Sir John McJack, "be I still the master here?"

"Mayhap, for the time." This with a grin.

"Then, mister, ye will give the men a round of the rum. And will ye bid the helmsman steer for the British Isles? There mayhap be some little creek that might be waiting there." He was removing his regalia. "I gives ye back your ship the now, and the saints shall bless ye for the lending of the same. Ye have served both well and good, both me and mine, for we were damned for sure before we found ye here. We were, at that!"

The captain grinned and bowed, while the ship bore north of east, clearing Cape

May by a moonlit mile. There where the "diamonds" slid in the ends of the waves, and clams lay helpless on the shore, where the *Phoenix* lay buried in the shoal and the white-bearded man beyond the dunes. The bones of the whales on the shore of the bay; the bones of a million red men in their little sandhills there.

McJack and Minyanata and Adrian and Yanata and the "Small One" — they stood on the stern and watched. They watched the land, that tree-line which made its shadow beyond where the surf would be, it seemed to be going away.

"I wonder," mused John McJack aloud, "where Nanquemoke be the now? The chief and his people?"

Silently Yanata pointed to the indefinite west: "Beneath the moon of the Manitou there."

"God grant them well!" pleaded McJack. "They be going afar, and the land be strange."

"And ye yerself," said the ship's captain, "ye be going, too, and to what ye cannot tell. Mayhap, things at home be worsened now, if the men of the king be at rape in the land. Ye have but lept from griddle to grate, at that! We cannot tell."

"Mayhap," admitted McJack. "But we will do as we have done afore: we will go and see, if the saints and all be willing. This be a wide, and a wild, and a worrisome world; it be, at that!"